PATRICIA WENTWORTH
RED STEFAN

PATRICIA WENTWORTH was born Dora Amy Elles in India in 1877 (not 1878 as has sometimes been stated). She was first educated privately in India, and later at Blackheath School for Girls. Her first husband was George Dillon, with whom she had her only child, a daughter. She also had two stepsons from her first marriage, one of whom died in the Somme during World War I.

Her first novel was published in 1910, but it wasn't until the 1920's that she embarked on her long career as a writer of mysteries. Her most famous creation was Miss Maud Silver, who appeared in 32 novels, though there were a further 33 full-length mysteries not featuring Miss Silver—the entire run of these is now reissued by Dean Street Press.

Patricia Wentworth died in 1961. She is recognized today as one of the pre-eminent exponents of the classic British golden age mystery novel.

By Patricia Wentworth

PATRICIA WENTWORTH

RED STEFAN

With an introduction by
Curtis Evans

DEAN STREET PRESS

Published by Dean Street Press 2016

Cover by DSP

First published in 1935 by Hodder & Stoughton

ISBN 978 1 911095 57 6

www.deanstreetpress.co.uk

Introduction

BRITISH AUTHOR Patricia Wentworth published her first novel, a gripping tale of desperate love during the French Revolution entitled *A Marriage under the Terror*, a little over a century ago, in 1910. The book won first prize in the Melrose Novel Competition and was a popular success in both the United States and the United Kingdom. Over the next five years Wentworth published five additional novels, the majority of them historical fiction, the best-known of which today is *The Devil's Wind* (1912), another sweeping period romance, this one set during the Sepoy Mutiny (1857-58) in India, a region with which the author, as we shall see, had extensive familiarity. Like *A Marriage under the Terror*, *The Devil's Wind* received much praise from reviewers for its sheer storytelling élan. One notice, for example, pronounced the novel "an achievement of some magnitude" on account of "the extraordinary vividness...the reality of the atmosphere...the scenes that shift and move with the swiftness of a moving picture...." (*The Bookman*, August 1912) With her knack for spinning a yarn, it perhaps should come as no surprise that Patricia Wentworth during the early years of the Golden Age of mystery fiction (roughly from 1920 into the 1940s) launched upon her own mystery-writing career, a course charted most successfully for nearly four decades by the prolific author, right up to the year of her death in 1961.

Considering that Patricia Wentworth belongs to the select company of Golden Age mystery writers with books which have remained in print in every decade for nearly a century now (the centenary of Agatha Christie's first mystery, *The Mysterious Affair at Styles*, is in 2020; the centenary of Wentworth's first mystery, *The Astonishing Adventure of Jane Smith*, follows merely three years later, in 2023), relatively little is known about the author herself. It appears, for example, that even the widely given year of Wentworth's birth, 1878, is incorrect. Yet it is sufficiently clear that Wentworth lived a varied and intriguing life that provided her ample inspiration for a writing career devoted to imaginative fiction.

It is usually stated that Patricia Wentworth was born Dora Amy Elles on 10 November 1878 in Mussoorie, India, during the heyday of the British Raj; however, her Indian birth and baptismal record states that she in fact was born on 15 October 1877 and was baptized on 26 November of that same year in Gwalior. Whatever doubts surround her actual birth year, however, unquestionably the future author came from a prominent Anglo-Indian military family. Her father, Edmond Roche Elles, a son of Malcolm Jamieson Elles, a Porto, Portugal wine merchant originally from Ardrossan, Scotland, entered the British Royal Artillery in 1867, a decade before Wentworth's birth, and first saw service in India during the Lushai Expedition of 1871-72. The next year Elles in India wed Clara Gertrude Rothney, daughter of Brigadier-General Octavius Edward Rothney, commander of the Gwalior District, and Maria (Dempster) Rothney, daughter of a surgeon in the Bengal Medical Service. Four children were born of the union of Edmond and Clara Elles, Wentworth being the only daughter.

Before his retirement from the army in 1908, Edmond Elles rose to the rank of lieutenant-general and was awarded the KCB (Knight Commander of the Order of Bath), as was the case with his elder brother, Wentworth's uncle, Lieutenant-General Sir William Kidston Elles, of the Bengal Command. Edmond Elles also served as Military Member to the Council of the Governor-General of India from 1901 to 1905. Two of Wentworth's brothers, Malcolm Rothney Elles and Edmond Claude Elles, served in the Indian Army as well, though both of them died young (Malcolm in 1906 drowned in the Ganges Canal while attempting to rescue his orderly, who had fallen into the water), while her youngest brother, Hugh Jamieson Elles, achieved great distinction in the British Army. During the First World War he catapulted, at the relatively youthful age of 37, to the rank of brigadier-general and the command of the British Tank Corps, at the Battle of Cambrai personally leading the advance of more than 350 tanks against the German line. Years later Hugh Elles also played a major role in British civil defense during the Second World War. In the event of a German invasion of Great Britain, something which seemed all too possible in 1940, he was tasked with leading the defense of southwestern England. Like Sir Edmond and Sir William, Hugh Elles attained the rank of lieutenant-general and was awarded the KCB.

Although she was born in India, Patricia Wentworth spent much of her childhood in England. In 1881 she with her mother and two younger brothers was at Tunbridge Wells, Kent, on what appears to have been a rather extended visit in her ancestral country; while a decade later the same family group resided at Blackheath, London at Lennox House, domicile of Wentworth's widowed maternal grandmother, Maria Rothney. (Her eldest brother, Malcolm, was in Bristol attending Clifton College.) During her years at Lennox House, Wentworth attended Blackheath High School for Girls, then only recently founded as "one of the first schools in the country to give girls a proper education" (*The London Encyclopaedia*, 3rd ed., p. 74). Lennox House was an ample Victorian villa with a great glassed-in conservatory running all along the back and a substantial garden--most happily, one presumes, for Wentworth, who resided there not only with her grandmother, mother and two brothers, but also five aunts (Maria Rothney's unmarried daughters, aged 26 to 42), one adult first cousin once removed and nine first cousins, adolescents like Wentworth herself, from no less than three different families (one Barrow, three Masons and five Dempsters); their parents, like Wentworth's father, presumably were living many miles away in various far-flung British dominions. Three servants--a cook, parlourmaid and housemaid--were tasked with serving this full score of individuals.

Sometime after graduating from Blackheath High School in the mid-1890s, Wentworth returned to India, where in a local British newspaper she is said to have published her first fiction. In 1901 the 23-year-old Wentworth married widower George Fredrick Horace Dillon, a 41-year-old lieutenant-colonel in the Indian Army with three sons from his prior marriage. Two years later Wentworth gave birth to her only child, a daughter named Clare Roche Dillon. (In some sources it is erroneously stated that Clare was the offspring of Wentworth's second marriage.) However in 1906, after just five years of marriage, George Dillon died suddenly on a sea voyage, leaving Wentworth with sole responsibly for her three teenaged stepsons and baby daughter. A very short span of years, 1904 to 1907, saw the deaths of Wentworth's husband, mother, grandmother and brothers Malcolm and Edmond, removing much of her support network. In 1908, however, her father, who was now sixty years old, retired from the army and returned to England, settling at Guildford, Surrey with an older unmarried sister named Dora (for whom his daughter presumably had been named). Wentworth joined this household as well, along with her daughter and her youngest stepson. Here in Surrey Wentworth, presumably with the goal of making herself financially independent for the first time in her life (she was now in her early thirties), wrote the novel that changed the course of her life, *A Marriage under the Terror*, for the first time we know of utilizing her famous *nom de plume*.

The burst of creative energy that resulted in Wentworth's publication of six novels in six years suddenly halted after the appearance of *Queen Anne Is Dead* in 1915. It seems not unlikely that the Great War impinged in various ways on her writing. One tragic episode was the death on the western front of one of her stepsons, George Charles Tracey Dillon. Mining in Colorado when war was declared, young Dillon worked his passage from Galveston, Texas to Bristol, England as a shipboard muleteer (mule-tender) and joined the Gloucestershire Regiment. In 1916 he died at the Somme at the age of 29 (about the age of Wentworth's two brothers when they had passed away in India).

A couple of years after the conflict's cessation in 1918, a happy event occurred in Wentworth's life when at Frimley, Surrey she wed George Oliver Turnbull, up to this time a lifelong bachelor who like the author's first husband was a lieutenant-colonel in the Indian Army. Like his bride now forty-two years old, George Turnbull as a younger man had distinguished himself for his athletic prowess, playing forward for eight years for the Scottish rugby team and while a student at the Royal Military Academy winning the medal awarded the best athlete of his term. It seems not unlikely that Turnbull played a role in his wife's turn toward writing mystery fiction, for he is said to have strongly supported Wentworth's career, even assisting her in preparing manuscripts for publication. In 1936 the couple in Camberley, Surrey built Heatherglade House, a large two-story structure on substantial grounds, where they resided until Wentworth's death a quarter of a century later. (George Turnbull survived his wife by nearly a decade, passing away in 1970 at the age of 92.) This highly successful middle-aged companionate marriage contrasts sharply with the more youthful yet rocky union of Agatha and Archie Christie, which was three years away from sundering when Wentworth published *The Astonishing Adventure of Jane Smith* (1923), the first of her sixty-five mystery novels.

Although Patricia Wentworth became best-known for her cozy tales of the criminal investigations of consulting detective Miss Maud Silver, one of the mystery genre's most prominent spinster sleuths, in truth the Miss Silver tales account for just under half of Wentworth's 65 mystery novels. Miss Silver did not make her debut until 1928 and she did not come to predominate in Wentworth's fictional criminous output until the 1940s. Between 1923 and 1945 Wentworth published 33 mystery novels without Miss Silver, a handsome and substantial legacy in and of itself to vintage crime fiction fans. Many of these books are standalone tales of mystery, but nine of them have series characters. Debuting in the novel *Fool Errant* in 1929, a year after Miss Silver first appeared in print, was the enigmatic, nautically-named *eminence grise* Benbow Collingwood Horatio Smith, owner of a most expressively opinionated parrot named Ananias (and quite a colorful character in his own right). Benbow Smith went on to appear in three additional Wentworth mysteries: *Danger Calling* (1931), *Walk with Care* (1933) and *Down Under* (1937). Working in tandem with Smith in the investigation of sinister affairs threatening the security of Great Britain in *Danger Calling* and *Walk with Care* is Frank Garrett, Head of Intelligence for the Foreign Office, who also appears solo in *Dead or Alive* (1936) and *Rolling Stone* (1940) and collaborates with additional series characters, Scotland Yard's Inspector Ernest Lamb and Sergeant Frank Abbott, in *Pursuit of a Parcel* (1942). Inspector Lamb and Sergeant Abbott headlined a further pair of mysteries, *The Blind Side* (1939) and *Who Pays the Piper?* (1940), before they became absorbed, beginning with *Miss Silver Deals with Death* (1943), into the burgeoning Miss Silver canon. Lamb would make his farewell appearance in 1955 in *The Listening Eye*, while Abbott would take his final bow in mystery fiction with Wentworth's last published novel, *The Girl in the Cellar* (1961), which went into print the year of the author's death at the age of 83.

The remaining two dozen Wentworth mysteries, from the fantastical *The Astonishing Adventure of Jane Smith* in 1923 to the intense legal drama *Silence in Court* in 1945, are, like the author's series novels, highly imaginative and entertaining tales of mystery and adventure, told by a writer gifted with a consummate flair for storytelling. As one confirmed Patricia Wentworth mystery fiction addict, American Golden Age mystery writer Todd Downing, admiringly declared in the 1930s, "There's something about Miss Wentworth's yarns that is contagious." This attractive new series of Patricia Wentworth reissues by Dean Street Press provides modern fans of vintage mystery a splendid opportunity to catch the Wentworth fever.

Curtis Evans

Chapter One

THE MAN turned at the end of the bridge and walked back. That he was committing an act of pure folly was, of course, perfectly plain to him, but at the moment that did not matter at all. All that mattered was that he should cross the bridge again.

He turned and walked back slowly in the teeth of the bitter wind. Overhead the sky hung low and dark, and the clouds were heavy with snow. It wanted half an hour to sunset, but the light was failing rapidly. It had not been really light all day, but he could still see the leaden flow of the river, with the ice clinging to its banks and a black mass of buildings rising up on either side like cliffs to meet the arch of the sky. The parapet of the bridge showed dark against the shadowed river. The woman's figure, bent above the parapet, showed darker still. She had not moved. He came slowly up the slight incline and saw that she had not moved at all. She stood as if she had been frozen there, a dark slender figure with bent head and drooping shoulders.

The man looked at her, frowning. He wore a rough sheepskin coat and cap, and the wind cut through them. The woman was thinly dressed. How much longer was she going to stand there? Till she froze where she stood? Perhaps that was what she was doing it for. In Russia nowadays no one cared what became of you. You helped to pull the car of the Revolution, or you crawled away out of its path to die.

He walked very slowly past her and then turned to look back. The act of folly was becoming more outrageous every moment. At a time when it was all important that he should melt inconspicuously into the background, here he was concerning himself with the affairs of a stranger. If he went on loitering like this, somebody would be tolerably sure to come along and notice him—and the one thing he could not afford was to attract notice.

He walked to the parapet and stood there a dozen feet away from the dark bowed figure. He could now see the line of her cheek and chin. She had a round cloth cap on her head. It hid her hair and her ears. Her eyes were open. The thin cheek and temple might have been cut from marble.

It was she.

He had, of course, known it all along. His heart gave an involuntary jerk. Talk of folly—what folly was there like this?—to be unable to pass a chance-met stranger seen half a dozen times in the streets of this Russian town, and, what was more, to be unable to think of her as a stranger. She bore the stamp and strain of utter poverty. He neither knew her name nor who she was. And the least turn of her head, the least movement of her hands, were as dearly familiar as if he had known her always. Well, there was no movement now. The stillness tugged at his heart. Ice is still, death is still. No living flesh should be as still as this. His blood stirred with something like horror, and before the horror had time to die he had crossed the space between them. The impulse carried him into abrupt low-toned speech.

"Why do you stand here in this freezing wind? It's too cold for you."

He spoke in Russian, and it was in Russian that she answered him. Without any turn of the head or change of expression she said.

"Yes, it is cold."

His heart jerked again. It was the first time that he had heard her voice. Drained and faint as it was, it could yet touch something in him which no sound had touched before. He stood looking at her, but she did not look at him. She looked at the snow-clouds and the river, but she did not seem to see them. Perhaps she watched the wind go by. He could see her eyes, and there was an awful patience in them. No one looks like that who has not grown used to pain. With a hot anger in his heart he said gently.

"It is much too cold for you. You should not stand here."

She turned her head a little then and gave him a tired, appraising look. Seen full face like this in the dusk, her face was all shadows. They lay heavily under the fine arch of the brow and in the hollows of the cheeks. She said, with a little more tone in her voice, as if she were making an effort.

"Why do you speak to me?"

If he had been looking for adventure, her look would have checked him, it was so remote. He said, almost roughly.

"You'll freeze if you go on standing here."

The faintest flicker of something that was not quite a smile touched the pale lips. He had a quick enchanted thought of what it would be to see her smile at him in joy. The thought sank down into the depths of him and stayed there. She said

"It would not matter in the least. Please do not trouble yourself about me." The words were Russian, but they came haltingly. The accent was not Russian at all.

He looked over his shoulder. They were alone upon the bridge. He completed his act of folly by stepping to her side and saying abruptly.

"You're English, aren't you?"

The voice and the English words struck against her numbness like a blow. They woke her to a faint tingling consciousness.

She said, "Who are you?" and spoke in English too.

With a complete absence of hesitation he put his life into her hands.

"My name is Stephen Enderby."

"English?"

"Of course."

"Is that why you spoke to me? Do you know me?"

"No, I don't know you—at least I don't know who you are. I've seen you. Does one have to know a woman to try and stop her freezing herself to death?"

If he had not been so near, he would have missed that second flicker of a smile.

She said, "I think so. It is very much one's own affair." And then, "How did you know I was English?"

He laughed. There was warmth and assurance in his tone.

"You don't speak very good Russian, and—I chanced it. And now that we are introduced, may I see you home, because you really oughtn't to be standing here in this wind."

For a moment she really smiled.

"Are we introduced, Mr Enderby?"

He laughed. The sound had a queer careless gaiety.

"Stefan Ivanovitch, if you don't mind. The other would probably mean a firing-squad if anyone heard you."

He saw her face change. It was as if all the shadows had deepened and frozen there. She swayed a little, and he put his hand on her to steady her.

"Then why did you tell me?" she said. "I'm a stranger. Why do you tell a thing like that to a stranger?"

His hand was on her arm. He felt it thrill as she spoke. She was very cold to touch, but it was not the coldness of death. Pain thrilled through her. He felt it under his hand. He said,

"No—you're not a stranger. I've watched you. Won't you tell me your name?"

She released herself and leaned against the parapet. The wind went past her. She said,

"My name is Elizabeth Radin."

Stephen laughed again.

"Now we're really introduced! Please may I see you home?"

"No, I don't think so, Stefan Ivanovitch." Her fingers lay on the cold stone and traced some pattern there. They were only half hidden by a tattered glove.

"Why?" said Stephen. He too leaned on the parapet. The river below them was unseen and the darkness had begun to close them in.

There was no answer. Her cold thin fingers moved upon the stone.

"Why?" said Stephen very insistently.

Elizabeth looked across the dark river. The black houses which stood over it like cliffs showed here and there a lighted pane. The wind went by. She said in a sweet, quiet voice,

"I haven't anywhere to go."

Stephen's heart gave a bound of angry excitement.

"What do you mean?"

"Just what I say, Mr Enderby—I beg your pardon, Stefan Ivanovitch."

Stephen caught her wrist.

"What nonsense is this?" Then he had his coat off and was putting it round her. "Here—slip your arms into the sleeves. It's a beastly fuggy old hide, but it will keep the wind out."

She had not known how cold she was till the warmth came round her. In these days, since Nicolas Radin's death, she had grown used to being cold. Life was one long nightmare. To freeze—to starve—perhaps to freeze to death...The sheepskin, warmed by Stephen's vigorous body, gave her a momentary sense of awakening. In the days before the nightmare began one had been warm and cared for. A shudder ran over her as she said very faintly,

"You mustn't give me your coat. You'll freeze."

"Not if we walk," said Stephen firmly.

He fastened the coat as if he were dressing a child and, taking her by the elbow, began to walk her down the incline towards the left bank of the river. He talked as they went, and his blood raced. The coldest wind in the world could not have frozen him just then. He was alive, warm, and dominant. He felt capable of striding straight on to the frontier and over it with Elizabeth in his arms. He had never been so happy in his life.

"Now," he said, "you'd better tell me why you haven't got anywhere to go. Then we can think what's the best thing to do. By the way, what were you going to do?"

"Stay there, I suppose."

He could only just hear the words.

"And freeze?"

"I suppose so."

He felt a boiling anger which merged into triumph. Freeze, would she? Not with him to take care of her! He laughed out loud. She had again that sensation of awakening. In the nightmare no one laughed. They starved, fought, agonized, intrigued, and died, but they didn't laugh. Stephen was talking in that warm, confident voice.

"Please tell me why you've nowhere to go. I'm all in the dark, and I can't help you while I'm in the dark. Why are you stranded here? What has happened? I'll be able to help you much better if I know."

They had left the bridge and were following the darkening road. Elizabeth said under her breath.

"I don't think anyone can help. I want to go home, but they won't let me go."

"You're English—you ought to be able to get away. Have you tried the proper people?"

"My husband was half Russian. He was a Russian subject. They say I've lost my British nationality. They won't let me go."

"Is your husband dead?"

"Yes," said Elizabeth. After a moment she went on, "He was an engineer. His father was Russian. He had the offer of a good job here. We were married and came out to take it up. It was all right at first. Then—" she hesitated—"things went wrong. Nicolas was accused of counter-revolutionary activities. They shot him."

Even through the thick sheepskin fleece she could feel the warm, strong pressure of his hand. They had turned out of the main road into a side road.

"What did you do?"

"I tried to get home, but they wouldn't let me go. They said I was a Russian subject. I don't know why they didn't shoot me too—it would have saved a lot of trouble. At least—I do know why. The Commissar Petroff had an old mother, and he wanted someone to look after her. She was bed-ridden, and he couldn't get anyone to stay with her, because of her tongue. He told me I might think myself very lucky to get the chance of establishing my revolutionary integrity. I hadn't any money, or any way of getting food, so I took the job."

"Well?" said Stephen.

Elizabeth shuddered.

"I can't talk about it. She was the most horrible old woman."

"*Was?*"

Elizabeth shuddered again.

"She died yesterday."

"And they turned you out?"

"No."

"Then—"

"The Commissar wished me to stay."

"You mean—"

"I thought I would rather freeze."

She felt that strong pressure on her arm again.

"Oh, you're not going to freeze. I've got a room—or to be quite accurate, a share of a room—and a share of my share is very much at your service. I won't offer to give it up to you, because I shouldn't like to leave you to fend for yourself amongst the other occupants. They're a queerish lot."

"Mr Enderby—"

"*Please!*" said Stephen.

"No—I mustn't say it, I know. I won't again. But I can't let you run yourself into danger."

"Danger?" He laughed like a schoolboy. "That's rather like telling a duck not to get its feet wet!"

"Do you mean you are in danger already?"

"Already—and all the time."

"Then I shall make it worse for you."

"No, I don't think you will. It wouldn't make any difference if you did. But as a matter of fact you'll be rather an asset. Anyone who was looking out for me wouldn't expect me to have a woman with me."

They turned to the left again and descended a narrow lane which ran down towards the river. It was now very nearly dark. The houses rose black on either side. The path was slippery with ice and trodden snow.

Elizabeth felt as if she were walking in a dream. Presently she would wake up and find herself on the bridge again with nowhere to go. Or perhaps this was the snow-sleep which has no awakening.

Perhaps she would just slip down, and down, and down into uttermost depths of unconsciousness...Perhaps...

Stephen felt her stumble. He threw his arm about her.

"What is it?"

There was no answer. If he had not held her up, she would have slipped from him and fallen. He lifted her and carried her into the house against which they stood.

Chapter Two

ELIZABETH OPENED her eyes. She was lying on a heap of straw and someone was rubbing her feet. Her eyelids felt very heavy. It was Stephen who was rubbing her feet. He must have taken off her shoes whilst she was unconscious. He was kneeling on the floor. As soon as he saw her eyes open he put a finger to his lips.

Elizabeth looked at him with wide, blank eyes. She was no longer unconscious, but she was not yet fully conscious. She could see and hear, but she did not think about the things which she saw and heard. They made floating pictures in her mind. Stephen's face was one picture. She had not really seen it in the dusk. Now she saw it quite clearly, for there was a light somewhere in the room and it shone on him. She did not see his rough peasant's clothes or the great square hands which were rubbing her feet. She saw only his face with its strong chestnut beard and vigorously curling hair, and between these the bold curve of the nose, the bronzed wind-beaten skin, and the bluest eyes she had ever seen.

She looked at this picture and found it a pleasant one. Then, shifting her gaze slightly, her mind received a second picture. There was a lamp hanging from the roof. It gave out a strong yellow light and a strong oily smell. Just below this lamp ran the dark line of a curtain.

Elizabeth shifted her gaze again. She was trying to think about the curtain. The lamp swayed slightly, but the curtain hung dark and straight. She began to wonder about it, and then quite suddenly her mind was clear and she saw that the curtain was a sack ripped open and hanging from a tightly stretched line of string. It screened the corner in which she lay. From the other side of it came the sound of voices and the shuffling of feet. She raised herself on her elbow.

Stephen put his finger to his lips again. Then he pulled the sheepskin coat over her feet and disappeared on the other side of the sacking screen.

Elizabeth sat up and stared about her. The place was warm, and she was warm. Her feet glowed from the warmth of Stephen's hands. It was weeks since she had been warm like this. Mingled with the smell of oil there were other smells. The reek of food, damp sheepskins, coarse unwashed human beings, and rank tobacco all helped to thicken the atmosphere. But it was warm. It was most blessedly warm. She pushed the straw up behind her back and leaned against it. What was to happen next seemed to concern her as little as if she had been in a theatre waiting for the curtain to rise upon the next act of some play the plot of which she did not know. She felt a faint curiosity, a faint thrill of anticipation, but no more. It was as if the events of that first act in which she had herself sustained so tragic a role, had brought her to an end of her capacity to feel. She leaned back against the wall, a mere spectator now.

Then the sack was pushed aside and Stephen came ducking under the line. He had a bowl of steaming soup in his hand, and as the smell of it rose up into her nostrils, Elizabeth felt a frightful pang of hunger. She could have snatched the basin from him and gulped like an animal, but she steadied her hands, and had parted her lips to say thank you, when he again laid a finger on his own. As she took the first delicious mouthful, he was speaking close to her ear.

"Don't speak. Your Russian won't pass muster. You'll have to be dumb. If anyone speaks to you, look vacant and shake your head."

A faint stab of fear pierced her indifference. Was he going to leave her? She looked at him across the bowl of soup with the question in her eyes.

He shook his head and put his lips to her ear again. His beard tickled her cheek.

"I won't be long. They won't meddle with you. They think you're my wife. Finish the soup, and I'll be back as soon as I can."

He waited till she had drunk it, and then pushed under the sacking again. One of the men in the room beyond said something which she did not understand, and the others laughed. Stephen laughed too, and then she heard the door open and shut again, and knew that he had gone. She found his words ringing in her head: "I'll be back soon"..."They won't meddle with you"..."They think you're my wife."...She pressed the straw into a pillow and fell asleep with her cheek on her hand.

She did not know how long she slept, but presently she was awake again. Looking down on her from over the top of the screen was a man with a wide pale face and ears that stuck out on either side of his head like bat's wings. She could see the lamplight through them, and the effect was fantastic in the extreme—the blunt, almost featureless face, crowned with a shock of fair hair, and those jutting blood-red ears. He called over his shoulder in a voice thickened with drink.

"Come and look at her for yourself then! I don't think much of Red Stefan's taste, I can tell you!"

Someone guffawed.

"You'll think something of Red Stefan's fist if you take liberties with his property!"

"Who's taking liberties? Who wants to take liberties either? Why, she's more like a bit of scraped bone than a girl!"

"Well, I've seen Red Stefan knock a man into the middle of the year after next for less than you're doing now."

Elizabeth heard the words and saw the face. She was still so dazed with sleep that she felt neither fear nor offence. She looked up with half opened eyes, and then she saw and heard something else. The door of the room was flung open. Someone came striding in, and over the head of the man who was staring down at her Stephen's face appeared. She had not realized how tall he was till then. He looked over the other man's head and, taking him by the bat-like ears, lifted him right off his feet. Elizabeth saw the white convulsed face jerk up, and down again. She heard his yell of anguish, the clatter of his feet upon the floor, and Stephen's great schoolboy laugh.

"Dance, little man, dance!" he said, and once again up came the face—up, and down again. Yell, scuffle, and laugh were repeated. There was the sound of a heavy slithering fall, and, still laughing, Stephen pushed under the sacking. With his fingers to his lips he said.

"He didn't frighten you?" And, as she shook her head, "He's like a bat—nasty, but harmless. He won't look at you again in a hurry. It's going to take him all his time being sorry for himself and telling the others how badly he's hurt. Now look what I've brought you."

He dropped a bundle on the floor, unrolled it, and showed her with pride a sheepskin coat and cap, and a peasant woman's skirt, blouse, kerchief and boots. The things were decent, but not new. "Better put them on," he said, dropping his voice until it only just reached her. "You won't want the coat in here, but you'd better get into the other things. Then give me what you've got on and I'll get rid of it."

She nodded, and he ducked under the sack and went out into the room. As she put on the things he had brought her, she could hear him chaffing the man whose ears he had wrung. He began to tell a story against him which made the other men laugh. There seemed to be two or three of them, and at least two women, from the voices.

Elizabeth rolled her old clothes into a tight bundle and waited for Stephen to come back. When he came he smiled approvingly, took her bundle, went off with it, and presently returned, breathing a little quickly as if he had been running.

"They're gone," he said at her ear. "I chucked them into the middle of the river beyond the ice. The current will take them away." He looked at her critically. "You haven't got the handkerchief tied right. It doesn't matter to-night. I'll show you how to do it in the morning. You'll remember not to speak—won't you? It's a whole heap safer for you—in fact it's the only way, because your Russian's really dreadful." He laughed a little. "It's dull for you, I'm afraid, not being able to speak. They've been congratulating me on getting a wife who can't give me a tongue-lashing."

Elizabeth smiled faintly. It warmed her to be near him. His good spirits, his strength, his easy friendly manner broke in upon the cold trance of loneliness and misery in which she had lived, moved and had her being for the last year. For his part, he was filled with a sense of triumph which he could hardly contain. To look at her sent tremendous currents of happiness swirling through him. He had got her, and he felt completely competent to keep her safe.

She had taken off her cap with the other things which she had worn, and he could see her hair—dark hair, as fine as silk, very thick, and cut irregularly as if she had tried to do it herself. She had grey eyes with a ring of black about the iris, which gave them a starry look, and her lashes were very fine and soft, and as black as ink. The arch of the brows made him think of wings. She was much too pale—much, much too pale. That damned Commissar must have starved her. Her cheeks had no business to fall in like that. But what a lovely line from cheek to chin. Her lips should be red, not faint and pale. They looked as if they held secrets which they would never tell. They made you wonder what the secrets were—sweet, wild, mournful, tender. Well, some day she'd tell them—to him. He meant to see about that. He said abruptly.

"Will you have some more cabbage soup?"

Chapter Three

IN THAT crowded room, with its heavy air and its rough snoring denizens, Elizabeth slept more peacefully than she had done for a year. Stephen lay stretched on the floor between her and the mixed company beyond the sacking screen. He had rolled up his coat for a pillow, and his head had scarcely touched it before his slow, deep breathing told her that he was asleep. The sound gave her a most perfect sense of safety. She thought how strange life was. A few hours ago she had been alone and in despair—most cold, most wretched, and most friendless. Now she was warm, and fed, and comforted. She had not really begun to think. She only knew that she felt safe. And so fell asleep.

She woke with a hand over her mouth and a voice at her ear. It was Stephen's hand and voice. He was saying "Ssh!" The lamp had been extinguished and it was quite dark. She ought to have been frightened, but she was not frightened at all. She blinked at the darkness and waited for Stephen to speak.

He said "Ssh!" again. And then, "Did I frighten you? I hope I didn't—but you were talking in your sleep."

He had taken his hand away from her mouth, but it rested on her shoulder. He felt the sudden upward leap of her heart. So she was afraid of what she might have said...He cast his mind back over the soft, rapid utterance which had waked him. And then she was whispering on a scarcely audible breath.

"What did I say?"

He patted the shoulder reassuringly.

"Nothing at all—just rubbish. But it won't do for the others to think there's been a miracle in the night. You've got to go on being dumb, you know. Now look here, I'm sorry I had to wake you, but it isn't worth while your going to sleep again. We're pushing off before dawn. There's a sort of wash-place along the passage. I'll light a candle for you as soon as we're outside. Don't be longer than you can help."

In the passage he lighted an inch of candle which he produced from an inner pocket, showed her the way to the wash-place, and then went back into the room. When she returned, he beckoned her behind the sack and produced with pride a bowl of coffee-substitute, some black bread, and, wonder of wonders, a boiled egg. The coffee was scalding hot, and the egg tasted better than anything Elizabeth had ever eaten. She had seen eggs in the last year, but she had not tasted one. The old Petroff woman had occasionally had an egg. When she had gobbled it up she would throw the shell at Elizabeth and tell her to fatten herself on that.

Elizabeth ate the egg and the black bread and drank the steaming coffee, and then sat on her straw bed and waited. Everyone in the room beyond seemed still to be asleep. They snored as noisily as animals. Elizabeth wondered how she had slept through such a chorus.

Stephen was away for a little time. When he came back he held her coat for her, and then, taking down the sacking, he rolled up the straw bed in it, tied it deftly with the string of the line, and signed to her to take up the candle and precede him.

At the street door he leaned his bundle against the wall and, taking the candle-end from her hand, blew it out, and after allowing a moment for the tallow to harden put it away in his pocket. Then the bundle was on his shoulder, and next moment they were out in the dark street.

To Elizabeth the darkness was absolute, but Stephen seemed to have no difficulty in finding his way. He took her by the arm and marched her up the lane at a good brisk pace, and presently she could see where the houses ended and the sky began. The houses were black, but the sky was only a very, very dark grey. There was no light in any window, and no star in the strip of sky.

They turned to the right and then to the left again. They were now out on the broad road which ran through the town. Elizabeth heard the sound of a horse shaking its head and the jingle of harness, and then they stopped just in time, as it seemed to her, to avoid running into a cart which was standing in the middle of the road. Someone moved in the dark and an old cracked voice grumbled.

"A nice time you've kept me waiting! If your wife don't get up any earlier than this, you'd better take a stick to her! Idle hussies, that's what the girls are nowadays! I tell you I'd have taken the stick to your grandmother for a lazy slut if she'd kept me about like this! And snow coming, as I told you yesterday!"

Stephen made no answer. He was loading his bundle into the cart, and presently when he lifted Elizabeth in she found she had a warm nest in the hay, with the sacking over all to keep the wind out. The grumbling voice went on for a while and then stopped. The harness rang, and with a jerk they were off.

It was bitterly cold, but not as cold as it might have been in November. There had been no deep snow yet, only a light fall, which had frozen, leaving the road hard. They went along at a good jogging pace. The houses fell behind. The snowy fields on either side seemed to give out more light than the heavy lowering sky. Elizabeth could just make out the driver's figure against the snow. Stephen looked back along their road and laughed.

"Now we can talk," he said cheerfully. "Old Yuri's as deaf as a post. If I were to let off a bomb just behind his back, he wouldn't hear it, so you needn't go on being dumb. Are you warm—comfortable?"

Elizabeth said, "Yes." Her voice was so low that Stephen laughed again.

"You needn't be afraid—he really can't hear you. Now don't you want to know who he is, and who I am, and where we're going? Because if I were you, I should be fairly bursting with curiosity by now."

Elizabeth smiled in the dark. It was rather a tragic smile. She could imagine Red Stefan's impatience with anything he could not understand. For herself, it mattered so little where she went or what she did. And then it came to her with the suddenness of a stinging blow that it did matter. Twelve hours ago she had asked no more of fate than a quiet corner to die in. Now, it seemed, she wasn't going to be allowed to die. Stephen hadn't the slightest intention of letting her die; she could see that. She was going to be made to live. Old deaf Yuri and his horses were carrying her to meet a new, troublesome, eventful, unescapable day. Perhaps it was a pity that Stephen had found her on the bridge. She might have been dead by now and all her troubles over. Something in her stirred a little scornfully. "How do you know they would have been over?" And right on that came Stephen's voice, saying.

"Wouldn't you like to hear the story of my life?"

Mere politeness would have compelled her to say yes. There was something eager and boyish in his tone. There was even a little of the same pride with which he had offered her the egg. It touched the springs of tears and laughter, and she said in a hurrying voice.

"Are you sure you want to tell it to a stranger?"

He said at once in a different tone,

"You are not a stranger."

"And at this time yesterday I didn't know that you existed," said Elizabeth. She could not see him, but at every jolt of the cart her shoulder touched his through the hay.

"What's that got to do with it?" he said. "I lived for six years in a man's house once, and we were strangers to each other all the time—always quite polite, you know. He was my guardian. Now I don't think I should ever be polite to you."

"Are you always rude to your friends?" said Elizabeth gravely.

He laughed.

"Well, you know what I mean. People are either your sort or else they're not. If they are, you can just be yourself, but if they're not, you keep on dropping bricks and having to pick them up again."

"And I'm not a stranger?"

"Did you think you were? Why, I told you my name straight away. I've never done that to anyone before—not when I was on a job, I mean."

"But why did you tell me your name?"

"Because I knew I could trust you, and I wanted you to trust me."

They jolted along for a minute or two after that, and neither spoke. Then Stephen said.

"I'd like to tell you what I'm doing here. It's quite interesting. We've got a long way to go, so we may as well talk. I'll tell you the story of my life, and then you can tell me the story of yours—that is, if you'd like to. And when we've finished both our stories, we can decide what we're going to do next."

Chapter Four

ELIZABETH FELT a little startled. He had seemed so calm and purposeful that she had made sure he had everything planned.

"Don't you know?" she asked.

"Not yet. But it'll be all right—something will turn up. We're out of that beastly hole of a town anyhow. Well now—shall I begin, or will you?" He sounded a little like the child who offers a ride on the rocking-horse which he is yearning to bestride himself.

She made haste to say, "You, please," and immediately he was in the saddle.

She was aware of him sitting up beside her in the straw, hugging his knees. His voice came from only a few inches away. When the cart went over a rut or a pot-hole, they were thrown together and then jolted apart again. He talked eagerly and as if it was a pleasure to him to be speaking English.

"I'm quite English, you know, on both sides. My father was killed in the Boer War. He was really an engineer, but he went out with a battalion of Mounted Infantry. When I was two my mother married a member of the Darensky family and took me with her to Russia. Paul Darensky had a big country place which he only visited once or twice a year. My mother was pretty and young and gay, and they both liked society, so they lived in Petrograd and entertained a great deal, and I ran wild on the estate with the peasants' children."

Elizabeth said almost involuntarily.

"Oh, poor little boy!"

"Why?" said Stephen. "I had a very good time. I was much fonder of my nurse than I was of my mother. She had a married brother on the estate, and his wife Katinka had about twenty children. I was friends with them all."

"I shouldn't have thought you'd have learned any English."

"I didn't. And then my mother suddenly got shocked at my being a little savage, and she went to the other extreme and got me an English tutor and a French governess." He laughed. "They amused each other at any rate—and I did learn French and English."

"Nothing else?"

"Oh, the usual things. Grant was quite an efficient fellow. He didn't bother me out of lesson hours, so we got on all right. Then when I was twelve, my mother died and I was packed off to my guardian in England. He was a cousin of my father's, and he had a big estate on the Devon-Somerset border. His name was Robert Carey, and we never stopped being total strangers, like I told you."

"Didn't you go to school?"

"Yes, *rather*. I'd have blown up if I'd had to stay there with old Carey. He sent me to Marlborough."

"How did you get on there?"

"Oh, I always get on. I had to knock one or two people down for calling me a foreigner, and then we were all right. I didn't have to see too much of old Carey, because I spent a good part of the holidays in Russia with Paul Darensky. He didn't take any notice of me, but he liked having me there. He'd been awfully in love with my mother and couldn't get over her death—just moped about on the estate and gave up all his friends. Well, when I was fourteen, the war started and I didn't go to Russia any more. My Lord—how fed up I got with old Carey!" He paused. "Now that's all very dull stuff. I hope you haven't gone to sleep. It gets more interesting as it goes on—at least I hope you'll think so. I wanted to enlist in '17, but old Carey swore he'd dig me out of any battalion I got into. And then the Revolution broke out over here. Kerensky had his shot at making a government, and in November the Reds got the upper hand and there was the devil to pay. The Army broke up, the men murdered their officers, the country estates were looted, and there was a ghastly mess all round. Paul Darensky was murdered on his own estate, and the house was wrecked. I was very glad my mother was dead. I didn't really know her very well, but she was too gay and pretty to be mixed up in that sort of thing, if you know what I mean."

Elizabeth said, "Yes, I know." She had a picture of a gay-winged butterfly blown away over the tree-tops before the forest was swept by a torrent of flame.

"Well," said Stephen, "that's all about that. In January 1918 old Carey had me into his study. There were two other men there, an old boy from the Foreign Office and a Russian. They said how-do-you-do to me, and then the Russian began to talk to me in Russian. I hadn't talked much for four years, but I got on all right. I don't forget things. After about five minutes he switched on to the Foreign Office bloke and said in English, 'That was all right—he could pass me as an educated Russian.'"

The cart jolted, flung them together, and flung them apart again. Stephen laughed and hugged his knees.

"The moment he said that, of course I saw what the game was, and I said, 'I can pass as a peasant too. Wouldn't that be useful?' The Foreign Office man came down like a cart-load of bricks on old Carey. 'What have you been telling him? You were not authorized to tell him anything at all!' Carey went as stiff as a ramrod and said he hadn't told me anything. I said, 'That's right, sir—I couldn't help guessing you were going to send me to Russia.' How could I, when he said I could pass, like that? What else could it have meant? They all had a good stare at me, and the Foreign Office man said, 'You're not slow in the uptake anyway. Can you talk Scotch as well as Russian?' I said I couldn't, and he laughed and said to the Russian 'Go ahead—try him with the peasants' talk.' I wondered how he was going to do it. I give him marks, for he really did it awfully well. He began by saying. 'Now, you're a groom, and I think you've been neglecting my horses.' And then he gave me a tongue-lashing, and I made the proper answers, excusing myself and swearing I'd done this, that and the other, just as I'd heard Paul's grooms do ever since I was a baby. Then he began to ask questions about the farm work—sowing, ploughing, reaping, cows, hens, pigs—the whole lot of it. I warmed up to it rather, and I did half a dozen different people—the fat pig man, and the very old man who knew more about cows than they knew about themselves, and so on. I did their proper voices. When I'd finished, the Russian kissed me on both cheeks and said—but if I tell you what he said, you'll think I'm boasting."

He heard Elizabeth's laugh for the first time, very soft and faint. He immediately wanted to pick her up and kiss her. And it would be so easy. No, not easy—impossible.

"Do you never boast?" she said, and the laughter was still in her voice.

"Oh, nearly always. A Russian peasant is a very boastful fellow, and I'm a Russian peasant about half my time. If I don't blow my own trumpet, people won't believe I've got one."

Elizabeth said, "I see—" She spoke quite gravely, but he thought she was still smiling. He hoped so, because he had an idea that she had forgotten how to smile. If he could make her laugh, she might think him as boastful as she pleased. He plunged back into his story.

"Well, after that they sent me to Russia. I was to be one of Katinka's twenty odd children, and I was to go to her father, old Yuri, who's driving us now. It was my own idea. Katinka used to talk about her father, but she hadn't seen him since she married, and I knew he wouldn't have the slightest idea how many children she had. I don't think she knew herself—she just went on having them. So, when I turned up in Yuri's village and said I was his grandson Stefan, neither he nor anyone else had the least doubt about me. I wasn't eighteen, and I looked younger, though I was so big, because my skin was very fair in those days. I used to have to keep it well smudged with dirt till it darkened a bit."

"What did you do?" asked Elizabeth.

"Not very much at first. I had to come and go, and get to know the ropes. Then they wanted to know about the Tsar and his family. You know all the rumours there were. Well, they wanted someone to go to the place and find out what had happened—whether they were really dead or not. And after that there were other things—getting people across the frontier, and, of course, making regular reports as to what was going on. I had to serve my two years in the Red Army and I was over here for four years straight on end, and then I was back in England for a bit. I've been backwards and forwards ever since. My riskiest job was working in a poison-gas factory at Trotsk." He laughed. "I was glad to get out of that with a whole skin, I can tell you!" After a pause he said, "I expect this will be my last job."

Elizabeth felt a thrill of superstitious fear. She said, "Why?" a little breathlessly. She could just see him now, black against the greyish white of the snow. The line of the horizon showed beyond his shoulder. It bounded an endless desolate flatness on which their cart must look like the merest speck. The sky overhead showed the approach of dawn. A yellowish tinge began to invade the grey. The horse's hoofs rang on the frozen snow.

"Why?" said Stephen. "Oh, just because...I don't want to go on being a Russian peasant for the rest of my life. I've saved a bit, and when old Carey died a year or two ago he left me a couple of thousand pounds and one of his farms. It was very decent of him, and I hope I haven't said anything about him that I oughtn't to. We just didn't talk the same language—that's all. I went into partnership with a cousin, Tom Carey, an awfully good fellow, and we've started breeding horses. Did I tell you I was pretty good with horses?"

"No, you didn't," said Elizabeth.

"Well, I am. It's part of my job really. You see I could go all up and down the country as a horse-doctor. I'd got to be something that would account for my being away a good bit. I took on cows and pigs as a side-line, and it was all very useful. I got quite well known. I might have been taken on as an *agronom* if I'd wanted the job—they go round lecturing to the peasants, you know. But that wouldn't have suited me. You can't just disappear if you're in a government job—and sometimes it suits me to disappear."

"I shouldn't have thought you'd want to be too well known."

He laughed, leaned close to her, and said in a loud stage whisper.

"Ssh! Not a word! I'm not always Red Stefan." Then, drawing back again, in a different voice, "Now it's your turn."

He was at once aware of a withdrawal. The silence between them seemed rigid for a moment. Then she said,

"I told you. There's nothing more."

Stephen's thoughts plunged and reared at that. Nothing more— when he wanted to know every single thing that she had ever thought or done. Well, some day she would tell him. He reined in those racing thoughts, and became aware that she was asking him a question.

"Where are we going?"

"To Yuri's village—for the moment. Afterwards—I don't know—it depends. I'm not quite sure how things are there just now. You see—" he leaned confidentially nearer—"I've been away all the summer. I only got back a week ago, and then I had to dig Yuri out and get him to come up to the town. He didn't want to a bit—he was afraid of a heavy fall of snow. But I had to have a good excuse to be there, so I got him to put a cartload of market stuff together and chance it. Of course he sold it pretty well. They tried to stop the peasants selling their own stuff, you know, but they had to let them do it in the end. There are too many of them. They can't shoot 'em all, and if they did, the rest of Russia would starve. So Yuri gets his price for butter and vegetables and eggs. As a matter of fact I had to be in Tronsk to meet the man who is going to take over my job. He didn't come, so they'll probably have to find someone else—"

"You mean—"

He nodded.

"I expect they got him. I was pretty sure of that by the second day, but I just felt I'd got to hang on. When I saw you on the bridge, of course I knew why. It was lucky you weren't a day later, because Yuri wouldn't have waited another twenty-four hours for anyone on earth. I expect he's right about the snow, but we shall get in before it comes."

She could see him quite plainly now. The road ran south and a little west, and the sullen dawn came up behind them, painting the sky just above the horizon with livid streaks. Everywhere else the clouds were of an even, impenetrable greyness. As they looked back along the way by which they had come, there was nothing to be seen but a vast plain thinly veiled in snow. When Elizabeth leaned sideways to the edge of the cart and looked past old Yuri's humped shoulders, there were, however, signs of broken ground and a sprinkling of trees with their branches stark against the snow.

As they came up with the first of the trees, she heard a loud cawing sound and looked about her for a sign of crow or raven. The sound came again, much farther off. And then, to her extreme surprise, a cuckoo called from a thicket on their right. She turned to Stephen and found him regarding her gravely.

"Did you know there were cuckoos in Russia?" he said, and before she could answer, the call came again, behind them. It hung on the frosty air, came more faintly, and died away.

Yuri looked over his shoulder, said something in a rapid mutter and, turning back, jerked at the reins.

"What did he say?" said Elizabeth. "Was it about the cuckoo? Did he hear it? I thought you said he couldn't hear anything."

Stephen nodded.

"He can hear one thing, but it's not the cuckoo. He was only saying something about the snow. He says he smells wind, and perhaps that'll carry it away. Do you know what the one thing is that he can hear? He lived up farther north when he was a boy, and he was chased by wolves. He was in a two-horse sleigh with two men, and when the wolves were gaining on them they chucked Yuri out. He was only a peasant child, you see. I tell you, some of those Russian nobles fairly asked for the Revolution. Yuri's father was a serf. They treated 'em like dogs, and after they were emancipated they cheated 'em right and left. It's only about twenty-five years since a peasant could be flogged by his master. If he died of the flogging, no one worried—there were lots of peasants."

"What happened to Yuri? How did he escape?"

"He shinned up a tree just in time, and the wolves followed the sleigh. He nearly died of the cold and the fright, and to this day he can hear a wolf's cry when he can't hear anything else. Look—you watch him!"

She looked round at Yuri's back. He wore a sheepskin coat and cap, very dirty, the cap pulled well down over his ears and the coat high about his neck. He drove in a hunched attitude and might almost have been asleep. As she looked at him, there came, as if from a long way off, a faint sound. Elizabeth found herself listening for it to come again, and when it came, a little louder, she felt as if a drop of ice-cold water had trickled down her spine. She had never heard a wolf's cry before, but with each repetition she found it more terrifying.

She turned quickly to Stephen and saw him looking away to the right with a set face. The sound was nearer now and louder. It was like a dog baying, and yet not like. It was sharper, higher, and it had the savage melancholy of hunger in it. Her heart began to thump against her side and a cold sweat of terror broke out on all her limbs. Suddenly the cry rang out so near that the horses shied violently and old Yuri, pulling on the reins with one hand, swung round in his seat and shook the other fist at Stephen whilst he poured out a flood of angry abuse.

Stephen broke into laughter. The cart swayed from one side of the track to the other, and whilst Yuri was taking both hands to the reins again, Stephen became suddenly aware of the fear in Elizabeth's eyes. In an instant he had both her hands in his.

"Were you frightened? What a brute beast I am! I wouldn't frighten you for the world—you do know that, don't you?"

Elizabeth felt utterly bewildered. The wolf's cry had ceased. Stephen was holding her hands and looking into her eyes. His were so blue and so near that she could not meet them. A giddiness came over her and her eyelids fell. In an instant he was holding her hands to his face, not kissing them, but pressing his forehead down upon them, whilst he held them in a grasp from which she had no power to withdraw. She felt as if her senses were leaving her, but his quick penitent words came through the faintness.

"Don't be frightened—you mustn't be frightened! I'd cut off my right hand before I'd frighten you. It was only a joke." Then he was looking at her again, and her eyes were open. "Please forgive me. I wouldn't let anything hurt you for the world. I never thought I'd take you in. I thought you guessed when I did the birds. Why, a cuckoo couldn't live here at all—it's only a summer visitor in England."

She said in a soft, confused voice, "The birds?"

"Didn't you really guess? That's a tremendously big feather in my cap."

She said the same words again. It was as if she couldn't move her mind to anything fresh.

"The birds?"

Stephen's heart cried out in him: "You're like a princess in a fairy tale—an enchanted princess who can't speak. Frozen—that's what you are—frozen with fear. And I helped to frighten you!"

Out loud he said, in the voice he would have used to comfort a child,

"Yes, the birds, and the wolf, and everything. It was me all the time. You won't be frightened any more, will you? Please, *please* don't be frightened."

"It was you?"

"Yes. I do it quite well—don't I? It wants an awful lot of practice. I started when I was only a kid. I can do a lot of birds and animals."

"But it sounded right over there."

He nodded.

"That's what takes such a lot of practice, getting it to sound from the right distance and direction—and you mustn't let a muscle of your face move, or it gives you away. You were looking at me when I was doing the wolf. It was pretty good to take you in when you were so close."

She drew her hands away from him. This time he let them go.

"It was stupid of me to be frightened, but—when I looked at you—you looked—as if we were in danger."

He laughed.

"All strong and silent! That was because I wasn't letting a muscle of my face move. Please forgive me for frightening you. You will—won't you?"

Elizabeth leaned back into the angle of the cart.

"It was stupid of me. I've always been frightened about wolves. Someone told me a story when I was a child—" A faint shudder ran over her. "If it had been anything else...I haven't really got anything much to live for—"

He could hardly catch the words. They came more and more slowly, as if she were tired out or half asleep. He frowned and stared out over the snow. So she hadn't anything much to live for...That was one of the things that had got to be changed. When people stop taking an interest in being alive, it doesn't take much to kill them. You saw that happening in Russia every day. The older people, the ones who weren't wanted because they didn't fit into the new Communist state—they just died, and nobody cared. He dared Elizabeth to die and slip away from him. She'd got to be disenchanted, waked up, made alive again. She needn't think he was going to let her go. He had got her, and he was going to keep her.

He began to think very seriously about the immediate future. They were going to the village. Well, when they got there, what next? Yes, that was the question—what next? He would like to give Elizabeth time to rest and get strong. The question was, could he afford to give her this time? Was it going to be safe? Well, that depended on two things. First, would Petroff take the trouble to try and trace her? He couldn't answer that, because Elizabeth hadn't told him enough about her relations with Petroff. He glanced at her and saw that she was asleep, her lashes very fine and dark against the whiteness of her cheeks. He leaned over and tucked the straw closely round her. The question about Petroff must wait.

The other question would have to wait too. It was a nuisance Yuri being so deaf. He would have to wait till they reached the village before he could find out whether Irina was there. If she was...

His frown deepened as he thought about Irina.

Chapter Five

THE VILLAGE stood bare of trees upon flat, open ground. There was a straggle of houses on either side of the one long street. There was a church with a dome like an onion. There was a big house, or hall, painted pink. The little houses were painted too, or washed with colour—green, pink, blue, and yellow, under eaves of bristling thatch. The small square windows stared blankly at the snow.

Elizabeth got down out of the cart and looked about her. She felt dazed and very cold. Stephen took her by the arm and led her into the hut before which they had stopped. An old woman who was tending the stove called over her shoulder in a high cracked voice with a nasal tone in it,

"Shut the door, whoever you are! What's the good of feeding the stove if the good heat is to be wasted?" Then, as she turned round and caught sight of Stephen, she gave a shrill cry, stretched out her arms, and ran to embrace him.

Stephen kissed her heartily, called her little grandmother, and with an arm still round her pulled her about to face Elizabeth.

"See what I've brought you! For ten years you've been telling me that I ought to be married."

The old woman stared at Elizabeth. She was a very ugly old woman, incredibly lined and wrinkled, but her eyes were bright and black. They gave her rather the look of an aged squirrel as she darted sharp suspicious glances at the stranger Stefan had brought home. All very well to tell him he should marry, but was this the strong strapping wench who was to save her old legs? Not she! A poor half dead looking creature to her way of thinking. A parcel of fools—that's what men were, and Stefan as big a fool as any of them for all he thought himself so clever. She stuck her old chin in the air and said,

"A wife, eh? Where did you get her from?"

"Picked her up in a snowdrift," said Stephen with a laugh. Then, as the old woman made an angry sound, "Well, she looks like it, doesn't she?"

"What's her name?"

"Varvara."

Elizabeth started slightly. She was Stephen's wife, and her name was Varvara, and he had picked her up in a snowdrift...What an odd dream to be having. But the hut was warm. Nothing else mattered very much. Her body felt light and strange, as if it might quite easily rise up and float away like a bubble rising in water. The hut was dark. Stephen and the old woman seemed a long way off. And then the darkness was full of coloured lights, out of the midst of which the Commissar Petroff's face appeared, looking angrily at her. She threw out her hands to ward him off, and knew no more.

Afterwards she could not remember very much about the next few days. She knew that she was ill, and that Stephen and the old woman were tending her. Sometimes she thought that she was dying, and once she heard the old woman say that it would be a kindness to let her die, and that for her part she didn't believe in flying in the face of Providence.

It was then that Stephen knelt beside her and took both her hands in his. He said in English, "Elizabeth—do you hear me?" and much against her will her eyelids opened and she looked at him. She couldn't see at all clearly. She wanted to shut her eyes and slip back into the shadows again, but Stephen wouldn't let her. She had to feel the strong clasp of his hands and to listen to what he was saying.

"Elizabeth—you're not going to die. Did you think I would let you? If you did, you were making a very big mistake. You are going to get well. Now drink this up and go to sleep."

She drank what he gave her, and slept.

When she woke again she was stronger. She lay with her eyes closed and heard the old woman talking to Stephen.

"Yes, yes, she will live—and I suppose you will think how clever you are to have cured her. Horses, cows, women—you can cure them all—can't you? And I suppose you think how clever you are. But I'll tell you what I think. I say that you never did a worse day's work than when you brought her to this house, and if we don't all live to be sorry for it, my name's not Akulina."

She heard Stephen laugh.

"Yes, she'll live," he said.

Akulina broke in with her angry grumble.

"And that's all you care about! Why didn't you leave her in the snow? Not that you need think I believe that story! But wherever you did pick her up, it's a pity you didn't leave her there."

"Come, come!"

She gave a sort of snort.

"Do you think I'm blind and deaf? Look at her hands and feet! Look at the underclothes she had on! Rags, to be sure, but silk. Either she's no better than she ought to be, or she's a *bourzhui*—and the one's bad enough for you, and the other's likely enough to get us all into trouble." She raised her voice to a high pitch of scorn. "Varvara indeed! And what was it you called her last night? And what kind of outlandish way were you talking to her? That's what I want to know!"

"Do you know the saying they have on the other side of the mountains, little grandmother?" said Stephen lazily.

Akulina snorted again.

"How should I know? Decent women stay at home and don't go where they're not wanted!"

"Well, they say there that when the devil wants a fine new crop of lies he sends round an old woman asking questions."

"Meaning I'll get lies for an answer—and from my own grandson too!"

Stephen's voice dropped to a warm, kind tone.

"You'll never have anything but good from me, little grandmother—don't you worry about that. But take care how your tongue wags outside, because—" he paused and a spice of malice crept into his tone—"*because* it would be very exciting for the village if you and I and grandfather were all stood up in a row in the yard and shot. But it wouldn't be quite so amusing for us."

Elizabeth fell asleep again and dreamed that she was standing against a white-washed wall to be shot. Her hands were tied behind her, and she felt cold and ashamed because she was in her night-gown and it was made of pink crêpe-de-chine with a low neck and no sleeves. It had slipped off one shoulder, and she could not pull it up again because her hands were tied. Someone called her name, and she saw the Commissar Petroff standing between her and the levelled rifles. He said, "Tell me the formula and I will save you." Then he smiled, and his smile was worse than his frown. She tried to scream, and suddenly the dream changed. She was running over the snow, and something was running after her. She heard the pad,

pad, pad of its feet, and she knew that it was a wolf. But when she looked over her shoulder it wasn't a wolf at all, but the Commissar Petroff, in a dark fur cap with two pointed ears. He caught her by the arm, and she woke screaming.

Everything was dark, and she didn't know where she was. Then Stephen's hand came out of the darkness and touched her. Afterwards she thought how strange it was that she should have known at once that it was Stephen who touched her. She caught his hand in both of hers and whispered confusedly,

"Has he gone? He frightened me—so."

Stephen's hand was very comforting to hold. He whispered back,

"Ssh! It's only Stephen."

She held his hand very tight.

"Has he gone?"

"There's no one here except Yuri and Akulina, and they're both fast asleep."

"I thought he was here," said Elizabeth faintly.

His other hand smoothed back her hair.

"There's no one here. I'm taking care of you."

"Oh...then it was a dream..." And then, "Where am I?"

"This is Yuri's house. It's the middle of the night. You've been ill."

"Yes," said Elizabeth. Then she shuddered a little. "He hasn't really been here? It was only a dream?"

"It was only a dream. Who were you dreaming about?"

"Petroff," said Elizabeth. "He wants me to give him the formula. But I can't—can I?"

"Of course you can't. Would you like something to drink?"

She drank what he brought her and went to sleep again, still holding his hand.

When she woke, it was daylight and her head was clear. She raised herself on her elbow and looked about her. A bed had been made for her on the lower part of the huge two-decker stove which occupied nearly half the floor-space of the hut. She had heard that

Russian peasants slept upon their stoves, and she had wondered what it would be like. There was straw under her, covered by a cloth. A blanket was over her. It was very warm and comfortable. The house had a partition running across it, but from where she lay she could see the door which led into the street, and on either side of it funny lop-sided windows, filled with clouded glass. Against the wall was a bench and what looked like an old-fashioned loom. In the corner above it an ikon, and in front of the ikon a small unlighted lamp. From the other side of the stove voices reached her—Stephen's voice and the old woman's.

"Came to the door as bold as brass!" That was Akulina on a high, angry note.

"And why shouldn't she?" said Stephen placidly. From the sounds, he appeared to be stoking the stove.

"Why shouldn't she?" Akulina became very shrill indeed. "In my young days a girl who thought anything of herself didn't go running after married men! Stood there in that doorway not half an hour ago when you were out getting in the wood, and 'I hear Stefan is back,' says she. 'Oh yes, he's back,' I said, and in she comes and shuts the door, which she might have done before if she was going to. 'And what can I do for you, Irina Alexievna?' I said. 'Is Stefan at home?' she says, and I said, 'No, he's not,' and looked for her to go, but she didn't budge. Mercy on us, Stefan, how do you suppose the wood is going to last the winter if you're so free with it?'"

Stephen laughed.

"I'll get you some more, little grandmother. Did Irina ask any more questions?"

Akulina snorted.

"She asked me if it was true that you were married, and I said it was. And then she asked after your wife, and I said she was ill, so then she stood over there and looked at her, and I could see she didn't think much of her. There she was, still asleep, but it was easy enough to see she wouldn't have been much more use if she was awake."

"Did she say anything?" Stephen's voice was a little hurried.

"How could she say anything when she was asleep?"

"No—*Irina*. Did Irina say anything?"

Akulina chuckled.

"Not she—not a word. Just stood there and looked. It's not very often that she hasn't got plenty to say, but just for once in a way she was as dumb as a calf."

"She didn't ask any questions?"

"I'm telling you she didn't. Just looked and turned round and went out of the house again. You may well be surprised, but that's what she did." She chuckled again. "Her that'll talk your head off any other time telling everybody how to do the jobs that they were doing before she was born or thought of! Why, last time she was here she as good as told me I'd get more eggs from my hens if I took up with some new-fangled notions she'd got hold of! I told her to go and talk to the hens, and see what they thought about it. 'They're fine talkers too,' I said, and she got red behind the ears and stuck her chin in the air and went off about my taking down the blessed ikon and putting a picture of Lenin in its place! Yes, she's got plenty to say for herself as a rule has Irina!"

Elizabeth felt suddenly giddy and lay down again. It troubled her to think that this Irina had stood there looking at her in her sleep. It was strange that she had not wakened. Strange? What was there that was not strange in this new life into which she had been plunged?

Presently Akulina went out of the house. As soon as she had gone Stephen came round the stove. Elizabeth raised herself again upon her elbow, and when he saw that she was awake he fetched her a wooden bowl of milk with an egg broken in it. She wondered how he had wrung these delicacies from Akulina. It troubled her, but she drank and felt stronger.

Stephen put away the bowl and sat down on the edge of the stove beside her.

"You're better," he said.

And Elizabeth said, "Yes."

He smiled very kindly.

"It was just shock, and cold, and not having enough to eat. You'll soon be all right. Now I want to talk to you before Akulina comes back, because there are things we must settle. She won't be very long, so we'd better get on with it. You needn't worry to talk—I'll do the talking. I only want you to listen and say yes, and no, and a few things like that. You're strong enough for that, aren't you?"

Elizabeth felt as if she were about five years old. She said "Yes," meekly, and when she had said it, her lips kept the faint shadow of a smile. He looked so large, sitting there with his blouse open at the neck so that the strong column of the throat showed. The bright chestnut hair which had given him his nickname curled vigorously. He looked the embodiment of cheerful health.

"All right," he said. "Now this is the first thing I want to say. There hasn't got to be any more of this dying business. It's no use, because I'm not going to let you die. You've had a good try at it, and it's got to stop."

"I didn't," said Elizabeth between tears and laughter. The calm way in which he was lecturing her, the kind look with its sudden embarrassing glint of tenderness, the very bright blue of his eyes, and those big square hands—she could have laughed, or she could have cried. How stupid to be so weak! But it was true that she had tried to die. His eyes accused her of lying. The lashes dropped over her own.

"I didn't."

"Oh yes, you did."

"It would save a lot of trouble," murmured Elizabeth.

"No, it wouldn't. You know, you're wasting time being obstinate like this. Akulina will come back before we've got anything settled. Now just listen to me. You want to die because you're feeling weak. That old Petroff woman starved you, didn't she?"

Elizabeth made no reply. It was all too bitter and too near. Bread of insult and water of servitude—bitter water and bitter bread.

"Now that's all over," said Stephen. "It's all over, and you've not got to think about it again. As soon as you feel stronger you'll want to live all right. You're not really a coward."

A tear crept down amongst the dark lashes.

"Perhaps I am."

"No, you're not. You've got plenty of grit, and I want you to show it. You see—" his voice changed and became warm and friendly—"you see, I want you to help me, and the very first thing I want you to do is to get well, because staying here isn't going to be very safe, and we can't get away till you're well enough. Am I tiring you?"

Elizabeth blinked away the tear.

"No. I'm stupid—I'll try and get well."

"Promise?"

"Yes."

He took her hand, held it for a minute, and then laid it gently down again.

"That's right! You're ever so much better, you know. Now listen! You can't be dumb here. For one thing, it'll make people talk too much. You know what villages are—everyone buzzing round and saying, 'Fancy—Stefan Ivanovitch has picked up a dumb wife!' And half the men asking me where you came from, and whether there are any more to be had." He laughed a little. "And then, apart from the gossip, it's no go, because you talked in your sleep and Akulina heard you."

"What did I say?" said Elizabeth, her eyes wide and startled.

"Nothing to matter."

"Did I speak English?"

"Akulina wouldn't know what it was. Besides, she won't talk. But I don't think you'd better be dumb—it isn't necessary. The talk here is a good bit mixed up anyhow. We're over the Ukrainian border, you know."

"Akulina talks Russian to you—"

"Yes. She's a Ruthenian, from White Russia. She was born and bred on the Darensky estate, and her daughter Katinka went back there when she married. Yuri is a Ukrainian. Are you any good at acting?"

Her lips moved into that faint smile.

"Yes, I think so."

"Very well then, here's your part. You come from East Russia. Your father and mother are dead, and you were trying to find your brother, who is in the Red Army. Your name is Varvara. You don't need to talk about any of this, but you've got to know it so as to have a proper background in your own mind. Whilst you're lying here, make pictures of your father and mother and the brother you're looking for. Your mother's name was Marya, and your father was Mikhail. Your brother is Ivan—you haven't seen him for two years. There aren't any more of you. Your mother's house was like this, only there was no partition and the stove was on the other side. Get it all into your head, and then talk as little as possible. You're very shy, and a little weak in the head."

Elizabeth's sudden faint laughter took him quite by surprise. He explained earnestly,

"I'm just thinking of what will be easiest for you."

Her laughter came with a rush. After a moment he laughed too.

"I say, I didn't mean it like that! Of course it sounds funny. But you see what I mean, don't you? It's an easy part to play really. You've just to say yes and no, and try to look as if part of you was somewhere else."

The laughter went out of Elizabeth and left her shaken. She said, "I'll try," and Stephen nodded encouragingly.

"It isn't the village people who matter so much," he said—"It's Irina. You'll have to be most awfully careful."

"Who is Irina?" said Elizabeth.

The question had been burning on her lips. They trembled a little when she had spoken, and she was angry with them for trembling. What did it matter to her who Irina was? She had come here and asked for Stephen. And why shouldn't she? *That was what Stephen had said—why shouldn't she?*

Stephen did not answer for a moment. Then he said, "We shall have to look out for her—she's clever."

"Who is she?"

He laughed.

"You might call her a sort of Communist missionary. She goes round amongst the villages trying to convert the old people and hotting up the enthusiasm of the young. I was hoping she wouldn't be here just now—we've had rather more than our share of her lately. Not but what we're very good friends and all that—" He broke off rather suddenly.

Elizabeth raised herself on her elbow. She looked at him, and he was looking away.

"What is she like? Is she young?"

He turned back, laughing.

"Oh yes, she's young—and most awfully good-looking at that. She's got the whole bag of tricks—brains, and looks, and most of the virtues. And that's why we've got to be careful. I've a great respect for Irina."

"You said you were friends."

He nodded.

"Oh yes."

With a little flush of effort she said,

"Wouldn't you like to tell her—we're not married?"

When Stephen stared, his eyes looked quite extraordinarily blue.

"Good Lord, no! I beg your pardon—but she's the very last person on earth. I say, what put that into your head? Did you think I was in love with her?"

"Why shouldn't you be?"

He frowned, and said with unexpected gravity,

"I'm not. Put it out of your head." Then he smiled again, a wide, amused smile. "I said we were good friends—not *friends*. There's a difference, you know. She's intelligent, and it's a God-send to have someone intelligent to talk to in a place like this—only I have to keep on taking care not to be too intelligent myself, and that's a bit wearing. We're not pals. We've really only got the colour of our opinions in common. I didn't get called Red Stefan just on account of my hair. No—we're fellow enthusiasts, and red-hot Communists. So if you hear me getting things off my chest like 'universal socialist materialistic ideology,' try and look as edified as you can, will you?—the dumb upward look of the neophyte in fact. Would you like to wash your face and hands? There's some hot water if you would."

Chapter Six

THEY WERE alone again in the afternoon, when Yuri was in the barn and Akulina was milking the cow. He asked her how she was, and she said, "Nearly well." All day the tides of strength which had ebbed so low had been flowing. She had slept a good deal and waked each time refreshed.

"To-morrow," said Stephen, "you must go out. They mustn't think we're hiding you. Are you quite warm?"

"Yes, quite," said Elizabeth.

She was sitting on the edge of the bed which had been made for her. The warmth of the stove struck pleasantly upwards through the earthenware platform and the straw that had been piled upon it. She felt weak, but relaxed and at peace. The terrible bitter strain of the past twelve months had been lifted from her.

Stephen was standing with his back to the door. The sole furniture of the room consisted of the bench and loom which she had seen when she first waked, together with a table and four, rude but solid stools. He took one of these stools and planted himself down upon it in front of her with his elbows on his knees and his chin in his hands. He appeared to be in deep thought. Presently he said,

"I ought to practise calling you Varvara."

Elizabeth's smile came quite easily. The lips that had been stiff and frozen were soft again. She looked down at him and asked,

"Is it difficult?"

"Yes," said Stephen, and plunged in thought again.

This was a new mood to her. If he had not wanted to talk to her, why had he sat down in front of her like this? But if he did want to talk to her, why didn't he begin? She couldn't really imagine that he lacked either words or assurance.

He hunched an impatient shoulder and said half angrily,

"Akulina will be back in a minute."

"Yes?" said Elizabeth.

"And I'm wasting time."

"Yes?"

"The fact is I want to talk to you, and I don't know how to begin."

Elizabeth looked at him in surprise. It was getting dark and she could not see his features very well. Was it possible that he was shy? She decided that it was not possible.

"The fact is," he burst out, "I've got to ask you some questions, and I'm afraid of upsetting you."

"Questions?" said Elizabeth slowly.

"Yes. You won't be upset, will you? I shall hate it if you are. I ought really to have asked you this morning, but then I thought, 'Suppose she faints again,' so I didn't do it. But I ought to have done it."

Elizabeth wondered what was coming. She shrank from these unknown questions, but in spite of the shrinking her mind was tinged with amusement. There was something boyish about his clumsy delicacy. And how like a man to be afraid that she would faint. She said,

"Please ask what you want to. I shan't faint."

He nodded.

"No—you're stronger." Then, with a blunt directness, "I want to know all about this Petroff affair."

Elizabeth started. The tinge of amusement faded. A tremor took its place. What he called the Petroff affair belonged to the nightmare region out of which he had carried her. To speak of it was to bring it back.

Stephen reached forward and took her hand.

"I've got to know," he said. "I can't keep you safe unless I know. I must know what to look out for. You see that, don't you?"

Elizabeth bent her head. He pressed her hand very hard indeed, and then let go of it rather suddenly.

"Well now, let's get it over," he said cheerfully. "To begin with, what's all this about a formula?"

She said the words after him with an involuntary shudder, whilst her hands went to her breast and pressed down upon it painfully.

"A formula?"

"Yes," said Stephen gently. "You said something about it in your sleep that first night in Tronsk, and last night you talked about it when you woke up."

"Did I?" The tremor was shaking her so much that the words shook too.

Stephen went down on his knees before her and took both her hands in his.

"Don't shake like that. Don't be frightened. I won't let anything hurt you—I won't really. Petroff shan't touch you. Is that what you're afraid of?"

She made a great effort and steadied herself.

"I'll tell you."

He had to wait after that, but he showed no impatience, only knelt there, holding her hands, not looking at her. She felt as if she were being held in a strong grasp on the edge of an abyss. She was to look over and tell what she saw there. She was just able to do this while he held her. If he were to let go, she would fall. She began to speak in a low faltering voice without any tone in it.

"We came out eighteen months ago. It was at the beginning of the summer. Nicolas had not lived in Russia since he was a boy. His father was Russian and his mother American. He went to college in America and took an American engineering degree. I met him out there. I was on a visit to the only relations I've got in the world. I'd been ill and couldn't work. They asked me on a long visit. I met Nicolas—" Her voice died away.

Stephen held her hands. After a moment she went on again.

"He had a friend in Russia—they were boys together. Alexis was an engineer too. He got Nicolas the offer of a job at Volkhov. We were both wild to go. Nicolas was very enthusiastic about the Five Year Plan and everything. But when we got there I began to be afraid. You see, he had the American outlook, the American point of view, but he hadn't the protection of being an American. He was a Russian subject. I used to tell him—but he wouldn't listen. He thought he was going to be able to make money. He'd got a new process—a new aluminium alloy. I don't understand these things, but it was going to make a lot of difference in making aeroplanes— they would be stronger and lighter. A man who died gave him the first idea, and he worked it out. There must have been other men in it too, but I don't know who they were. He used to talk to me about it and say what a lot of money we should have when we got back to America. He was going to make some excuse and throw up his job. He didn't seem to understand what a frightful risk he was running. And then all of a sudden something must have leaked out. They sent for him. They asked him if he had a new process. He said no. They let him go that day. He came in and told me he was going to try and get away in the night. He said he couldn't take me—I should be safer where I was. But before he went he made me learn the formula of his process. He said if he didn't get away and I did, I could sell it and it would provide for me. He made me swear that whatever happened I wouldn't give it to *Them*. I learnt the formula by heart. He didn't dare put it on paper. He told me to say it over every day so as not to forget anything. I think I could say it in my sleep."

"You did," said Stephen.

He felt her shudder.

"I know."

"Go on."

She shuddered again.

"Nicolas went away. It was night. I never saw him again. He was taken—and—shot."

Stephen looked up for a moment. His eyes were wild and bright, but when he spoke his voice was very gentle.

"Did you love him very much?"

Elizabeth looked down into the abyss. Her own personal tragedy had been swallowed up there. She had not loved Nicolas Radin, but she had mourned for him. She had loved someone whom she thought was Nicolas, and she had found herself married to a Nicolas who became more and more a stranger. She thought of this self-centred, moody being, with his impatience, his hot fits of anger and his cold indifference, his disregard of her warnings, and she felt again the pang with which she had parted from her first romantic dream. The dream was not Nicolas, but she had once thought it was.

Stephen looked down again.

"Please go on. We haven't much time."

Elizabeth's voice became a mere whisper.

"Next day Petroff came," she said, and paused on that. It was a long pause, but at last she went on. "He said Nicolas had been shot as a counter-revolutionary—and all his papers belonged to the State. He took everything. Next day he came back. He asked me about the aluminium process. He went on asking me until I fainted. They scraped the walls and pulled up the floors, but they didn't find any more papers. I told them Nicolas never wrote anything down. If it hadn't been for the process, I think they would have just turned me out to starve like they do if they don't think you are any use to them, but they wanted the process very badly. They didn't think I knew anything, but they weren't quite sure...Petroff took me to Tronsk where his mother was. He told me I was lucky to be housed and fed in return for looking after her." She gave the faintest, saddest ghost of a laugh. "She didn't feed me very much."

His hands tightened over hers.

"Is there any more? You'd better tell me everything."

Everything? Twenty-four hours in a day—seven days in a week—four weeks in the month and two or three days over—twelve months to make up the year. And every hour of every day filled with the petty, senseless cruelties of an old woman to whom these cruelties were meat and drink.

"Tell me," said Stephen.

She shook from head to foot.

"I—can't. She made me feel—degraded. It was like living in a sewer."

Stephen said one word very low.

"Petroff?"

She never knew what a relief her answer brought him.

"No—not like that—no." She breathed quickly and went on. "He didn't come much—only now and then. I think they stopped bothering about the process. I was just a useful slave. Then about a month ago Petroff was there for a week. He took more notice of me. I got frightened. One night I woke up saying the formula aloud. I had to sleep with the old woman. Petroff was in the next room. He didn't hear me, but after that I was afraid to go to sleep till he had gone. A week ago he came back. In the evening the old woman said, 'I wish you'd bring a gag for this foreigner of yours! She keeps me awake all night talking in her sleep.' It wasn't true of course, but she must have heard something. Petroff made a disgusting joke, but afterwards they sent me out of the room and talked. When I came back, he began about the formula again. He said, 'My mother says you say the same thing over and over again, and she doesn't think you're saying your prayers.' Then he battered at me with questions. I don't know why I didn't tell him the formula and have done with it, but I'd promised Nicolas, and then—they hate everyone so, and they talk all the time about World Revolution. It kept coming to me—if they get the process and it helps them to make these stronger, lighter aeroplanes, what will they do with them? That used to haunt me, and I got as if I *couldn't* speak. I only wanted to die. That night the old woman was taken ill. There wasn't time for anything except nursing her. Petroff was unhappy. He cried and behaved like a child. When she was dead, he said how lonely he was, and that I must take care of him, because his life was very valuable to the Cause. He said if I told him the formula he would marry me, but in any case I must be kind to him and comfort him, because he was all alone. He got very drunk, and I ran out of the house...Then you found me."

There was just a moment when the silence seemed to Stephen to be ringing with the words he must not say. Yes, he had found her, and he would keep her. The words rang in his head, and rang in the silence. Elizabeth was aware of them, as someone who is quite deaf may be aware that the air is vibrating with the clamour of unheard bells. She was disturbed without knowing why. But it had been a relief to speak—the greatest relief that she had known for more than a year. The burden of her secret knowledge had been lifted. Stephen could carry it now.

Chapter Seven

THE SNOW did not come. A bitter wind blew, and the sky was heavy and dull.

Elizabeth's strength came back to her. She was astonished at the number of hours she could sleep. She went out next morning into the yard which lay behind the house. There was a rough barn with a diminished store of fodder for the one cow, which was the last pride of Akulina's heart. Once she had had three; now it was as much as they could do to keep even one alive through the winter. She grumbled on about the old times and the new without waiting for any reply. She did not trouble herself to be at all discreet. If she couldn't say what she liked at her time of life and in her own backyard, things had come to a pretty pass. Indeed that was just what they had come to. What was the use of sweating and straining to grow crops for *Them* to take away and hand over to townsfolk who had never done an honest day's work on the land in their lives? "And if you hide a bit of corn to keep you alive through the winter they go on as if you'd done murder." As if it wasn't hard enough to get a living anyway, with neither of them as young as they were and Katinka so far away that she might just as well be dead. "Those who have ten children can have them all under one roof, but when you've only got one she's bound to go as far away as she can." She and Yuri had had other children, but they had lost them all, and now, when she could have done very well with a good strong girl about the house, Stefan must needs go and bring home a useless dreep of a creature with about as much colour and strength as a tallow dip which has been left out in the August sun.

Elizabeth endeavoured to placate her.

"I'm getting stronger."

"With those hands? What work have they ever done, I should like to know!"

"I can sew," said Elizabeth.

"And embroider?"

"Oh yes."

"And what's the good of that, now there's no cloth to be had? Even if one had money to buy, the government shop is only open one day in the month—and the good-for-nothing rubbish they sell!" She made a gesture of contempt. "We used to weave our own cloth, but *They* won't have it. Fine new times—that's what I say! You've no clothes but what you stand up in, I suppose?"

Elizabeth shook her head.

"When I married," said Akulina with pride, "I'd a Sunday dress as well as a working one, and I had two embroidered handkerchiefs. I have them still. In those days stuff was made to last, not to fall to pieces when it had been worn three times."

While she grumbled, Elizabeth was thinking. Her bad Russian would be less noticeable in a village where a mixture of Russian and Ukrainian would probably be quite usual. She must say as little as possible of course. Perhaps she wouldn't have to go out much.

She found next day that she would have to make a public appearance. There was to be a special broadcast at the Soviet House, when a speech by Voroshiloff would be received. To stay away would be to expose oneself to a charge of being lacking in Revolutionary ardour. Red Stefan's wife must be above suspicion in that respect. She could at any rate hope to be lost in a crowd, since the whole village would be there.

They walked up the road to the pink-washed building which Elizabeth had seen standing out amongst the village houses on the day of their arrival. It contained a fair-sized hall furnished with benches. At the far end was a platform upon which there were a couple of chairs, a table, and a wireless installation. From the wall a picture of Lenin looked down, symbolically draped in red, with the blood-coloured star of the Revolution above, and the hammer and sickle below. Under this portrait was a second small table, on which reposed Lenin's works—the Scriptures of the new State.

The room seemed quite full as they came into it. It was lighted by unshaded wall-lamps with reflectors, and the smell of soot and oil mingled with the smell of sheepskins, tobacco and unwashed clothing. As they entered, the village schoolmaster was concluding a speech which was evidently intended as a stop-gap, for at intervals he turned from the audience to fidget nervously with the wireless controls, when a loud roaring sound supervened. Each time he did this he explained all over again that there was some trouble with the transmission, after which he continued his speech, which was all about the blessings of education. He was a thin, worried man with a weak, worried voice. No one appeared to be taking the slightest interest in what he was saying. He did not even seem to be interested in it himself. The other chair on the platform was occupied by the village President, a grey-haired man with a fine head.

When the schoolmaster turned again to the wireless, Yuri, who had been gazing morosely at the President, remarked in a perfectly audible voice,

"That man cheated me over a cow thirty years ago, and there he sits in a fine chair as if he were a Commissar!"

The people in front of him turned to look, the President opened his mouth to speak, and with a sudden blare from the loud speaker Voroshiloff was addressing them from Moscow. Whatever his natural voice might have been, under the technical defects of the instrument and the schoolmaster's inexpert fumbling it had become a super-voice—enormous, tinny, raucous. It bawled out a sentence about World Revolution and ceased abruptly. A horrible crackling took its place.

The schoolmaster fiddled with the controls, and was evidently about to resume his seat, when a woman pushed through the crowd and, springing on to the platform, turned to face the room. After one glance Elizabeth did not need Akulina's disgusted "Of course she must come shoving in" to tell her that this was Irina. She was tall and well made. She wore the blouse and skirt of a peasant woman, but she wore them with ease and grace. A scarlet kerchief was knotted at her breast, but her head was bare. It was a well shaped head, covered with thick glossy black hair. Elizabeth, gazing at her curiously, received an odd sense of shock. Stephen had said that Irina was good-looking. Good-looking? She was beautiful. She was perhaps the most beautiful person that Elizabeth had ever seen. From that dingy ill-lit platform her beauty bloomed like a flame. That was what she reminded Elizabeth of—a dark and vivid flame. She had a lovely oval face with regular features and large dark eyes. But the burning and the beauty came from within. It shone through her and seemed to light the hall.

She began at once in a clear ringing voice which completely drowned the schoolmaster's attempt to finish his last sentence.

"If we cannot hear Voroshiloff, we can hear Lenin. We can hear the voice of the Revolution speaking in our own hearts and being echoed back from millions of other hearts, not only in the Union of Soviet Republics, but from the world outside, where a million million workers hail the rising of our Red Star and lift up their right hands to join with us in the overthrow of the bloody monster of Capitalism. We aim at the dictatorship of the world proletariat and the dictatorship of the world proletariat is an essential condition precedent to the transformation of World Capitalist Economy into Socialist Economy. The federations of republics will grow into a World Union of Soviet Socialist Republics uniting the whole of mankind under the hegemony of the International Proletariat."

Her voice had a singular dominant quality. Elizabeth saw all the faces in the hall lifted. People who had been fidgeting and whispering now stared in the direction of the platform.

"The bourgeoisie," declaimed Irina—"the bourgeoisie resorts to every means of violence and terror to safeguard its predatory property. Hence the violence of the bourgeoisie can be suppressed only by the stern violence of the proletariat. The conquest of power by the Proletariat is the violent overthrow of bourgeois power and the destruction of the Capitalist State."

The long words rolled over the listeners' heads. Except for a few of the younger ones—little Octobrists of eight or nine, adolescent Pioneers, Young Communists—they neither understood nor wished to understand what Irina was saying. It all sounded very fine and grand, and it was doubtless pleasing to *Them*. In the old days you had to stand well with the land-owners, the people up at the big house. Now they were gone, but there were new masters. The peasant always has a master. Whether you use two flat stones, which is the oldest way of all, or a piece of noisy machinery, which is the very newest, it matters little to the grain which is in process of being ground.

The room was warm and full of the satisfying smell of oil. Irina's voice was mesmeric. She talked about the Agricultural Front, about the Five Year Plan, about the necessity for communizing everything—The Collectivized Farm was essential—resistance to Collectivization must cease—only by way of the Collective Farm could true Socialism be established and the needs of the Proletariat satisfied. At the mention of the Collective Farm a slight glaze filmed the eyes of the listeners. Elizabeth was aware that Irina no longer held them spell-bound. Some deep, instinctive resistance made itself felt.

As Irina paused on a period, Akulina said in a bitter whisper, "Cock-a-doodle-doo! When a hen takes to crowing she's ready for the pot!"

Her neighbour on the bench, a little bent old woman, gave a brief cackle of laughter. She stared inquisitively past Akulina and Yuri at Stefan and the new wife he had brought home. She chuckled again and poked Akulina with her elbow.

"Those crowing ones don't always catch the men," she said.

Akulina snorted. Whatever else Varvara was, she was at least quiet in the house. She said so, not troubling whether her words travelled beyond old Masha or not.

The little old woman giggled.

"To have that one in the house would be like having an earthquake there!" She indicated Irina with a jerk of her chin.

A boy with a wild, thin face had jumped up on a bench in the front of the hall and was talking fervently but not very audibly about the Young Communist movement. The fidgeting had begun again, and a buzz of talk. The two old ladies continued their conversation with a good deal of enjoyment.

Irina remained upon the platform. Standing beneath the portrait of Lenin, she surveyed the inattentive audience with an air of disdainful impatience.

"Looks at us as if we weren't good enough to tread on!" was Akulina's comment.

Masha nodded.

"She'd have had your Stefan fast enough if she could have got him. It wasn't for want of trying if she didn't. What's this girl like that he's married? She looks a quiet one, as you say."

"Oh, she's quiet." Akulina's tone was disparaging in the extreme.

"Any dowry?"

"Who has a dowry nowadays, when we're all stripped to the bone? Three cows I had, as you know—and how we're going to get the one that's left through the winter—"

"Is she any good in the house?" pursued old Masha.

Yuri had gone to sleep. From across him Stephen caught enough of the women's conversation to make him uneasy. Masha was the most inquisitive old woman in the village, and would undoubtedly pass on all she could glean to her six daughters-in-law, and all her neighbours. The gleaning would be well garnished.

The Young Communist was still addressing a completely inattentive room. Stephen thought it was time to make a diversion. He jumped on the bench and began to sing *The Red Flag* in a fine rolling baritone. At the first note Irina's expression changed. Exaltation replaced disdain. Springing to the front of the platform, she joined in the song. It was immediately taken up by all the younger part of the audience.

The trivial nursery-rhyme tune went with a swing. Elizabeth's fancy gave it its original German words. The deserted lover naïvely addresses a fir-tree:

"O fir-tree, oh, fir-tree,
How green are your leaves—"

He contrasts them with his sweetheart's fickle behaviour:

"O maiden, O maiden,
How false is your heart!
You swore to me when I was lucky.
Now I am poor, you throw me over.
O maiden, O maiden,
How false is your heart!"

It was a far cry from this pastoral simplicity to the angry passions of *The Red Flag*, yet these had an ugly naïveté of their own.

She looked up at Stephen towering above her, and thought how strange it was to see him swinging his arms in time to the rhythm and throwing a world of revolutionary fervour into his fine voice.

When the song was finished, there were cries of "More!" and "Go on, Stefan!" A girl of about seventeen began to sing, but she was hushed down. Stefan was evidently a popular performer, and there were demands for favourite songs. In response to one of these he gave a highly dramatic rendering of a folk-song about a man who was hunted down by a wolf. It was rather a blood-curdling performance, and old Yuri woke up to mutter, and mumble disapproval.

When the last "Yoi-hoi!" had died away, Stephen jumped down from the bench, to find Irina at his elbow. Elizabeth had seen her leave her place on the platform and make her way towards them with an uneasy sense of danger. When she saw her standing by Stephen, the thought of how well matched they were passed through her mind like a draught of cold air. She was as finely made for a woman as he for a man. Her head rose above his shoulder, while her dark hair and eyes and warm, vivid pallor were in perfect contrast to his blue eyes and ruddy colouring.

Irina addressed him at once with an air of intimacy.

"That was well sung! We have missed you here—I have missed you. There are many things which I would like to discuss with you. You have not been in Moscow?"

He shook his head.

"Oh no. Have you?"

Irina dropped her voice.

"Yes—and there is much to tell you. There are great developments coming." Her eyes glowed as she spoke. "But we can't speak of that here. We must meet and talk."

As she spoke, the schoolmaster came nervously up. At close quarters he was astonishingly like an ant. His hands moved continually like antennae. His long bony neck would have looked better in a collar. He had with him a female ant, whom Elizabeth immediately guessed to be his wife. They wore the same large convex glasses and cut their hair in exactly the same way, but the eyes behind the female glasses were less worried and more watchful. They shook hands with Stephen, and next moment Elizabeth was being presented as Varvara Ivanovna and his wife. Behind his fatuous smile of the new-made husband, Stephen watched her with apprehension. Would she pass? Or would there be something which would set Irina's keen wits to work—guessing?

He looked, and saw a pale mask with vacant eyes and a mouth that dropped at the corners. When the schoolmaster and his wife spoke to her, she fingered her skirts and looked down.

Stephen nudged her.

"Where are your manners? You should say how-do-you-do to my good friends Anton Ilyitch and Anna Stefanovna." Then, over her head, he explained, "She has never seen so much company before."

Through her down-dropped eyelids Elizabeth was aware of Irina's scrutiny. She smiled a faint, empty smile, hung her head, and twined her fingers in her skirt. It would be as well not to show more of her hands than she could help. They were roughened by work, but they were too small and fine for a peasant. She did not like Irina's silence. She was more aware of it than of the conversation between Stephen and the others.

Irina broke it at last.

"Are your parents alive?"

Elizabeth shook her head. Strangely and suddenly the question touched a hidden spring of pain. Her parents had died in the same year ten years ago when she was only fourteen. Such an old wound to hurt again in this keen way. No acting could have served her like the tears which came stinging to her eyes. Some of them brimmed over and rolled down her cheeks. She lifted a fold of her skirt and wiped them away.

"They are dead?" said Irina. "It is very foolish of you to cry. Old people are a burden to the State. It is we who are young who have to fight in the battle of World Revolution." She turned to Stephen. "I am going now, and you can walk back with me. Anton and Anna will not be home just yet, so we can talk undisturbed."

"Look at that!" said old Masha in a scandalized whisper. "Not a week married, and she carries him off as bold as you please, and his wife stands there as limp as a bit of potato-peeling and lets her do it! Why, I'd have had my two hands full of her hair if it had been me! What's the matter with her? Isn't she right in the head?"

Akulina shrugged her shoulders.

"She's a poor creature, and the Lord knows why Stefan picked her. But that's a man all over—so long as the girl's his own picking, she's all right for him."

Elizabeth sat down on the end of the bench. Under the twisted folds of her skirt her hands were clenched. Her anger surprised her. She tried to argue it down, but it remained. If she were really Stephen's wife, she could not be angrier. It was a self-evident absurdity that she should be angry at all. She had no longer the slightest inclination to weep. Her eyes were dry and hot. She made her face as blank as possible and stared sullenly down into her lap.

Stephen walked over the frozen snow with Irina. She lodged in the schoolmaster's house, an arrangement which was the source of much watchful suspicion on the part of the schoolmaster's wife, and of a mixture of self-conscious terror and vanity in the schoolmaster himself. That so beautiful a person as Irina, and one who was said to have the ear of influential Comrades in Moscow, should have her name linked with his, that Anna should make him jealous scenes about her, was both flattering and alarming.

Irina began to talk about him at once.

"Anton is becoming quite intolerable. Because I discuss things with him he seems to think that I am in love with him. And as for Anna, she's so jealous that I should not be surprised if she became insane."

Stephen wondered if she was as cold-blooded as she sounded.

"Perhaps it would be better not to make her jealous."

"Jealousy is madness," said Irina calmly. "I am not responsible for Anna's fancies. I am glad that you are back, so that I may have someone rational to talk to."

"I do not think I shall be here for long," said Stephen.

"You move about too much. Soon it will not be so easy to do that. There is to be an internal passport system. That is to get rid of the remnants of the proscribed classes, who have swarmed like parasites into the towns. Everyone will have to have papers, and it will not be so easy to get about."

"Yes, I have heard that. It will be a very good thing," said Stephen indifferently.

Did she mean anything? Was it a warning? An internal passport system was going to make his work about a hundred times more difficult and dangerous than it was already. It was going to make getting Elizabeth out of the country something very near an impossibility. The answer to that was, "Hurry, hurry, hurry! Get a move on! Get her away and over the border before they can get their passports going."

Irina said, "You are very silent."

That wouldn't do. No, by gum, it wouldn't. He said the first thing that came into his head.

"Sometimes one doesn't want to talk."

"When one is with a friend—yes, I have felt that too. In a true friendship like ours, where there is a common ideology, words are not necessary, yet sometimes they give one pleasure. You do not imagine—" She broke off without finishing her sentence.

"What were you going to say?"

"It was about Anton. I do not wish you to think that I have a particular friendship for him. Physically, he repels me."

Stephen was not surprised to hear it, but he found the trend of the conversation a little alarming.

"Whereas you," said Irina in a clear ringing tone which she did not attempt to lower—"you, of course, have always attracted me."

This being one of those remarks to which it is difficult to think of a suitable answer, Stephen made no answer at all. If Irina meant to make love to him, it was going to be a damned difficult situation to handle—difficult, but neither so difficult nor so dangerous as an inquisition upon Elizabeth.

Irina's clear voice flowed on.

"I would not accept a marriage relationship which was founded on physical attraction alone—you must not think that of me. There must be community of ideas and a common devotion to Soviet Socialist ideals. I should consider a union of these three elements necessary for happiness in marriage. In fact, they constitute love as I understand it."

"That is very well put," said Stephen.

"Yes," said Irina. "We have that community of ideas—I have often noticed it. Why did you marry this girl Varvara, with whom you have not an idea in common? I do not mind telling you that it has lowered you very much in my esteem."

They had arrived at the schoolmaster's house. Irina opened the door, walked in, and began to light the lamp. When the wick flared it threw her shadow upon the opposite wall. It hung there, very tall and black, like something that menaced them both. She slipped the chimney over the flame, straightened herself, and went on as calmly as if there had been no interruption.

"Is your marriage a registered one?"

Stephen shook his head. Lies were awkward things and apt to trip one up. He told no more of them than he could help. The fact that his marriage was unregistered would shock no one except a few of the older people in the village.

"Perhaps we shall register it—I don't know."

"Why do you not come in and shut the door? Whether you register your marriage or not is nothing to me—you must understand that."

"How could it be?"

Irina looked at him with contempt.

"Now you are not being honest. When two people are friends, the bad conduct of one must concern the other."

"I am sorry you should think my conduct bad," said Stephen in his most matter-of-fact voice. He did not wish to have a scene with Irina, but he could see that she was heading that way. Perhaps it would be better to have it out with her and get it over.

Her eyes flashed dark fire.

"You make a low animal marriage like that, and you do not expect me to think your conduct bad?"

"A man must marry some time."

Irina lifted her head. The shadow moved behind her on the wall.

"And you choose this Varvara for your life-companion. What a companion!"

"I had better go," said Stephen.

He turned to the door, but she was there before him. She leaned against it with outspread arms and barred his way.

"Irina—let me go!"

Her arms fell. She said,

"You have gone already."

As this, unfortunately, was not the literal truth, he was obliged to wait until she chose to let him pass.

"Our marriage would have been a true companionship." There was no flush upon the even whiteness of her skin, but her eyes blazed. "Did you not know that I would have been your wife?"

"Come, Irina!" said Stephen. "What is the good of all this? Since I have a wife, we cannot be married."

"A wife!" said Irina bitterly. "A half-witted creature whom you picked up no one knows where!"

"Come, come," he said—"she is my wife. There is no use in this."

The fire went out of Irina's eyes.

"Why did you do it?" she said.

Stephen shrugged his big shoulders.

"How can I tell you that?"

There was a moment of silence. She stepped away from the door and stood at the table with her shoulder turned to Stephen. In a lower voice than he had ever heard her use she said,

"The wife of a kulak said to me last year, 'It is my turn to-day, but it will be yours to-morrow.' They were turning her out of her house. She said to me, 'You'll be unhappy some day.'"

For the first time Stephen felt moved. He said,

"I'm sorry, Irina."

She went on speaking as if she had not heard him.

"Another person's conduct should not be able to make one unhappy. That is a weakness." She looked suddenly over her shoulder and said, "Do you love me?"

Stephen said, "No."

"Why?"

"How can I say? I don't know why."

She beat with the flat of her hand on the table.

"Do you love—her?"

He made a gesture with his hands.

"Irina, what is the good of asking such questions? You are hurting yourself, and you are hurting me. Let us be good comrades as we were before."

"No—that is impossible."

"Why should it be impossible?"

She turned away from him and looked down at her own hands. Then quite suddenly she faced him again.

"Divorce her!" she said.

Stephen turned on his heel and went out.

Chapter Eight

AKULINA WAS grumbling when Stephen came home.

"Click-clack and waste of time—that's what I call your meeting! And wanton behaviour on the top of that! Idleness breeds mischief! I've no patience with it. These winter evenings when the beasts are bedded, young women ought to be weaving, not standing up on a platform making eyes at the men. And as for you, Stefan, you ought to be ashamed of yourself. You'll be in trouble if you don't mind what you're doing, and you won't be the first—no, nor the last either. And her to come in here and tell me to take down the blessed ikon! As if it wasn't enough that we don't light the lamp in front of it any more—and I hope Those above don't hold it up against us! And as if that wasn't enough, in she comes and says, 'You ought to take it down and have a picture like mine.' And I can well believe that there are doings in any room of hers which she wouldn't want a blessed saint to be looking at! But praise God that's not the case in this house, and never will be whilst I'm in it!"

Akulina tossed her head and began to clatter about the stove. She opened the narrow door and a red glow shone from it. Stephen brought wood without speaking and stoked the fire. Akulina banged the door again.

"*Superstition!*" she said. "Oh, that's a great word with them—isn't it? Superstition, superstition, superstition—everything's superstition you can't see with your two eyes every day of the week and twice on Sundays! Cackling geese! I could tell them a few things—yes, that I could! Why, there was what happened to my own father, and my mother never let him hear the last of it, though it happened before they were married."

"You can't tell *them*, but you can tell us," said Stephen.

Akulina was mixing something in a bowl. She stirred vigorously and tossed her head.

"You may believe it, or you may not, but this is what happened."

The lamplight was yellow in the small room. Yuri lay on the upper tier of the stove, smoking. The smell of the rank tobacco and the faint blue of the smoke hung overhead. Stephen sat up to the table. He had a piece of hard wood in one hand and a knife in the other. Elizabeth, from the edge of her bed, wondered what he was going to do with the wood.

Akulina went on stirring and talking.

"It happened when my father was quite young. His father was a serf on the Darensky estate, and his mother had been foster-mother to the young prince, so they were foster-brothers and of the same age, and when the young prince went to and fro to his estates in the north he used to take my father with him as his body-servant. It was a very fine place for shooting and hunting. They used to be there every summer. Well, one day when my father was about two or three and twenty years old, he was riding alone in the forest with the prince. They were a long way from the house—perhaps half a day's journey, perhaps more—and they were in the deep forest, just the prince and my father and no one with them. So then they came to a clearing where there were wild raspberries growing, and in amongst the raspberries there was a young girl, and she was picking them into a basket of fresh green leaves. She didn't look up for the horses, but went on picking. The prince called out to her, but she took no notice. She went on picking the raspberries into her basket. My father said she was the prettiest girl he had ever seen—yes, and stuck to it too in spite of my mother's tongue. He said her cheeks were as red as the raspberries, and her mouth like fresh raspberry juice, only redder still. Well, the prince was angry because she took no notice of him, so he told my father to go and fetch her. In those days if a young prince had a fancy to a girl he took her, so my father left his horse standing and began to push his way through the raspberry brake. The prince sat there and watched him, and this is what he saw. As soon as my father got within catching distance, the girl ran behind a bush. My father went after her, and there was the prince sitting on his horse, waiting. Presently he called, and no one answered him and no one came. He took my father's horse by the bridle and rode round to the other side of the clearing in a great anger. He rode, and called, and shouted for an hour, but there was neither hair, hide nor hoof of my father nor of the girl, so he said 'Devil take them both!' and rode away home." She turned to the stove and arranged her mixture in four flat cakes to bake.

"That's not the end of the story," said Stephen. His piece of wood had taken a rough animal shape. There was the outline of a head and paws.

"The end?" said Akulina as she scraped her bowl. "Where should I be if that had been the end of my father? No, praise God!" She let go of the spoon to cross herself.

"What happened?" said Elizabeth.

"You may well ask. The prince was in great anger, and if my father had come home that night, anything might have happened. But he didn't come home that night, nor the next, nor the next, nor the one after that. They sent out men to search for him, but they couldn't find him, and what's more, they couldn't find that clearing where the raspberries grew. So then the prince left off being angry, because he thought his foster-brother had been torn in pieces and devoured by some wild beast of the woods.

"A month went by—yes, it was a whole month—and the prince went hunting with his cousin who had come there to visit him. They were separated from the men who were with them...No, I don't know what they were hunting. The forest was full of beasts, and they could hunt what they liked. My father said it was the finest place for hunting he had ever seen. Well then, all of a sudden they came out into a clearing, those two, and in a minute the prince knew the place. There was the raspberry brake, only there was no more fruit in it and the leaves had begun to wither. And there was the bush where he had lost my father. He called out to his cousin to tell him that this was the place. And he had no sooner done that than the bush stirred and out from behind it came my father. He came pushing through the brake, and the prince's cousin slashed at him with his whip and gave him every bad name he could think of. But the prince never spoke a word until my father had come up close to him, and then he said, very cold and stern, 'Where have you been, Ivan?' My father stared at him as if his eyes would drop out of his head. 'You sent me to fetch her, little brother,' he said. 'I didn't tell you to take a month over it,' said the prince. And the prince's cousin said, 'Why do you talk to the fellow? Tie him to your stirrup and gallop him home. That's how I'd deal with a runaway.' The prince didn't take any notice of him. He was looking at my father. 'Why did you do it?' he said. 'And where have you been all this month that we've thought you dead?'

"My father said that when he heard that word it was like a brand of hot iron on the top of his head. He put his hand on the horse's shoulder to keep himself from falling down. 'A month, little brother?' he said. 'It was just now—and you sent me, and I came back again. And where did *he* come from?' said my father, looking at the prince's cousin, a big man, very strong and ugly, sitting up on his horse and scowling like the devil. 'Look at the raspberry brake,' said the prince. He took my father by the shoulder and turned him round. And there were the leaves withering and the fruit all gone. When my father saw that, he became very much afraid. 'The leaves!' he said. And the prince said, 'It's a full month, Ivan. Where have you been?' Well, to the last day of his life that was just what my father couldn't tell. He went after the girl, and when they were behind the bush she smiled at him and took one of the raspberries out of her basket and set it against his mouth, and from that moment he didn't know anything that happened until he heard the prince's voice calling out, 'This is the place.' And when he heard that, he came out from behind the bush just as I've told you. There were people in our village said that he had run away with the girl and stayed with her as long as she would have him, but that is not true, and a wise woman told my father that it was a lucky thing for him that it was only the one raspberry he tasted, for if he had had more, the devil would have had him, and no chance of his ever coming back."

"Did he get into trouble?" said Elizabeth.

"Oh no," said Akulina cheerfully. "The prince was his foster-brother and very fond of him, you see. But my father would never eat a raspberry to the day of his death."

"It's a good story," said Stephen. He looked across at Elizabeth and his eyes twinkled. He seemed very strong and merry, sitting there carving his bit of wood.

"It's a *true* story!" said Akulina with a toss of the head. "And it's black shame on you, Stefan, to sit there and doubt your own great-grandfather's word. Where would you have been if he had stayed with the raspberry witch, I should like to know."

"Not in this room," said Stephen. "And that would have been a pity—wouldn't it?"

He looked again at Elizabeth, and Elizabeth looked down into her lap. "He looks at every woman like that," she said to herself. But she didn't mean every woman, she meant Irina.

Akulina's scolding voice broke in.

"No good comes of despising one's parents, I can tell you that, unless they should be evil-doers and witches—and praise God that's a thing we've never had in our family, unless it was my father's cousin that married a woman from over the Lapp border, and then it was only his mother-in-law, and that doesn't count for any kin to us."

"Was she a witch?" said Stephen.

"Was she!" Akulina's tone became very shrill indeed. "Everyone knows there are a lot of witches in Lapland, and only a man that was looking for trouble would have gone there for a wife."

"Tell us about it, little grandmother," said Stephen. "I don't know that story."

"What's the good of telling stories to people who don't believe them?" said Akulina. But when she had had a look at her baking, she came and sat down on one of the stools and went on talking. "An unbelieving lot—that's what this generation is. And what the next will be like, the Lord knows. Praise God, I shan't be here to see it."

"Varvara will believe every word you say," said Stephen—"and so will I."

Akulina snapped her fingers.

"Do you think I believe you? But this is the story, and the man it happened to was your great-grandfather's own cousin, the son of his father's brother. Mikhail was his name, and he was a forester on that estate I told you of up in the north."

"Prince Darensky's estate?"

Akulina nodded.

"He was a forester and he lived in a hut in the forest, and that's where he brought his Lapp wife and her mother. The girl was well enough, as I've heard, but the old woman had witch written all over her. Mikhail would have gone to her funeral with a light heart, I can tell you. Not one hand's turn did she do to earn her keep. In summer she'd sit in the open door muttering to herself, and in winter she'd lie on the stove and sleep. Well, one summer's night Mikhail woke up, and when he put out his hand to find his wife, she wasn't there. He called out, but there wasn't any answer at all. He unfastened the door, and as soon as he did that, something ran over his foot. There was a gust of wind that pulled the door out of his hand and slammed it, and when he turned round, there was the old woman looking at him with eyes like a snake. 'What is it?' she said. 'Where's my wife?' said Mikhail. 'Where are your eyes?' said the old woman. And with that he looked again, and there was his wife lying down in her usual place. He went up close, and for all he could tell, she was asleep, but when he put his hand on her, he could feel that she was breathing quickly, as if she had been running. He looked at the old woman again, and she had her hand at her mouth. There was a sight of something green between her fingers like a fresh-plucked leaf, and he could see her jaws working as she mumbled it, and all the time she kept her eyes on him.

"Well, Mikhail didn't say anything, but he thought a good deal, and he took notice that the moon was full that night.

"A month went by and the moon was full again. The old woman, who had seemed to have new life in her after the last full moon, had come to be so feeble that Mikhail was in great hopes that she wouldn't last much longer. On the night of the full moon his wife made him a stew with savoury herbs. He was just thinking how good it was, when he remembered that she had given him just such a stew on the night of the last full moon, and after that he didn't eat any more of it. They all lay down to sleep, but Mikhail set himself to stay awake. Well then, he couldn't do it. He was so drowsy that his eyelids wouldn't stay open, and when he pinched himself he couldn't feel the pinches. He heard the old woman say, 'Run, honey-mouse, run!' and with that he fell into a deeper sleep than he'd ever been in in his life.

"He couldn't say how long he'd been asleep, when something waked him. He didn't know what it was, but he felt afraid. He jumped up and got a light. His wife was lying there asleep, but the old woman had her head up looking at him as she had done before, and between her lips there was the end of a green leaf. 'Where did you get that leaf?' said Mikhail. 'You're dreaming,' said the old woman, and the leaf was gone, because she'd swallowed it. And when he put his hand on his wife, her breath was coming so fast that it frightened him."

"Where had she been?" said Elizabeth.

Akulina got up, opened the oven door, turned her cakes, and came back again.

"Well may you ask," she said. "Yes indeed—where had she been? That was what Mikhail was asking himself every minute of the day. At one time he was ready to drag his young wife by the hair and hit her head with a stone until she told him, and at another he could have taken his axe to the old woman. He told my father it was like a dozen devils talking in his head. In the end he ran away from them and went to the priest in the next village, who was a very holy man, which is more than you can say about all of them. The priest listened to what Mikhail had to say, and when he had finished, he told him what he must do. So Mikhail went home again, and when his wife came out to meet him, he spoke kindly to her, and that night he praised her cooking and they were merry together. So things went on towards the next full moon. The old woman had been brisk and spry enough the first part of the month, but come to the end of it, she began to pine and dwine again. So they came to the night of the full moon. The young wife cooked such a supper as would make any man's mouth water, but Mikhail restrained himself. He made believe to eat, but neither bite nor sup of that cooking passed his lips. When the time came to sleep, he lay down in his place with his wife beside him. He closed his eyes, but this time there was no drowsiness in him, he was broad awake. He said over and over to himself the words which the priest had taught him, and every now and then he put out his hand to feel if his wife was there. It must have been about midnight when he heard the old woman stir. She put up her head and began to mutter like someone talking in her sleep. Then all at once she called out clear and shrill, 'Run, honey-mouse, run!' and with that something ran over Mikhail in the dark. He stared at the door. It did not fit quite close, and the moon shone in along the sill two fingers wide. He saw something small and black run through the crack, and when he put out his hand to feel for his wife, she wasn't there.

"Well then he knew what he had to do, because the priest had told him. He went out of the house in haste and barred the door on the outside with the bar of wood which he had made ready, and when he had done that, he filled all the crack between the door and the door-sill with the clay which he had kneaded and mixed with the holy water which the priest had given him. And after that he took in his hand a bowl with the rest of the holy water in it and waited for what would happen next. It was very bright moonlight. The hut stood in a clearing, and the moon was over the trees. There was a bush beside the door, and Mikhail stood behind the bush with the bowl of holy water in his hand. Whether the old witch inside got the smell of it or not, he couldn't say, but presently he heard her get up and move about. She came to the door and tried it, and found it fast. He heard her go dragging back to her place again. He might have been waiting an hour, or maybe two, when a wind came blowing between the trees. It made the sort of sound that you don't like to hear when you are out alone, and it was colder than a summer wind ought to have been. It came in three gusts and died away again. And the first thing Mikhail heard after that was a little scratching sound like a dry leaf moving on the ground. He looked round the bush, and there was the smallest, prettiest mouse he had ever seen trying to get in under the door. It had pale honey-coloured fur and black eyes, and it held in its mouth a fresh green leaf. Mikhail saw it run to and fro along the sill scratching with its paws, and every time it touched the clay he had kneaded with the holy water, it let out a squeak and ran backwards. From inside the house Mikhail could hear that the old woman was moving again. He heard her move, and he heard her claw at the door to get it open, and he heard her call 'Come, honey-mouse, come!' And with that he threw the holy water which he had in his bowl, souse on to the creature that was scrabbling there at the sill."

Akulina paused and looked round her with an air of triumph.

"Souse," she said—"right onto the door-sill and onto that honey-mouse creature. And what happened then? Mikhail told my father that his heart turned right over inside him with fright. He heard his wife scream as if she was being murdered, and he heard the old woman screech like a lost soul, which is just what she was. He heard her fall down inside the door, but he stood where he was and couldn't move, because there was his wife stretched out as if she was dead, with her forehead on the door-sill and her two hands catching at the posts. After a while he stooped down and turned her over. She looked as if she was dead, and in her mouth, clenched fast between her teeth, there was a fresh green leaf. He had a great work to get it from her, and it wasn't a job he'd any fancy for, but in the end he managed it. Then he unbarred the door and went into the hut. The old witch lay dead upon the threshold. He stepped over her and went to the hearth and burned the leaf to a white ash before he did anything else. When he had finished doing that, he turned round, and there was his wife smiling at him, and yawning. 'I feel as if I had run a hundred versts,' she said. 'You may have run five hundred for all I know,' said Mikhail, watching her. And that was all she ever said about the matter. She didn't shed any tears for her mother, and you may be sure that Mikhail didn't. And she made him a good enough wife after that—at least Mikhail made no complaints. But witchcraft will out, and it was a daughter of hers who bewitched the monk Boris."

Stephen's carving was now quite a recognizable bear. He looked up from putting in the eye to say,

"What story is that, little grandmother?"

"One you won't hear to-night," said Akulina.

She withdrew the cakes from the oven, set them on the table, and poked up Yuri, who had fallen into a doze.

Elizabeth ate her cake and wondered what it was made of. Rye, grit, chaff were all possible ingredients. But it was crisp and hot. Very dry, though. It was like an echo to her thoughts when Stephen said,

"Come, little grandmother, give us some cheese. This is too dry alone."

"Cheese!" said Akulina in a scandalized tone. "Are we to eat roubles? Or do you wish it to be talked of in the village, so that people may say we are kulaks and throw us out to starve? Cheese indeed!"

"Oh, I'm Red enough to be able to eat a bit of cheese without getting into trouble," said Stephen, laughing. "Besides, who's to know?"

Akulina tossed her head. Her black eyes snapped.

"That you may well ask! There is an eye at every chink and an ear at every crack in these bad days. Who was there to say that Nikita had grain hidden under the floor of his barn? Did I know it, or any honest person in the village? Yet someone tells *Them.* Nikita is turned out and his house pulled down—yes, the very timbers are taken, and he and his wife and their four children are driven away, God knows where. Without a doubt they have all perished. What hearts of stone *They* must have to do such things! There was that poor Anna with a baby at her breast and another that could only just walk, and two older children, and all of them screaming and wailing and begging for mercy. Your fine friend Irina went by and heard them. For once she was silent and had nothing to say. We were all there, weeping with Anna and trying to console her—but what can you say to one who is being driven out to perish with her children? All at once Anna screamed out, 'It is you who have brought this on us!' and she pointed with her finger at Irina. 'Why do you come here to destroy us? One day you will be punished for this—yes, one day you too will be unhappy!'"

"Was it Irina who told?" asked Elizabeth in a tone of horror.

"How should I know?" said Akulina crossly. "Someone told, and therefore six persons must perish. Even the worst of the old landlords didn't do such a thing as that. And it was his own grain, that he had sweated for, ploughing, sowing, reaping, storing. And for what? That he and his family might perish! Why should we grow grain any more or make a little cheese? Perhaps it will be our turn next. Perhaps you yourself, who are so Red, will go to *Them* and say, 'Yuri and Akulina have cheeses stored in the thatch of their house.'"

Stephen burst out laughing.

"Let us at least eat one of the cheeses now before all these things happen," he said.

Akulina went away grumbling, but she brought out a cheese, and a bottle of the forbidden home-brew.

"Since you have had a wedding without a feast, you may have a feast without a wedding," she said.

Yuri drank most of the liquor, which had a strong and horrible smell. When he had emptied two bottles of it, he told them the whole story of how the village President had cheated him thirty years before. It was over a black and white cow, and he had never got his own back. He went on telling the story until he fell asleep.

When she had cleared away, Akulina filled the lamp in front of the ikon and lighted it. "After such talk of witches and were-mice, I'll run no risks for this night," she said. She crossed herself and genuflected before the ikon.

When the other lamp was extinguished and all in the house was dark, the red light burned with a steady glow. Elizabeth found it comforting. She watched it until she fell asleep.

Chapter Nine

SHE AWOKE with a start. For a moment she was back in the room which she had had to share with Petroff's mother, rousing, as she had been roused a dozen times in every night, to go here, to go there, to fetch this or that, to trim a lamp or light a fire, to prepare food, and all the time to be called every foul name. Then she was on her straw bed in Yuri's house, very warm and safe, with the red lamp shining before the ikon in the corner and Stephen saying her name:

"Elizabeth—are you awake?"

At first she could not tell where she was. There was a faint crimson twilight round the lamp, but the rest of the room was quite dark. Then he spoke again, and she heard him move. He was quite close to her. He said,

"Are you awake?" and after a pause he repeated her name— "Elizabeth."

She raised herself then and asked,

"What is it?"

"May I talk to you?" said Stephen. His voice sounded very near indeed, but she couldn't see him. "It's a most awful shame to wake you up, but it's so much the safest time to talk. It would take a bomb going off right under them to wake either Yuri or Akulina. Do you mind terribly?"

Elizabeth said, "No."

It gave her the pleasantest sense of intimacy to be talking with Stephen like this in the night. She tried to remember her pride and anger of the night before, but sleep had flowed over it and washed it away. It is very difficult to feel proud and sleepy at the same moment. A safe, friendly feeling filled the room. The strong rhythmic snoring of Yuri and Akulina did not disturb it in the least.

"You see," said Stephen, "I went up and had a talk with Irina, and she told me one or two rather disturbing things. She's just got back from Moscow and she's well in with the Party there. Things are going to be tightened up in the passport line. That's one reason for getting you away as soon as possible. Another is the weather.

Then there's this business of Nicolas Radin's aluminium process—I wanted to ask you about that. Does Petroff definitely know you've got it by heart?"

A cold shiver went over Elizabeth. Why must they talk about Petroff? She said falteringly,

"No—I don't know—I'm not sure—he thinks—"

"That means he's not sure. And he thinks—what does he think?"

"I don't know. He thinks—I know—something—"

Stephen was silent for a minute. She thought he was sitting on a stool drawn up close to her bed. His voice came from a little above her when he spoke.

"Well, it all comes to this—how keen is he? Will he just cut his losses and get on with his job, or will he go on trying to find you?"

"If he doesn't think I'm dead, he'll try and find me."

"What makes you think that?"

"I don't want to think it," said Elizabeth with a flutter in her voice.

Stephen's voice came warm and kind.

"Don't be frightened. Try and tell me why. It's important."

She drove herself to speak of what she hated to recall.

"When they shot Nicolas, they shot the other men who were in with him. He couldn't have made his experiments alone. They shot them all. Petroff wasn't there. He came next day, and he was very angry. He said they'd bungled badly. He said the process would be very valuable. You know how they think the whole world is plotting to attack them—he talked a lot about that. He said if they had these strong, light aeroplanes, they could attack first."

"How did he know so much?"

"They had a spy among the men. The spy didn't know what the process was, but he knew what it would do."

"So you think Petroff is really keen?"

Elizabeth said, "Yes."

"Then we ought to get off as soon as we can—next time Yuri goes to market, I should think, if you're strong enough."

"I'm quite well."

"You're better. You did very well this afternoon. You acted very well. Irina didn't suspect anything."

"Are you sure?"

Elizabeth had not been sure. It had seemed to her as if those bright dark eyes had looked her through and through.

"Oh yes, I'm sure. She thinks you're just a very low type of peasant—a barbarian." He laughed a little. "That's what Varvara means, you know. It sounds pretty, but it means a barbarian—the same as Barbara. I don't know why I hit on it for you, for I can't get my tongue round it."

"Can't you?"

"You know I can't. I just don't call you anything."

"You called me Elizabeth just now," said Elizabeth to herself.

There was a pause. Now that her eyes were more accustomed to the darkness, she could just see him as a dense shadow in the dark room. The little red light shone like a star above his shoulder. Elizabeth was glad that Akulina had lighted it to-night. She said, to break the silence,

"Akulina puts a red light under her ikon, and the Communists put a red star over Lenin's picture. It's funny—isn't it?"

Stephen looked over his shoulder and then back again.

"Akulina frightened herself with her own stories. She was like a child, afraid to go to sleep in the dark. She knows dozens of stories and she loves telling them. She likes frightening herself, I think. Do you know what you reminded me of the first time I saw you?"

This was abrupt, even for Stephen. If Elizabeth had not so very much wished to know what it was that she reminded him of, she could easily have gone on talking about Akulina. Instead there was one of those pauses. To Stephen it was not a pause at all, because his thoughts were on that first picture of Elizabeth and the inner vision it had given him. To Elizabeth it was a hush of suspense.

Stephen looked at his picture.

A cold street and a lowering sky, and a long line of people waiting for the scanty bread of the Revolution, a great many of them old, because if you had a relation past work, she had to pay her way by standing in the bread queue while the able bodied attended to their jobs. All looked hungry, cold, and pinched. Elizabeth stood far down the line. She would have a long time to wait before she got her ration. He saw her most vividly—the set of her head, the line of cheek and chin, the arch of the brow, the frozen patience in which she stood. Something kindled in him at the very first look. It was like the lamp which Akulina burned before her ikon. But it never went out.

When Stephen had finished looking at the picture in his mind, he said,

"Three or four years ago I was waiting at the edge of a lake. I had to meet a man, and he was late. It was very cold. There was a lot of cloud in the sky, and a wind, and it had begun to freeze hard. I was looking at the water, and all of a sudden I saw a star in it. The wind had moved the clouds and the star came through—I could see it in the water. It wasn't bright like a star ought to be on a frosty night. It looked as if it were drowned. That's the word that came into my head about it, you know—drowned. Just for a moment I couldn't think why it looked like that. And then, of course, I realized that it was because the lake was skinning over. The star was drowned under the ice. When I saw you the first time, you were standing in a bread queue in that beastly thin dress of yours with the wind cutting like a knife. As soon as I saw you, I thought about that drowned star, because that's what you looked like—as if the ice were freezing over you."

Elizabeth felt most oddly touched and embarrassed. There was not the slightest emotion in Stephen's voice. It was exactly the same voice in which he would have made a remark about the weather. It did not change in the least when he said without any pause,

"You're sure you'll be strong enough to travel in a day or two? I don't want you to be ill again."

"I shan't be ill again. I feel—different."

She had been starving for more than bread. Stephen had fed her—comforted, protected, shielded her—given her kindness. What sort of ungrateful stone had she got for a heart, to be proud and angry because he had another friend? Perhaps he had been friends with Irina for years. And why not? The heart which she accused did not really feel at all like a stone. There was a new warmth about it. It shrank and trembled in a most unstonelike way.

"It's a funny thing about revolutions," said Stephen cheerfully— "they always seem to lead to bread queues. They had them in the French Revolution, you know. The Soviets have a lot in common with the French Revolution people—bread queues, and a currency that's so depreciated that outsiders won't look at it, and laws to prevent people getting out of the earthly paradise they've made. They had paper francs in Paris—*assignats* they called them—and if you emigrated, or tried to emigrate, you went to the guillotine. Here they walk you down into a cellar and shoot the back of your head off. I like non-revolutionary countries best. It'll be jolly to get out of this—won't it?"

Elizabeth did not answer for a moment. Then she said in a voice he could hardly hear,

"Shall we—get—out?"

"Of course we shall. What do you think?"

"You're sure?"

"Of course I'm sure." He felt for her shoulder in the dark and patted it. "Go to sleep and don't worry."

She heard him climb back to his place again and lie down. In less than a minute his breathing told her that he was asleep.

She lay in the dark and felt safe. Presently she would sleep, but not yet. It was so long since she had felt safe like this. The image of Irina had ceased to trouble her. She drifted into a dream of flowery meadows where she walked knee-deep and listened to the singing of larks. It was a very pleasant dream.

Chapter Ten

STEPHEN WAS in the barn next day, when Irina walked in. She stood and looked about her for a moment before she spoke.

"What a waste all this sort of thing is! A barn like this half empty—these little foolish strips of cultivation, divided and redivided so that it would be impossible to use machines upon them!" She made a gesture with her hands as if she were throwing something away. "What can one do? I am so disheartened that I could cry. I felt I must talk with you or I could not have enough courage to go on."

Stephen was quite willing to talk. Irina was just back from Moscow, and what she had to say might be interesting.

"What is the matter?" he said.

She laid her hand on his arm without any trace of self consciousness.

"You know how I have worked on the Agricultural Front. Before I came to this district I was in the Caucasus—before that near Minsk. I helped to organize the Collective Farms in each district. Does anyone think it was pleasant work? Where it was possible to persuade, I persuaded, but where force was needed, force had to be used. How do you suppose I bore to see houses pulled down, people thrown out, or to hear women shrieking and cursing me? Is that pleasant? I bore it because I could see the end—the whole country collectivized—the old dirty houses and the old dirty people swept away—the small narrow fields, the little miserable barns like this, the two or three starveling cattle, all gone. And instead—what?"

"I'm a public meeting, and she's addressing me from the platform," said Stephen to himself.

"What?" repeated Irina in a rapt tone. "The whole land cultivated by tractors—obsolete methods replaced—Collectivization everywhere—improved stock—hygienic buildings—nurseries for the children—and cultural opportunities for all!"

"It's a great idea!" said Stephen with enthusiasm. "What's gone wrong with it? Why are you discouraged?"

"Why? You know—or you ought to know. Where were you all this summer? If you were going up and down the country, what did you think of the Farms—the Collective Farms? What did you think of the crops—the output—the agricultural conditions?"

Stephen shrugged his big shoulders.

"Not too good," he said. "They are letting the weeds get ahead of them, and that's the devil. They are lazy. They grow enough to feed themselves and don't trouble about the workers in the towns."

Irina made a passionate movement.

"There—you have said it! But this laziness and apathy have not just grown of themselves—they have been fostered. Counter-revolutionary influences have been at work. There are class enemies on the Farms." Her eyes glowed. "I said I was discouraged, but what's the use of being discouraged? I was whining, and Lenin said, 'Never whine! We must fight!' You know I have just been in Moscow. They told me there what is to happen." She dropped her voice to a lower tone. "It was a great blow to me, because they will go no further with Collectivization. You know how I had set my heart on a Collective Farm here—the plans had been passed and the site chosen. Well, that's all put an end to. I tell you I could have cried. But they're going to tighten things up in the existing Farms. They are planning special police to deal with them. Counter-revolutionaries are to be detected and punished with the utmost severity."

"That sounds all right," said Stephen heartily.

"Yes, I was wrong to be discouraged. It was my own fault. After we had talked last night I was so discouraged that it would have been a pleasure to die. That was because I had been thinking about personal happiness, and a good Communist does not care about that, but only about the Cause."

Stephen nodded gravely.

"The Cause should always come first," he agreed. He wished very much that Irina would take her hand off his arm. Instead she pressed it with a good deal of warmth.

"Yes, yes—how well you put it! That is what makes the bond between us—to both of us the Cause comes first."

"Yes, naturally."

Irina leaned against the arm she was holding.

"The Cause still comes first with you then?"

"Of course it does."

"You have not put a personal affection in its place?"

"*I?* What a question!"

She took a half step back as if about to loose her hold, but instead of doing so she pressed suddenly near again.

"Is it her eyes you prefer to mine?" She said the words as if they were forced out of her. Her face flushed, and her own eyes, large and brilliant, were fixed upon him in an imploring look.

"You have very fine eyes," said Stephen impartially.

Irina caught her breath. She said,

"Is that all you have to say? Am I to make an inventory in order to find out what makes you choose a half-witted peasant girl like this Varvara? It must be something that you see in her—something you find lacking in me. I ask you to tell me what it is. Is that too much to ask?"

As she spoke, Elizabeth came into the barn. She saw Irina with her hand on Stephen's arm, her face a little flushed and her lips moving in low, earnest talk. She would have liked to turn back, but Akulina had sent her for an apronful of straw, and if she went back without it, there would be questions. Besides, the slow-witted Varvara would not be supposed to notice anything. With a dull and listless air she crossed the barn and began to pull at the straw.

Stephen came over to help her, and Irina followed him. When Elizabeth turned to go, she stopped her. Seen in the light of day, there was something in the girl that might attract a man. She had fine eyes, if they had not looked so vacant. She had small hands and feet, and a certain grace. Irina said abruptly,

"Where do you come from? What is your village?"

Elizabeth gave her a blank stare. Since she had no idea what she should say, it seemed the best thing to do. Perhaps Stephen would come to her rescue.

Stephen did. He laughed till the rafters rang, and said,

"It's a good joke your asking her that, because she doesn't know. You see she doesn't come from a village at all. Her father was a forester, and the nearest village was so far away that she was waiting to go there till it was time for her to be married." He put a rough arm round Elizabeth's shoulders and gave her a shake. "And that's why you're so shy, my little pigeon—And then her father and mother died, and she started out to look for her brother who had joined the Red Army, and as she hadn't the least idea where he was, she hadn't much chance of finding him, and it was a real bit of luck for her finding me."

"Was her father a kulak?" said Irina, still staring.

The well-to-do peasantry upon whom the Revolution had made special war had been driven out of their holdings in thousands all over Russia. This girl with that undefined look of being different might be the daughter of such a family, crazed perhaps by her sufferings. There are many crazy people in the Revolutionary paradise. Women who have seen their homes burned down, their husbands shot, and their children starved to death are often not quite sane afterwards.

Stephen laughed again.

"A kulak's daughter? What an idea! Didn't I tell you her father was a forester?" He let go of Elizabeth and gave her a push. "Run along with that straw, or my grandmother will scold, and when my grandmother scolds it's all we can do to keep the roof on."

As Elizabeth ran out, he began to pile up the straw which she had pulled down. As he worked, he sang in his big rolling voice:

"Let the red cock crow on the Kulak's roof!
Pull down the beams of the Kulak's house!
Let the red cock crow!
Let the red fire glow!
Pull down the beams of the Kulak's house!"

"What is that song?" said Irina.

He looked over his shoulder and saw that she was pale.

"It's a very good song. There's another verse." He went on singing:

"Let the red cock crow on the Kulak's roof!
Pull down the walls of the Kulak's house!
Let the red cock crow!

Let the red Cause grow!
Pull down the walls of the Kulak's house!"

"Where did you get that song?" said Irina.

Stephen turned round laughing.

"I made it. Don't you think it goes well? I knew you'd like it."

Irina stamped her foot.

"I hate it!"

He came over to her and took her by the shoulders.

"Was it you who reported Nikita for hiding grain?"

"No!" said Irina violently. She wrenched away from him and went back a step or two. "Why should you say such a thing? Why should you think I would do such a thing?"

Stephen looked mildly surprised.

"Why should you be angry with me? Wouldn't it have been your duty to report him if you knew that he was hiding grain?" He whistled the air of the song he had just sung—*Pull down the beams of the Kulak's house.*

"Be silent!" said Irina passionately.

Stephen stopped whistling.

"You are not a good Communist if you are sorry for kulaks and grain-hoarders," he said contemptuously. "I suppose it was Nikita's wife Anna who frightened you by saying it would be your turn to be unhappy one day."

"She did *not* frighten me!" said Irina with heaving breast.

Stephen pressed his advantage.

"I should never have thought that you would have been superstitious, Irina. To be afraid of a poor, silly, demented woman's curse!"

Irina was frightfully pale.

"She did *not* curse me!"

"Well, it sounded very like it to me. Isn't it cursing to wish anyone unhappy?" He shrugged his shoulders. "There are curses I'd prefer to that myself."

"I tell you she did *not* curse me!"

"All right," said Stephen cheerfully—"you didn't report Nikita, and Anna didn't curse you, and you're not superstitious, because none of us have any superstitions left. It's a wonderful world—isn't it?"

He turned back to the straw and sang again:

"The red cock crows on the kulak's roof."

Irina rushed out of the barn.

Chapter Eleven

STEPHEN CAME back into the house and found Elizabeth alone there. She was looking pale and troubled.

"That's all right," he said. "But we must get away. She's a heap too interested in you."

Elizabeth had turned away. She said without looking round,

"What happened? What did you say?"

Stephen laughed a little grimly.

"I pulled off a good rousing counter-attack. I asked her if it was she who reported Nikita for grain hoarding. Akulina was talking about it last night."

"Was it Irina?" Elizabeth's tone was low and horrified.

"I don't know. I expect so. She'd look upon it as a duty—you've got to remember that—a painful duty."

Still without looking round, Elizabeth said,

"She wouldn't find it a painful duty to report me."

"I don't know," said Stephen. "I don't believe she'd know, herself. Most of the time she's a set of copy-book maxims for Young Communists, very handsomely bound, but every now and then a streak of something real crops up, and then I'm sorry for her because she doesn't know what to do with it."

Elizabeth went over to the old-fashioned loom and stood there fingering it.

"It would be better to tell her that we are not married."

"Why?"

"It would be better."

He came and leaned against the wall beyond the loom so that he could see her face.

"Why do you want to commit suicide?"

She lifted her eyebrows.

"I don't."

"Telling Irina we're not married would be suicide—for both of us. And a nasty, painful, lingering suicide too—weeks in a buggy Bolshevist prison, a lot of beastly interrogations—they're great on third degree—and a nasty, messy execution at the end of it. I could do it much better with a revolver if you're really set on it. Of course it would annoy Akulina very much to come in and find our corpses on the floor, because she takes a good deal of pains to keep things clean. I expect you've noticed there aren't any insects, and that's more than you can say about most peasants' houses."

Elizabeth looked up, met his teasing eyes, and quickly looked away. She frowned a little and said,

"When we were talking on the bridge, you said—I should be— rather an asset." She hesitated curiously over the words. "You said anyone who was looking for you wouldn't expect you to have—a woman with you. I've wanted to ask you about it. What did you mean? Are people looking for you?"

"They're not looking for Red Stefan," he said with a laugh. "I didn't mean that. We'd be badly up against it if they were."

"What did you mean?"

"I told you I was in Tronsk to meet a man who was taking over my job. When he didn't come, I was pretty sure he'd been done in. Well; they might have known he was going to meet someone, and that would mean they'd be keeping their eyes skinned for anyone who was hanging around in Tronsk without a good excuse. They might have come to wonder why Red Stefan was kicking his heels there. But if he was there to pick up a wife, that let him out. That's what I meant."

"I see," said Elizabeth. She smiled suddenly and sweetly. "I don't know if that's true, but I should like to think it was."

"Oh, it's quite true," said Stephen. Then, with one of his abrupt turns, "I didn't tell you that I knew Petroff, did I?"

She was really startled.

"No—you didn't."

He looked pleased.

"I know him quite well. We're almost bosom companions. You see, I saved his life."

"Why did you?"

"I didn't know what a nuisance he was going to be. It was in the early days at Magnitogorsk. The whole place had run out of vodka—and you know what Petroff is when he can't get vodka. I had two bottles, and he swore they saved his life."

"I didn't know you'd been in Magnitogorsk."

"Oh, I've been in lots of places," said Stephen cheerfully.

It came on to snow that evening and snowed all night. An hour before the snow began Irina left the village for the nearest Collective Farm, which was about ten versts away. The schoolmaster drove her over, and his wife was quite certain that he would be snowed up at the Farm with Irina and unable to return. All the women agreed with her that this was what Irina had intended. Akulina did not scruple to assert that she had caused the snow to fall—how, or by what arts, it was not for a God-fearing woman to say.

In the morning there was a frozen whiteness everywhere under a heavy lowering sky. Stephen and Yuri went out to make a path to the cow-shed and the barn. Presently Stephen came back alone.

"We're off," he said. "Yuri's getting out the sledge. He's grumbling like anything, but he's really quite pleased, because he'll get a fabulous price in Tronsk for Akulina's eggs and a couple of the cheeses they've been hiding. The hens have laid so well this week that if they were anyone else's, Akulina would say it was witchcraft."

The sledge was much more comfortable than the cart had been. It ran smoothly over the crisp snow, under which lay buried the ruts and pot-holes of their journey from Tronsk. Yuri drove. The horse went gaily to a tinkling of bells. Elizabeth, well wrapped from the biting cold, found herself strangely happy. Pleasant to be flying along like this—pleasant to be leaving the village behind—pleasant to be getting away from Irina. Before she knew what she was going to say, she had spoken Irina's name.

"Irina—why did she go away like that?"

"She went to the Collective Farm," said Stephen without any expression in his voice.

"Why?"

He shrugged his shoulders.

"She often goes there."

Elizabeth had a quick, vivid memory of what she had seen when she came into the barn—Irina holding Stephen by the arm, leaning to him, speaking low and earnestly, with the glow in her cheeks which gave her a warmer beauty. Why had she begun to speak about Irina? If there was something between her and Stephen, he would not tell her. Why should he? She was just a stranger whom he was befriending at a great risk to himself because she was his countrywoman. Why should he tell her about his private affairs? She felt suddenly cold and desolate. A shiver ran over her, and at once Stephen asked,

"Are you cold?"

"No."

"You shivered."

"I'm not cold."

Stephen considered this for a moment. Then he said,

"Have I made you angry?"

"Of course not."

He pursued this line of thought.

"You sounded angry."

It would be quite dreadful if he were to think that she was angry about Irina. She said quickly in a laughing voice,

"You don't know how I sound when I'm angry."

Stephen said, "No—that's true." And then, with one of his sudden changes of subject, "I want to talk to you about Petroff. Do you mind?"

He was really thinking that he should like to see Elizabeth angry, because that was a way he had not seen her yet. Every fresh way of seeing her was something added to the picture in his mind. Anger is like a lightning flash; it reveals with an intense, brief light. He would like to see Elizabeth by that revealing flash. Only of course he would rather the anger should not be directed against him. Petroff stepped naturally into his mind as an altogether suitable person for Elizabeth to be angry with. Let Petroff be struck by the lightning, and more power to it. He smiled affably as he said,

"I want to talk to you about Petroff. Do you mind?"

At any other moment Elizabeth would have minded. She would not, perhaps, have said so, but she would have winced a little. At this moment, and as an alternative to Irina, Petroff was positively welcome. She said quite truthfully,

"No, I don't mind."

Stephen leaned back beside her.

"Well then, I've been thinking a lot about Petroff's position. You see, the whole thing is a good deal like that game called devil-in-the-dark. I don't know if you ever played it. You put out all the lights, and one person is *He*. The others are all trying to get out of the room without being caught. You have to listen like mad and guess where *He* is, and what *He's* doing, before you move a step. That's why I want to talk about Petroff—I've got to guess what he's likely to do. To begin with—is he in love with you?"

Elizabeth's lips lifted a little.

"I shouldn't call it that."

"Well, it's more a question of what he would call it—isn't it?"

"He called it being in love," said Elizabeth.

"Sometimes that sort of thing is just a passing fancy with a fellow like Petroff, but sometimes it takes a pretty strong hold. I'm awfully sorry to bother you about this, but you're the only person I can ask—I can't very well go to Petroff. I hope you don't mind."

"Why should I mind?" said Elizabeth. Petroff was no longer the last horror of a nightmare. She had come out of the dream in which he had troubled her, and he simply did not matter any more.

"Well then, have you any idea how deep this went with him?"

Elizabeth's brows drew together.

"I don't really know. I should say not very deep. But he likes getting his own way. I've heard him boast that nobody ever got the better of him."

"You think he'd try and find you?"

"I think he'd try and find the formula."

"Yes—if he thought you'd got it. He really does think so?"

"I don't know. He may have been trying to torment me. I don't know. I believe he does think I know something."

Stephen nodded thoughtfully.

"Then I figure it out this way. He'll try very hard to find you. He's not in terribly good odour at present—I've heard that from more than one quarter. A lot of the Communists in power are very strict about things like drink, and it's perfectly well known that Petroff is a good deal too fond of the vodka bottle. If he hadn't been a really clever mining engineer, he'd have got the sack long ago. If he could produce a new aluminium alloy which would assure them a lead in the manufacture of aircraft, it would be bound to give him a new lease of political life. That's how it looks to me. So when I heard he was down at the Collective Farm, I thought we'd better get a move on."

Elizabeth drew a sharp breath of dismay.

Stephen nodded.

"I heard yesterday."

"The farm Irina went to?"

"That's the one." He laughed a little. "An old lady who lived near my guardian in Devonshire used to say, 'Compliments pass when gentlefolk meet.' She was about a hundred."

Elizabeth's eyes were on him, wide and startled.

"Do they know each other, Irina and Petroff?"

"Oh Lord, yes! Irina knows everyone. She was one of the people who told me that Petroff was for it unless he mended his ways."

"I see—" said Elizabeth.

Petroff and Irina—Irina and Petroff...The names linked themselves in her mind. And Irina had gone to the Collective Farm.

Stephen's voice came through her thoughts.

"I wanted to ask you about that formula. You haven't got it written down anywhere?"

"No. Nicolas said it wouldn't be safe."

"Yes—he was right. You wouldn't know how to hide it." He paused, and then added briskly, "But I should."

Elizabeth looked at him in surprise.

"Do you want me to write it down?"

"Yes, I think so."

"Why?" said Elizabeth.

Stephen was silent.

Elizabeth fixed her eyes on him.

"Do tell me why you said that."

"Well, it's rather difficult to explain. I was thinking you might easily forget a bit of it—and—several other things like that."

"What sort of things?"

He shook his head. Impossible to tell her just what their chances were of getting clear, or that he might use the formula to bargain her free. It wasn't that he had thought out any plan. It was merely the old sense that knowledge was power.

Elizabeth looked away across the snow for some time. Little feathery clouds blew up from the horse's hoofs. The bells on the harness tinkled. The runners of the sledge made a soft crunching sound as they slid over the snow and pressed it down. There were no other sounds. Everything beyond them was cold, still, and empty—life, and growth, and fertility all frozen. But in Elizabeth herself they had suddenly, wonderfully quickened. The frost was all gone from her heart; just in one moment the last of it had broken and dissolved in a strange warmth and confusion of thought and feeling. She felt as if it were about to sweep her away. Her hands clasped one another beneath the sheepskins. She closed her eyes for a moment.

At once Stephen was asking her,

"What is it? What's the matter?"

She looked up at him then, a strange bewildered look.

"What were we talking about?"

"Are you all right? Why did you shut your eyes like that? We were talking about the formula."

"Yes," said Elizabeth—"the formula. You wanted it?"

She had quite forgotten why Stephen wanted it, and it did not matter in the least. She had a most overwhelming desire to give him whatever he wanted. If it had been the heart out of her breast, it would have been a little thing, and this longing to give would be still unspent. The formula was like a mere speck of dust caught in a torrent. If he wanted it, it was his. Whatever he wanted of her was his already, given with both hands and a heart that asked only to go on giving.

She told him the formula in a soft, steady voice, repeating it as she had learned it from Nicolas Radin's dry and shaking lips. Poor Nicolas! She thought of him with a great softness of pity. She said the words he had taught her without missing a syllable. She repeated the figures, the instructions, the explanatory details. How many hundreds of times had she said them over in her mind—as she walked along a lonely street, as she stood silent in the bread queue waiting for her poor ration, or at night whilst the old woman snored beside her in the dark? It was as if they had been frozen into the ice about her heart. Now, on this new warm flood, they came pouring out. Only she could still control her voice. The outpouring was in thought alone. The words came in a quiet, measured order, whilst her hands held one another hard and her eyes looked away across the snow to the grey horizon. For Elizabeth it flamed with all the jewel colours of sunrise.

"You've got an awfully good memory," said Stephen in an admiring voice.

He had produced pencil and paper. She found him looking at her with a gratified air.

"Do you mind saying it all over again? I want to write it down."

Elizabeth didn't mind how often she said it. She wanted to do what Stephen wanted her to do, and to unpack her mind of this dangerous secret stuff gave her a sense of pure relief. She gave the words and figures again with a slow, meticulous accuracy and watched him write them down.

When he had finished, she asked him,

"Where will you hide it?"

Lovely to feel that it was no longer any affair of hers. But just for curiosity's sake she might ask her question.

Stephen said, "Hush!" and bent a frowning face over the paper. His lips moved in a soundless mutter. He made horrible faces like a schoolboy.

Elizabeth regarded him with tenderness. Men never grew up. No, that wasn't it—the man you loved never grew up. Behind the grown-up make-believe there was the dear funny little boy whom his mother had loved. Perhaps some day there would be another little boy, very dear and funny, with bright blue eyes and an inky frown.

Stephen's frown went suddenly. He looked up with a beaming smile, and Elizabeth repeated her question.

"How are you going to hide it?"

He burst out laughing and tapped his forehead.

"Here," he said, and began tearing the paper into tiny scraps which he tossed out upon the snow.

Chapter Twelve

IN THE STABLE behind the tumble-down pot-house where Yuri unharnessed his horse it occurred to Elizabeth for the first time that she did not know where they were going. Perhaps at the back of her mind she had taken it for granted that they would go back to the room to which Stephen had taken her on the first night. It appeared, however, that she was mistaken. Stephen when asked where they were going said that he didn't know. After which he linked his arm in hers and marched her out into the street.

"Are we not going to the same place as before?"

He shook his head decidedly.

"No. It's not fit for you—and it's dangerous."

"Are we just going to walk about the streets?" said Elizabeth demurely.

Stephen laughed.

"Would you like to? I don't trust you, you know. You might just slip away into the snow and get lost. There's not much more of you than a snowflake. Would you like some hot coffee?"

Her lips trembled into a smile.

"I might like the moon."

He patted her arm.

"Oh, you'll get the coffee all right. Here—there's a short cut down this alley. It takes us in by the back way."

"But in where?"

"It's a café. I'll have to leave you there whilst I go and prospect. I think I know someone who will lend us a room, but it might be dangerous to take you there till I'm sure the coast is clear."

They turned out of the alley into a yard. A path had been cut through the snow to a door in the wall of a ramshackle house. On this Stephen knocked. It was opened by a middle-aged woman with a face heated and reddened by cooking. She beckoned them in, shut the door again, and began to scold Stephen for coming in that way. Talking and scolding all the time, she took them across the kitchen and up some steps, at the top of which she left them. The scolding voice retreated. They were in a narrow, dark passage where Elizabeth could see nothing. She pressed involuntarily against Stephen, and for a moment his arm came round her and held her there. He said something under his breath, but her heart beat so loudly that she lost the sense of what he said. It was just Stephen's voice which came to her, low and moved. And then a door in front of them was pushed open and a tall, thin man in the dress of a waiter stood aside to let them pass.

They came into a room with alcoves on either side and small tables everywhere. Stephen took her across to one of the alcoves, ordered coffee, and when the waiter had gone put the money to pay for it into her hand.

"Now all you've got to do is to sit here till I come back. Keep turned away from the room and drink your coffee. No one will notice you. I shan't be longer than I can help." He spoke in Russian, and his voice was as cool and practical as if there had never been that moment in the passage. Then he was gone, threading his way among the tables and disappearing through the door by which they had come.

Elizabeth was glad to be alone. Her heart still beat, and all her thoughts were in confusion. That half embrace had most deeply and sweetly troubled her. She needed time to steady herself again. She leaned her elbows on the little table and hid her eyes. When the waiter put the cup of coffee before her she looked up with a start. She paid him and, taking up her cup, she sipped from it and began for the first time to take in her surroundings. She had thought the room empty, but four or five of the tables were now occupied by quiet people who ate and drank either in silence or with some scarcely audible murmur of speech. Opposite the door by which she and Stephen had come in was an open archway partially screened by curtains. It appeared to lead to an outer room.

Elizabeth drank her coffee. After one glance over her shoulder she kept her face from the room. Presently she found that she could see without being seen. On the wall of the alcove a little above her head was a small mirror in a cheap wooden frame. It was tilted at such an angle that it reflected the curtained arch and about half the room. She sat with her chin in her hand and watched the reflection. Every now and then the curtains in the mirror would part and someone would come through them into the picture—a man with grey hair and a broken nose; an elderly woman with bowed shoulders and a lagging step, in a fur-trimmed coat of incredibly old-fashioned cut; a young man with light, restless eyes; and others. Sometimes they stayed in the picture, sitting down at one of the small reflected tables to eat and drink like the people of a dream. Sometimes they passed across the picture and disappeared from it into some unseen corner of the room. They came for the most part singly, and went, as they had come, without speech or greeting.

Elizabeth's thoughts began to wander. She looked for Stephen's return and feared it. His touch had moved her so deeply that their next meeting would be full of strange emotions and possibilities. She longed for him to come, and she dreaded his coming. She felt as if she knew neither herself nor him—as if they had suddenly lost their old selves...Something new lay just beyond this moment.

She looked up from her thoughts into the mirror and saw the curtains part.

Irina stood between them.

The floor seemed to tilt under Elizabeth's feet. The room reflected in the mirror was tilting too. In a moment the chairs, the tables, the silent guests would begin to slide down that tilting floor towards the curtains between which Irina stood, tall and dark and beautiful, with a scarlet handkerchief knotted at her throat. There was a mist round her. Through the mist Elizabeth saw the curtains move. It was Irina who moved them, thrusting at the heavy folds with a strong bare hand. The room beyond showed through the gap, incredibly far away.

Irina turned and spoke over her shoulder to someone in that faraway room. There was a sound in Elizabeth's ears like the sound of a high wind, but Irina's voice cut through it clear and hard.

"This way, Petroff. There is plenty of room in here, and it is warm."

At Petroff's name Elizabeth found herself on her feet. The floor still tilted. The noise in her ears confused her. A kind of panic courage carried her towards the door by which she and Stephen had come in. She mustn't run. She must be quick without seeming to hurry. She must keep her back to the curtain through which Petroff might come at any moment. If he saw her, she was lost. She mustn't think about Petroff or she would go sliding down that tilting floor right into his arms.

She reached the door. Opened it. Shut it behind her.

In the dark passage she stood, drawing the long breaths of a hunted creature. Her heart still beat and her knees shook, but the floor was steady under her feet. She began to run, and then, remembering that there were steps ahead of her, pulled up with a hand on the wall at either side of the narrow passage. She had stopped only just in time. One foot was over the edge of the topmost step. For a moment all her weight came on her hands. Then, as she steadied herself, someone came running towards her out of the darkness. She had no time to draw back, to turn, or to flatten herself against the wall. Someone large and black loomed up, bumped into her, caught her off her feet, and carried her with a half stride along the passage. An overwhelming rush of happiness swept her clear of all her terror and confusion, because at the first touch she knew that it was Stephen who held her.

They met where they had parted—for, to Elizabeth, they had parted when his arm had loosed her here as the waiter opened the door. But if they had parted on an emotion, they met in an adventure. Each said the other's name in a laughing, breathless whisper.

"Stephen!"

"Elizabeth!"

"Stephen—"

"Where are you running to?"

"We *must* run. Petroff is there with Irina."

He gave a long, soft whistle.

"The devil he is! Did they see you?"

"I don't know. I didn't dare look. I got to the door—somehow."

All this time she was in his arms, held close whilst they whispered. There might not have been any danger in the world. To Elizabeth there was only Stephen, and to Stephen only Elizabeth.

Then in a moment everything changed. With a smothered laugh he set her on her feet, swung round with her, and ran her down the stairs, through the passage, and across the kitchen. Either the red-faced woman had never stopped scolding, or Stephen's second irruption had started her off all over again. She seemed to be saying the same things that she had been saying when they came in, and in exactly the same angry, dreary voice. Stephen banged the outer door upon her and her complaints and the warmth of her stuffy kitchen, and they were out in the wintry dusk with the sky dark over them and a faint glimmering light striking up from the fresh-fallen snow. The path that had been cut through it to the yard gate was like a strip of black carpet spread for them to walk on. Actually they ran, and came, still running, out of the gate and round the corner into an empty street.

"Well, that's that," said Stephen cheerfully. He dropped his arm from Elizabeth's waist and hurried her along with a hand at her elbow. "Petroff couldn't have seen you or he'd have been after us by now. Tell me about it."

Elizabeth told him. Then she said,

"How did they come there? Were they following us? You said they were at the Collective Farm."

"Yes—I've got to think that out—it's important. By the way, I've found a room all right. It belongs to the man I told you about, Boris Andreieff. He's a very hot Red, so it'll be a good place for us to stay. It was a bit of luck catching him, because he's just off to Moscow to attend a Party meeting. He's one of the Reddest friends I've got. Well, now about Petroff and Irina—I should think Irina went pelting off to the Farm in a temper. I don't suppose she went specially to see Petroff, though of course she knew he was there, because the person who told me was the schoolmaster, and he'd naturally tell Irina too. She may have gone specially to see Petroff, but I don't think so. I don't think she suspected enough for that. I think she was just in a generally angry, irritated, suspicious state of mind." He spoke as if he was thinking aloud. Then he gave a kind of half laugh and turned to Elizabeth. "I'm only guessing, but when you know people you can generally guess right. Let's go on guessing. I think Irina got to the Farm and started grousing to Petroff about how uncollective the peasants were, and what a lack of Party enthusiasm there was. That's not guessing, because she always does that when she can get anyone to listen to her. And then, I think, she probably went on to grouse about me—what a pity I didn't go to an agricultural college and get a government job, and what was I thinking about to go and pick up with a woman whom nobody knew anything about, a half-witted creature who couldn't put two words together, and all that sort of thing." He patted her arm encouragingly. "I say, you don't mind, do you—because you did act it most awfully well."

"No, I don't mind," said Elizabeth in a dreamy, contented voice.

Stephen patted her arm again.

"It was a compliment really. Anyhow I meant it to be a compliment. Well, then I expect Petroff asked questions, and Irina probably described you enough to make him prick up his ears. They couldn't get over last night because of the snow, but I rather guess they took a drive this morning—and thank the Lord they just missed us. I had a feeling we'd been long enough in that village. Well, they found we were gone and they came along after us. It's all guessing, but that's how I think it was. I don't see any other way of it, unless they're not thinking about us at all. I think they are, but perhaps they're not. We're feeling awfully important to ourselves, but it's just on the cards that they're not giving a damn for us. Irina often goes off into the blue when anything has put her out, so it's quite likely she got Petroff to give her a lift and came here to work things off. She's got friends in Tronsk."

Elizabeth was not really caring very much about Irina and her tempers. One thing that Stephen had said was giving her a curious thrill of surprise. He said they were feeling very important to themselves, and—this is where the thrill came in—it was true. It was such a long time since she had found anything in herself which could interest anyone, because she had been dead, and the dead are not interesting. At Stephen's words she became aware that she was alive, and not only alive but full of a vivid, vital interest in herself, and in Stephen, and in the world which surrounded them.

They turned another corner and went in at the door of a dark, forbidding house four stories high. None of the bare, blank windows showed any light. They climbed a black stair to the third storey, where Stephen produced a key and unlocked the door which faced them. She heard him moving, but could see nothing until a match spirted and gave her his face suddenly like a picture on the dark. He was lighting a lamp, and in a moment the dull yellow glow showed a good-sized room with a large window, a bed in the corner, and an old comfortable chair. A stove, which had been allowed to go out, still radiated a little heat, and to anyone coming in from the street the room felt warm.

Stephen turned from the lamp and shut the door. He emptied his pockets and put on the table bread, tea, cheese, and a chunk of cold sausage, after which he set himself to stoke the stove, filled a kettle, and put it on to boil.

Elizabeth became aware that she was very hungry.

Chapter Thirteen

WHEN THEY had eaten, Stephen went out. He had talked cheerfully throughout the meal, but his talk somehow gave Elizabeth the feeling that she was being shut out. She felt vaguely rebuffed. She wanted to know what he was thinking and planning. She was quite sure that behind the talk his mind was busy with plans. When he got up to go, she got up too and stood in his way, one hand upon the door.

"What are we going to do?" she said.

"I don't know," said Stephen—"Get away from here as soon as we can."

"How soon can we get away?"

"Not to-night, I'm afraid."

She felt a little shock of surprise. She had not thought of going on that night, but when he spoke of it the desire to go swept over her like a sudden gust of wind. It shook her, and she was afraid.

"No, I don't think we could get away to-night," Stephen repeated. "I've got one or two things to see about. I hope you don't mind being left. It won't do for you to go out and risk being seen. I hope Irina didn't see you."

Elizabeth hoped so too. Her hand dropped from the door. She was chilled and weary. She stood aside for Stephen to pass. Then all at once, with his hand on the latch, he turned round and came to her.

"Will you rest?"

"I'm not tired."

They stood for a moment close together without speaking. Then Stephen took both her hands in his and lifted them to his lips. He kissed first one and then the other. Then he let them go and ran out of the room and down the stair.

He was in a state of extreme exhilaration as he came out into the cold street. He had held Elizabeth in his arms, and she had let him kiss her hands. Of course holding her in his arms had been more or less of an accident, but if she had been offended she wouldn't have let him kiss her hands. The question was, had she let him kiss them, or had he just kissed them? A moment ago he had been sure; now he wasn't. After all, how could she have stopped him? He had just grabbed her hands and kissed them. It was a very disquieting thought, and he must be more careful another time. It would be horrible if Elizabeth were to think that she couldn't trust him.

He had got as far as this in his thoughts, when he heard Irina's voice. He had come the width of three houses from Boris Andreieff's lodging and he was just about to turn the corner, when from the other side of it he heard Irina speak his name. She said "Stefan," and he did not wait to hear what else she said.

Irina being one of the two last persons on earth whom he desired to meet at this moment, he swung round and dived into the nearest doorway. It stood recessed under a half porch, and, flattening himself against the door with his face towards it, he waited for Irina to pass by.

She did not pass. She turned the corner, still talking, and there stood no more than a couple of yards away, the centre of a group which, from their voices and the sounds of their feet, must consist of some half dozen men. The street was very dark. The shadow of the porch was opportune. Stephen hoped for the best. Having tried the handle and found that the door was fast, he could do no more. If he were seen, it would be only as a shadow, an unknown man entering or attempting to enter an unknown house. Even Irina would not stand talking at a street corner for long in this bitter weather.

All this was in his mind as one thought.

He pressed against the door, wondered what Irina had been saying about him, and heard a man say,

"We're not to go in?"

Irina's voice answered him.

"No, no, of course not."

Another man said,

"I don't see why."

"Why?" Irina's tone was sharp. "Haven't I told you why?"

A third man said in a slow, drawling manner,

"Alexis must always be told a thing three times. That is what he calls being thorough."

The others laughed. There were certainly half a dozen of them.

"I don't see why," said Alexis obstinately.

"Haven't I told you I'm not sure?" said Irina.

"I thought you said you were sure." Alexis sounded a little sulky.

Stephen could hear Irina stamp her foot on the snow.

"I am sure in myself—I have told you that! From the moment I first saw her I said to myself, 'There is something wrong there. Stefan is not the man to marry like that.' And when she could not tell me the name of her village, then I began to think indeed. And when Comrade Petroff told me about the woman he was looking for, I was sure in myself that this Varvara must be the one, so we came here after them. Then, half an hour ago, when I met Vera and she told me she had seen Boris Andreieff at the station and that he said he had lent Stefan his room, I thought at once, 'Now we have her!' Only we mustn't run any risk. She must be watched so that she can't get away."

"But still I don't see why we are to wait outside," said Alexis.

"Alexis never does see anything," said the man with the drawling voice.

Irina stamped her foot again.

"How many times am I to tell you that it is Comrade Petroff who must identify her? You will wait on the stair and see that she does not go out. As soon as you are there I will go for Petroff. If she is not the woman he is looking for, there is no harm done—we have only paid a friendly call upon our friend Stefan and his wife. If she is the woman, then Petroff can deal with her. She is a counter-revolutionary and a *bourzhui* who has been withholding valuable information from the state."

"But still I don't see—" began Alexis.

Irina interrupted him furiously.

"Do you want Stefan to break your head? He probably will if he's at home. It might be better for you not to be in such a hurry. He doesn't like being interfered with, you know."

"If it comes to head-breaking, a bullet can do more damage than a fist." This was a dry voice that had not spoken till now.

They were armed. It was, of course, to be expected, but it was a death-warrant to any hope of getting Elizabeth away. If he had had a pleasant vision of knocking the conspirators' heads together two by two, chucking them down Boris Andreieff's conveniently steep stair, and carrying Elizabeth off in triumph over their silly prostrate bodies, it did most definitely drop down dead at the realization that these Young Communists were in possession of fire-arms. The young man with the dry voice sounded as if he would have a steady hand. Alexis, of course, could be trusted to miss anything he aimed at.

Alexis was saying,

"But if she is a counter-revolutionary—"

"Oh, go home, Alexis!" said the man with the drawling voice.

"There's no need to get your head broken until Petroff has said what she is," said Irina. "You stay on the stair till he comes. Once Stefan knows what she is, he will be on our side. He's a good Communist. It is the woman who has deceived him!"

The feet moved on, tramping the snow. The voices became fainter and were lost.

Ten years in the Secret Service trains a man to think rapidly and to make lightning decisions. Before the sound of the tramping feet had died away Stephen knew what he must do. He began to run in the direction from which Irina and her friends had come. Irina would not run. She would go with the men as far as the door of Boris' lodging. There would probably be a little more talk. Alexis would almost certainly delay the proceedings still further. Irina rarely missed any opportunity of holding forth. It might be another five minutes before she would start to fetch Petroff. In any case he had the legs of her and could count on getting there first. He spared no time to wonder what he would have done if he had not known where Petroff lodged. He did know, and the knowledge was to save them.

He came to the house with his part ready conned. Petroff had a three-roomed flat on the second floor. As Stephen knocked on the door, his ears cocked for the sound of Irina's step on the stair behind him, it came to him that this had been the door of Elizabeth's prison. Here she had lived in torment for a year. Here the old woman had bullied and starved her.

A voice shouted, "Come in!"

He opened the door and went in, his mind very clear and angry. The door led directly into a room from which other doors opened, one on either side. In the middle of this centre room was a large table littered with papers. Petroff sat at the table, but he was not occupied with the papers. He had a bottle in front of him and a glass in his hand. The room stank of vodka and the smoke of a rank cigar.

With a beaming smile Stephen rushed upon him and wrung him by the hand.

"Do you remember me, Comrade—Red Stefan? Yes, yes, of course you do—and Magnitogorsk—and the vodka! Well, well, well—that was a good meeting, wasn't it? And the vodka was good vodka! You were pleased to see me that day—eh, Comrade? And to-day you'll be even better pleased—unless I have made a mistake, and I don't think I have."

Petroff pushed back his chair, but he did not push it much farther from the table. He pushed it so that his hand could with one movement reach the revolver which he kept in the top right-hand drawer. He was not at all drunk. He had not had time to get drunk. He had merely taken enough vodka to make him feel that he was more than a match for Red Stefan.

Stephen saw the movement and laughed. He leaned on the table with an air of genial friendliness.

A man of stout build this Petroff. A little softer than he had been at Magnitogorsk. No—decidedly he had not improved. He had always had Tartar eyes and a face that looked as if someone had been careless with it. Now he had, in addition, an air of having gone to seed.

"What do you want?" said Petroff, his hand at the drawer.

Stephen laughed again.

"What do you think? You'll never guess, so I must tell you. You're looking for a woman, aren't you-counter-revolutionary with important information?"

"Who told you that?" said Petroff sharply.

Stephen made a fine vague gesture.

"Some comrade—I don't know—it might have been Irina. Could it have been Irina?"

His ears were strained for the sound of Irina's footsteps. Yet he must not hurry too much. Petroff was no fool.

"It might have been Irina." Petroff's tone was noncommittal.

Stephen nodded.

"Or it might have been some other comrade. Anyhow I heard it, and—now see if you are not surprised—I believe I have found her, this counter-revolutionary of yours. What is her name?"

Petroff had opened the drawer. His hand was on the revolver. His shallow, slanting eyes watched Stephen's face.

"Her name is Elizabeth Radin."

Stephen looked first puzzled, then excited.

"She called herself Varvara to me. And I married her. Think of that, Comrade! I found her wandering about in the streets like a half-wit and took her off to my village—never suspected anything till she began to talk in her sleep, and then I thought to myself, 'Oi, oi! What's all this?'" He laughed boisterously. "It's a funny business—eh, Comrade?"

Petroff kept his hand on the revolver.

"What did she say?"

"One night she said your name—'Petroff'—just like that."

Petroff reached his left hand for his glass and drank.

"She said my name?"

Stephen slapped his thigh.

"If I was a jealous husband, Comrade, what should I make of that? She said your name, and something more. She said, 'Petroff wants it,' and then she screamed out, 'No—no—no!'"

Petroff set down his glass again, empty.

"You're sure about this?"

"Sure? Of course I'm sure! That's why I'm here. I didn't say a word even to Irina. I just brought her along for you to have a look at her."

The door at the foot of the stair opened and shut. That would be Irina. All right, let her come. He'd beaten her. There was nothing to spare, but he'd done it.

Petroff was saying,

"Here? She's not here?"

Stephen leaned towards him eagerly.

"No, no, she's at Boris Andreieff's lodging. He lent us the room. I left her there and came to fetch you—"

Feet on the stair, and a knocking on the door...Irina.

"You'll have to identify her," said Stephen.

The knocking went on.

"Come in, if you want to!" shouted Petroff.

The knocking stopped. The door was flung open and Irina ran into the room.

Chapter Fourteen

STEPHEN SWUNG round on his corner of the table and stared at Irina with a most convincing surprise. Petroff stared too.

After all, Irina had run. Her breast heaved, and her cheeks glowed with an unwonted colour. At the sight of Stephen she came to a standstill a yard from the open door and stood there angry, breathless, and beautiful.

With a welcoming shout Stephen sprang at her and linked his arm in hers.

"It never rains but it pours! Here you are—and in the very nick of time!" He kicked the door shut, laughed noisily, and pulled Irina towards Petroff. "You're full of visitors to-day, Comrade. But I can always go if I am in the way. You and I have had our talk, so if Irina wants to talk secrets to you, I can make myself scarce. All I've got to say is, you're a very lucky man, and I wouldn't mind being in your place."

Irina pulled furiously away from him.

"What are you doing here, Stefan Ivanovitch?"

He made a laughing gesture.

"Just having a little talk with Comrade Petroff."

Her eyes blazed on him.

"What have you been talking about?"

"Why not ask him?" said Stephen.

Petroff had withdrawn his hand from the top right-hand drawer. He did not think he was going to need that revolver. The little scene interested him, but he had the feeling that it was time for him to take part in it. A cleverer man might have gone on listening, but Petroff, though no fool, had his weaknesses, and one of these was a disposition to hold the centre of the stage. He took his cue now with alacrity.

"Yes, why not ask me?" he said.

Irina was a very handsome young woman, but she was just a little too bossy for his taste. The equality of women was all very well, but a girl like Irina didn't stop at that—She wanted the upper hand all the time. He felt decidedly grateful to Stefan. It wouldn't do Irina any harm to be taken down a peg or two.

"Well?" said Irina defiantly. "What has Stefan been saying?"

Petroff smiled, showing teeth blackened by tobacco.

"He has been telling me that he has found Elizabeth Radin."

"What?" said Irina in angry amazement. She stared at Stephen and put a hand on the table as if to steady herself.

"He has found Elizabeth Radin," said Petroff.

Irina's voice sank to a sharp whisper.

"What?"

Stephen slapped his thigh and shouted with delight.

"It's a joke—isn't it? But you haven't any idea what a good joke it is. Lord—how you'll laugh! Shall we tell her, Comrade? I think we'll have to, because she'll never guess."

He came and sat on the edge of the table and leaned confidentially towards Irina.

"I've found Elizabeth Radin. And who the devil do you suppose she turns out to be?" He drummed with his heels against the table leg and thumped an emphatic accompaniment upon the paper-strewn table top. "Guess—guess—*guess!* No, you can't guess—nobody could—so what's the good of trying? Oh my Lord—it's funny! I'll have to tell you. She's my wife Varvara. Just open your mouth and swallow that down if you can! Elizabeth Radin is my wife Varvara!" With a final bang he made the papers fly and the ink jump in Petroff's ink-well. "What do you say to that?"

For the moment Irina had nothing to say. She stood in a staring amazement which had no words.

Stephen sprang off the table and smote Petroff on the shoulder.

"There, Comrade—what did I say? She is so surprised that she can't say a single word. Irina without a word to say! Did you ever think you would see that? I shall certainly stick a feather in my cap." He clapped Petroff's shoulder again. "Tell her it's true, Comrade, or she won't believe it."

Stephen's hand was heavier than Petroff cared about. He pushed back his chair again, wincing.

"He certainly says his wife is Elizabeth Radin," he said drily.

Irina leaned still more heavily upon the table. She removed her gaze from Stephen and looked at Petroff.

"Did he come here to tell you that?" she said in a low voice.

Petroff gave a brief nod.

"He came here to tell you that?" she repeated.

Stephen threw back his head and laughed.

"I said you would never guess! How could you? No one could have had the least suspicion. I had none myself until she began to talk about Comrade Petroff in her sleep—and, as I was saying to him, there might have been more than one explanation for that. Even Commissars must relax sometimes—eh, Comrade? But it wasn't exactly love-words she was saying in her sleep." He pursed up his lips and winked at Petroff, after which he burst out laughing again. "Just think of me picking her up so innocently and believing everything she said! She pitched a good tale, you know—I'll say that for her—about her father and mother being dead, and a brother in the Red Army she hadn't heard of for two years, and couldn't I please help her to find him. Well, there's no harm done, but it'll be a joke against me for the rest of my days. Divorce is easy—that's one thing. And as we never even registered, well, there's an end of it."

Irina jerked herself upright and came to him, moving stiffly.

"Do you mean that?"

"Do I mean what?"

"That there's an end of it."

"Do you think I'd stay married to a counter-revolutionary?" His voice was hot with rage.

"Don't be angry, Stefan." Irina spoke quite humbly.

"Then don't make me angry! How would you like someone to say you'd marry a counter-revolutionary?"

The colour rose in Irina's cheeks. She laid a hand on his breast and said,

"Don't be angry, Stefan."

Petroff might not have been there at all—a circumstance very annoying to Petroff. He thought it time to intervene. He rose to his feet and rapped on the table.

"It remains to be seen if this Varvara really is Elizabeth Radin. What is the good of talking about it? I must see her. If she is Elizabeth Radin, she must be arrested without delay. Whilst we are wasting time she may be making her escape."

Irina laughed, and for that laugh Stephen came near to hating her.

"No, no, she won't get away—I've seen to that. There are half a dozen Comrades on the stair waiting to see that she stays in Boris Andreieff's room until you come. She won't get past them—you may be quite sure about that. There are six of them, and they are armed."

"That was well thought of," said Petroff. "I will get my coat and we will go at once."

He hurried into the next room, leaving the door open.

Irina turned searching eyes on Stephen's face. She did not touch him, but they were so close that if he had bent his head, they might have kissed.

"I knew you didn't love her," she said.

Chapter Fifteen

ELIZABETH SAT in Boris Andreieff's room in the shabby, comfortable armchair and waited for Stephen to come back. It was an ugly room with high, bare walls which at some very distant date had been washed pink. Dirt and age had now converted them to the semblance of some ancient map. Here a trail of smoke simulated a mountain range, there a long crack did duty for a river, whilst holes in the plaster might have been lakes. The original pink, lingering where a picture, now removed, had protected it, looked as ghastly as rouge on an old woman's face. The room contained no single object which was not of a utilitarian nature except the inevitable portrait of Lenin. The window, which looked upon the frozen river, was curtained against the cold with hangings of a stuff so aged that its original colour could no longer be discerned. It reminded Elizabeth of a London fog, and at once there leapt up in her a sickness for home—London mud under her feet, and the smell of a London fog, queer, sooty, cold. What a ridiculous thing to feel homesick about!

She laughed at herself, and came back.

If the room was ugly, it was warm. The stove was giving out a good heat, the lamplight softened the bare outlines, and the chair was really comfortable. It was more than a year since she had had any privacy, more than a year since she had sat alone in a room like this with the freedom of her own thoughts. She was not really in a hurry for Stephen to come back. They had lived at such close quarters that she felt a need to step back and look at him.

She began to go over everything that had happened from the time of their first meeting. Strange meeting. Strange life together. Strange prelude to another life. She had been so frozen, so nearly dead, that it was as if he had brought her up from the grave itself. If it had not been for him, she would have died on that first night when she had run from Petroff's lodging into the bitter streets. If it had not been for him, she would have died on that other night in Yuri's hut. She thought of him with a little trembling laughter at her heart. He was so big and sure, so strong and yet so gentle with her, and as naïve as a boy. In one and the same breath he would tell her she was like a frozen star and ask her if she would like some more cabbage soup. Stephen was always practical.

She went on thinking about him until a sound on the stair broke in upon her thoughts. She sat up and listened. She had not expected Stephen back so soon. And then, all alone as she was, she blushed, because she did not really know how long she had been dreaming about him.

She got up and went to the window. If this was Stephen, he should not find her watching the door for him. Instead she lifted the curtain and looked at the frosted pane. The river was there beyond, all frozen now. She could not see it, but she knew that it was there. This, then, must be one of those tall dark houses at which she had stared from the bridge. It was so curious to think of herself as she was then, shelterless and without hope, and to come back to this new self, sheltered, and with new hope springing.

She turned from the window at what she took to be his step. Or was it only the stair creaking? Old stairs did creak, and this house must be very old. She let fall the curtain, crossed the floor, and opened the door a little way. There was no light anywhere. The open space was a handsbreadth of darkness.

She stood there listening, with one hand on the door and one on the jamb, and it seemed to her as if the darkness were coming into the room.

It was a darkness full of sounds—an unquiet darkness—a whispering, shuffling darkness. There was no word spoken, no sound of which she could say, a foot moved, or one man jostled another. Yet, standing there with the wide black crack between her right hand and her left, Elizabeth knew that there were men upon the stair. Three, four, five, six...How could she tell whether there were four or six of them? More than three, and not more than six. What did it matter how many there were? She would be as surely trapped by two as by a dozen. And there were more than two. The sounds were not all the same sounds. The whispers were different whispers.

Elizabeth's left hand, which held the door, began very slowly to push it to. The handsbreath of darkness became a finger's breadth, and then was altogether gone. The door was shut. Her hands groped below the handle, found the key, and turned it in the lock. Then she went back from the door as far as the table and leaned upon it. The lamp which stood there made a warm glow against her shoulder and her neck.

Elizabeth leaned upon her hands and bit into her lip, Presently she put up her right hand and wiped away a drop of sweat which was running down her cheek. She had locked the door—an old frail door, with an old frail lock. How long would it keep anyone out? No, not anyone—any six.

An old German nursery rhyme came humming through her frightened thoughts:

Ach du lieber Augustin, Augustin, Augustin.
Ach du lieber Augustin, alles ist hin.
Rock ist weg,
Stock ist weg,
Mädel ist weg,
Alles ist weg—
Ach du lieber Augustin, alles ist hin."

Everything's gone—everything's gone—everything's gone...

"Ach du lieber Augustin, alles ist hin."

And then:

"Rock ist weg,
Stock ist weg,
Mädel ist weg—"

What would Stephen say when he came back and found her gone?

Everything gone—everything gone—everything gone...

"Ach du lieber Augustin, alles ist hin."

The rhythm came with the beating of her heart, and louder, louder, louder. She could neither think nor move. Breathless, she could only wait for the door to be broken in.

And then, as she stared at it, she saw the handle move. The latch rattled, the handle moved again.

All at once Elizabeth became able to think and speak. The tune stopped beating out its jingle of words amongst her disorganized thoughts. It was as if a very loud noise had suddenly stopped.

The handle of the door was shaken. She said in a quiet voice,

"Who is there?"

And Stephen said,

"Open the door—it's me."

A warm weakness flowed over Elizabeth. She had forced herself to such a pitch of self-control, and the danger it was to meet had dissolved unmet. It was as if she had nerved herself for some terrible fall, only to find that the imagined precipice was an illusion. She was so shaken with relief and happiness that for a moment she could not move. Then she ran to the door and turned the key.

The door was pushed open so roughly that she was flung backwards, and at once the room was full of people—Stephen, Irina, Petroff, and half a dozen young men pushing eagerly past one another till the last of them was in and the door slammed to.

Elizabeth stood where the thrust of the door had sent her, and looked on this unbelievable scene. She saw Irina who hated her, Petroff from whom she had fled, and a Stephen whom she did not know. A Stephen whose arm was linked with Petroff's as he shouted noisily,

"There, Comrade! There she is! And it's for you to say *who* she is. She's my wife Varvara all right, but if she's your Elizabeth what's-her-name, you're welcome to her, and I'll call it a good riddance."

There was a murmur of talk among the Young Communists. Petroff shook off Stephen's hand and came forward, those shallow Tartar eyes of his fixed maliciously upon Elizabeth. As he advanced, she went back step by step until the wall stopped her, her eyes glassy, her hands palm outwards as if to fend him off. When she reached the wall, she braced herself against it. Her hands fell to her sides. She waited for what would come next.

Petroff came to within about a yard of her and said,

"You've been in a great hurry to change your name, haven't you?"

Stephen looked over his head and laughed.

"I was right then. Didn't I say so? It would be a good joke against me if I hadn't found it out for myself. She is really your Elizabeth Radin?"

Elizabeth held up her head and looked at Petroff. She could not look at Stephen.

She heard Petroff say, "Yes, she is Elizabeth Radin," and at once the room was full of loud buzzing voices. Irina talked, the Young Communists talked, Stephen shouted, and Petroff, coming quite near, said in a tone which somehow pierced the noise,

"What a fool you were to run away!"

The word echoed bitterly in the lost and arid place where Elizabeth's consciousness struggled with the approach of darkness. A fool ... a fool who had climbed up a little way out of the pit, only to slide back again—and deeper. No, she had not climbed, she had been drawn up, and the hand that had drawn her up had thrust her down again—Stephen's hand. She shuddered from the thought that she had clung to it. It fell now on her shoulder with a heavy grip.

Stephen, still laughing, shook her a little.

"Well, what's to be done with her, Comrade? Here she is!"

At his touch Elizabeth screamed. It was the faintest of sounds, no more in reality than a sharply drawn breath of agony, but it rang in her own ears as a scream. It drowned Stephen's voice and Stephen's words. It was the last thing she heard, because in that moment the darkness fell.

Chapter Sixteen

ELIZABETH OPENED her eyes because a bright light was shining on them. She shut them again quickly because the light hurt her. It continued to shine through her closed lids. After a moment she put up her hand to shield her eyes, and with that movement consciousness flowed back and she was aware of her body again. She was lying down...on a bed...her hands and feet were cold...the light was shining on her eyes...

A shiver ran over her. She raised herself on her elbow and once more opened her eyes. She was lying on a narrow bed in a square white-washed room. There were more beds like the one she was lying on—three or four more. An unshaded electric light hung from the ceiling.

Elizabeth frowned, raised herself a little more, and looked about her. There were three other beds. On the edge of one of them a young woman sat looking at her. She had a foolish flat face, rather light eyes, and hands with stubby fingers and bitten nails. There was a finger at her mouth most of the time. She looked over her shoulder and said,

"She's awake, Marfa."

Elizabeth sat up and saw a little old woman peering at her.

"Where am I?"

She felt sick at the sound of her own voice, because it brought back to her those other voices—Irina's—Petroff's—*Stephen's*. She said the words again, because she had stammered over them the first time.

"Where am I?"

The old woman went on peering. The young one said,

"Prison."

Elizabeth repeated the word as if saying it to herself:

"Prison—"

She sat on the edge of the bed and put her feet to the floor. She felt giddy when she moved. When her head was clear again she became conscious of some relief. If this was a prison, it was at least a clean and decent place. It was, she discovered, a woman's ward in the ordinary civil prison, and for this she felt thankful. The lot of the political prisoner was generally cast in fouler places. Stories she had heard of horrible over-crowding, filth and vermin came back to her as she looked at the neat beds, the whitewash, and the well scrubbed floor.

Her two companions were serving sentences, one for selling illicit vodka—all intoxicants being a government monopoly—and the other for murder. It was the young woman, Anna, who was the murderess. She had got tired of looking after some aged relative and had strangled her. She spoke of it without a trace of compunction. For the rest she seemed a stupid, amiable person who could talk by the hour about nothing. The old woman never spoke at all. Her grey hair fell over her eyes in an unkempt tangle, and through the elf-locks she watched Elizabeth's every move with the suspicious air of an animal.

"He was a big man, that one who carried you in," said Anna presently—"a fine man, though I don't like red hair myself. They say you can never trust a red-haired person."

Elizabeth winced. Stephen had carried her in. She had trusted him with all her heart. She winced now at the thought that he had touched her. Her sheepskin coat and cap were laid at the foot of the bed. Was it Stephen who had put them on her before he carried her through the cold streets? Or was it Petroff, who would not want her to die until she had given him the formula?

"He carried you as easily as if you were a baby," said Anna—"and took off your coat and cap and laid you down on the bed. There was a dark man with him—a Commissar. I have seen him before. His name is Petroff. He took hold of your wrist and felt it, and said, 'Is she all right?' And the big man took hold of your other wrist. There they were, one on either side of you, like two dogs with a bone. Then the big man said, 'So you don't want her to die, Comrade?' And that Petroff said, 'Not just yet.' 'Oh, you needn't be afraid—she won't die,' says the big man, and with that he laughs and lets go of your wrist. Is he your lover?"

"I have no lover," said Elizabeth.

Anna bit a thumb-nail which was already down to the quick.

"Well, I wouldn't have a red-haired one—you can't trust them."

Elizabeth sat and stared at the wall, and thought how she had trusted Stephen. She had given him her trust and her friendship. She had been ready to give him her love—if he had wanted it. She wondered whether it would hurt more to think that he had not wanted it at all, or that he had wanted it lightly for the pleasure of a passing moment. As the thought shaped itself, she knew the answer. She could bear the thought of his indifference. *She knew very well that he had not been indifferent.* The pain of her wound was the pain of knowing that he had wanted her, and, wanting her, had held her cheaply—a mere pawn, to be sacrificed without compunction the moment the game or his safety demanded the surrender of a piece. She would do him the justice to suppose that it was the game to which she had been sacrificed. She would try and believe that. Her wound would ache a little less bitterly if she could imagine some motive not altogether ignoble.

Then, sharply and suddenly, she remembered that she had given him the formula.

Chapter Seventeen

THERE FOLLOWED a night of moments lengthening slowly into hours. The moments were so long that time had no measure left by which to mete the hours. Yet in the end a slow, cold daylight broke upon the ward. The walls changed imperceptibly from black, through all the shades of grey, to a clear, staring white.

There was water to wash in. Elizabeth washed. There was her bed to make. She made it. Then she sat down again and stared at the wall, whilst Anna told her long stories about her relations, her friends, her acquaintances, and their friends, relations, and acquaintances.

Elizabeth did not listen, but every now and then a sentence reached her mind:

"So then he took a knife and stabbed him...

"It was a neighbour's child and it ran away into the forest...

"After that Nadashda had three more husbands, but she wasn't happy with any of them..."

It did not matter to Anna that Elizabeth was not listening. She talked on with great enjoyment.

It was about four in the afternoon that the summons came.

Elizabeth had lost count of time. There had been two meals. She had eaten, but she could not have said what it was that she had eaten. Anna had talked incessantly. And then the door was unlocked and a wardress told her to put on her coat and cap.

"Are they going to shoot you?" said Anna, with an interested stare. "You're a *bourzhui*, aren't you, and a counter-revolutionary? It's a pity to put on a good coat to be shot in. Blood never really comes out."

In the corridor there were three men in police uniform. They closed round her, one going in front and two behind, and so down a flight of steps and out into the street. She wondered if they were going to shoot her without a trial, or whether some travesty of justice would come first and the shooting afterwards. She had given Stephen the formula; there was therefore no further reason for keeping her alive. She had heard of so many summary executions that she did not doubt she was going to her death.

She felt a curious indifference. It was growing dark. The wind blew out of the north. Now and again a tiny stinging point of snow touched her face. Her feet were cold and so heavy that she could hardly lift them. She wondered whether they had far to go, and whether they would shoot her in the open or drive her down some cellar stair. She felt a sick horror at the thought of the cellar.

She had not been noticing the way they took. When they stopped before a door, her heart turned over. Now it would come—now, in the next few moments.

The door opened. One of the men went in, and she followed him. There were two steps down, which she took instinctively, because in the old house where Petroff had his flat there were two steps down as you come in. Her feet had grown accustomed to them. She drove her nails into the palms of her hands. This time she must not faint. It was just the waiting that was dreadful. She would probably not feel the shot.

And then all at once she was walking, not downstairs, but up, and she knew why she had found the steps familiar. This was the house in which she had lived for a year. Even in the heavy dusk she would have recognized it if her thoughts had not taken her so near death as to make all other impressions meaningless. The fear of death slipped away and another fear took its place. Her foot stumbled and she was thrown against the man on her right. He took hold of her roughly and pushed her on. They continued to mount the stairs.

In the middle room of the flat above Petroff was drinking scalding tea well laced with vodka. A large samovar steamed pleasantly upon a side-table. Petroff sat in his writing-chair, his tumbler of tea all mixed up with a froth of papers. On the opposite side of the table Stephen bestrode a wooden chair. He had a smoking glass in his hand. He drank from it and set it down.

"Of course it's all the same to me what you do with her, and whether I go or stay."

"You've said that before," said Petroff.

"Of course I've said it before—and I shall go on saying it. You can't say a true thing too often, can you? Hi, Comrade, how many of these little glasses does it take to make you drunk—fifty or a hundred?"

Petroff shrugged his shoulders.

"Help yourself," he said. "I'm not here to get drunk—I'm here to find out what this woman knows."

"Well then, but have you thought of this, Comrade? She's a cunning one—as cunning as they make them, I should say. Suppose she only *pretends* to tell you what you want to know. Have you thought of that? She might do it, if she thought it would save her skin. And that, Comrade, is where I come in. You bring her in here, and you tell her, 'There's your husband who heard you talk in your sleep, and if you alter so much as a single word he'll know it, and then it'll be no good pleading and asking for mercy, because you won't get any.'"

Petroff frowned at his steaming drink.

"That is not badly thought of," he said.

"I have these ideas," said Stephen. "Sometimes they come to me when I'm drunk, and sometimes when I'm sober. Just now I'm not as drunk as I'd like to be. That's the worst of having a head like mine—it costs such a lot to get drunk. This vodka isn't as good as the stuff I had in Magnitogorsk."

"Oh, be quiet!" said Petroff, and with that there came a thumping on the door. Stephen swung round and watched it open. The man who had knocked came into the room, and behind him two others with Elizabeth between them. One of them held her by the arm. There were blue marks like bruises under her eyes, and her face was quite white. The eyes themselves had a frozen look of fear. All her movements were slow and stiff.

"Leave her and wait downstairs!" said Petroff sharply.

Stephen leaned over the table and began to whisper.

"Do you really want them to wait? I shouldn't have said you did. It may take some time to make her speak, and they're an interfering lot. Why not say you'll ring them up when you've finished with her? They'll be glad enough not to wait about in the cold."

"Hold your tongue!" said Petroff, pushing back his chair.

He went over and spoke to the men at the door.

"It will not be necessary for you to wait. It may take me some time to interrogate this person. I will telephone for an escort when I have finished with her."

The man he addressed looked sulky.

"We have orders to wait."

"Very well then, wait!" said Petroff with a shrug of his shoulders. The man hesitated.

"If you take the responsibility—" he said.

"I do not care whether you wait or not!" said Petroff, and slammed the door.

Elizabeth heard their feet go clattering down the stair, and then Petroff's hand was on her shoulder.

"Well now, my girl—are you going to be sensible?" he said.

Stephen got up and pushed his chair towards her.

"Let her sit down—let her sit down, or she'll be fainting again. She's got a most cursed aggravating way of fainting just when it's inconvenient. Do you hear that, Varvara? None of your fainting tricks here—they won't do you any good. Have a drink and brace up! And if you tell Comrade Petroff what he wants to know and ask him nicely, perhaps he'll let you off without a firing-party this time, and you can go and look for that brother of yours in the Red Army that you told me about." He laughed heartily at his own joke and, still laughing, filled up his glass at the samovar and pushed it into Elizabeth's hand.

The smell of the spirit sickened her, and she set it down on the table. She had sunk down upon the wooden chair and sat there looking at Petroff, who had resumed his seat and was facing her across the littered table. He leaned back as if to show how much at ease he was and addressed her in a judicial tone.

"What Stefan says is to some extent true. If you are going to be sensible, I daresay I can do something for you."

Elizabeth stretched out her hand for the glass she had refused. At the sound of Stephen's voice a kind of inward shivering had come upon her. It was the cold, she told herself, it was the cold...But if she was to answer Petroff, she must get the better of it. She lifted the glass to her lips and drank. The tea was scalding hot. There was not so much vodka in it as she had supposed. She steadied herself and, with her cold hands clasped about the warmth of the glass, said,

"What do you want?"

Petroff's lip lifted in a sneer.

"What innocence! You know very well what I want, and I can assure you that I mean to have it. I know that you have Nicolas Radin's formula, and you'll save us both a lot of trouble if you'll hand it over quickly."

So Stephen had not given him the formula. The knowledge put a little heart into Elizabeth. She could still fight if there was something to fight for. She lifted her head with a touch of pride and said,

"What do you mean?"

Petroff flung himself forward and banged on the table.

"What do I mean? You have the nerve to ask me that! Do you suppose you're going to get away with that sort of bluff? No, no, my dear, it's not good enough. You shouldn't have let yourself talk in your sleep. First my mother hears you, and then your husband. Being a good Communist, he comes and tells me. So now you know where we are. Come now—you ought to be grateful to me instead of sulking. You'd have been in a filthy political cell if it hadn't been for me. I've got a special authority from Moscow to deal with your case, and I don't mind telling you why. *They want that process of Radin's.* I'm going to tell you just how badly they want it—badly enough to stretch a point and let you go if you'll give it to me, and badly enough to break me if I don't get it out of you. There—you can't say I haven't been frank with you. And if you think for about half a minute, you'll see how much chance you've got of keeping a secret which means life and death to me. I'm bound to have it—*bound*—and I'll stick at nothing to get it."

His narrowing eyes held hers. His voice became a mere rasp. He threw back his head and laughed a little.

"There are ways of making people speak, you know."

There was a silence. Stephen stood at the corner of the table, his eyes going from one to the other, like a man watching a game.

When the silence had lasted for a little while, he leaned forward, picked up the vodka bottle and tipped it up over Petroff's glass. The colourless liquid gurgled out, and Petroff said,

"Hi—that's my glass!"

Stephen picked it up, laughing.

"I'll put a drop of hot tea in it. You'll be dry enough before you're through with Varvara, I can tell you. One of those quiet obstinate ones—that's what she is—the sort that wears a man down and makes his throat as dry as a lime-kiln. Next time I shall pick a talker—a good lively girl who'll say what she's got to say and get it off her chest. I've had enough of these sulky ones." He was at the samovar as he spoke.

"Don't drown the vodka," said Petroff without taking his eyes off Elizabeth.

She sat looking past him at the curtained windows. She would do anything rather than look at Stephen. And then she *was* looking at him, because he had come round behind the table with the drink in his hand. He leaned over Petroff's shoulder and set it down. And then, as he drew back, his fist shot out and struck the Commissar behind the ear. It happened so quickly that it left Elizabeth dazed. She had no time to cry out. One moment Petroff was staring at her out of his narrow, slanting eyes, and the next he was face down amongst the litter of his own papers, his body sprawling and his arms shot limply out across the table.

She found herself on her feet without knowing how she had got there. Stephen was picking Petroff up and laying him down on the floor. He said in his natural voice,

"Lock the door, will you."

And all at once the nightmare was over. Warmth and courage came back to her. She ran to the door, locked it, and then came back again.

Stephen had been tying Petroff up in a quiet, methodical manner. There was already a gag of cotton waste in the Commissar's mouth and a good wide bandage to keep it there. These things had emerged from a capacious inner pocket, which further provided a length of good stout cord. This went to the binding of Petroff's hands and the securing of his ankles.

Stephen looked over his shoulder at Elizabeth and laughed.

"That's done his job!" he said. After which he picked Petroff up and carried him into the back room.

He came back alone.

"We've got to hurry," he said. "It's a nuisance about the police. We'll have to go out of that back window. There's a bit of sloping roof that might have been made for us. I'm afraid those policemen are going to have a long cold wait."

As he spoke, he was taking a canvas roll out of his pocket and opening it. It seemed to contain some very odd things. He picked out a stick of shaving-soap, a razor, and a pair of scissors. Next he filled the empty glass with boiling tea and spread newspapers over the floor and upon the table. A pocket mirror came out of the roll and was set up. Kneeling down before it, he began to remove his beard, using the scissors first and the razor afterwards.

Elizabeth watched him, leaning on the table. The nightmare had gone, but it was just as if a very loud noise had suddenly stopped, or as if she had been in frightful pain and all at once the pain had been wiped away. There was a feeling of almost dazed relief. She could not really think; she could only feel that the pain had gone.

She watched Stephen.

He looked younger without his beard. Her eye was pleased by the shape of his chin and the clear, firm line of the jaw.

He looked round at her suddenly with a frown.

"Why did you look like that when you came? Nobody's hurt you?"

(Nobody—Oh. Stephen!)

"Oh no," said Elizabeth.

"Then why did you look like that?" said Stephen, scraping away at his cheek.

Elizabeth was silent. The situation was beyond her. How could she say, "I thought you had betrayed me?" And yet what else was there that she could have thought? What did she think now? Quite frankly, she didn't know. Only the nightmare seemed to have broken and released her.

Stephen had finished shaving. He dived into his pocket and brought out a wig of unkempt black hair. He put it on, adjusted it carefully, and then repeated his question.

"Why did you look like that? Did you think I'd let you down?"

Elizabeth had no answer.

Stephen picked up a stick of something that looked like putty, nipped a bit out of it, and proceeded to alter the shape of his nose by giving it a higher bridge.

"I'm sorry if you thought that," he said. "You see, I ran into Irina and her crowd of Young Communists just after I left you. The Young Communists were on their way to keep guard over you whilst Irina went to fetch Petroff. They didn't see me, so I thought I'd better get going before Irina did."

He poured away nearly all the tea, added some dark powder to what remained, stirred it with the handle of Petroff's pen, and began to apply the stuff to his face. It gave him the skin of a gipsy, and he further added to the effect by running his hands over the none too scrupulously tended floor and then smearing his face with the resulting grime. Darkened lashes and a pair of bushy black eyebrows made him the complete ruffian.

"Now for you," he said. "I'm afraid I'll have to make you a bit dirty. Don't look till I've done with you."

Elizabeth sat down. She shut her eyes when she was told to shut them, and felt Stephen's fingers busy with her face. He was staining her skin as he had stained his own, rubbing the stuff well in and then dabbing things here and there. He talked all the time.

"I was afraid you might think I had let you down, but of course I hoped you wouldn't. If I hadn't got to Petroff first, he'd probably have arrested me too. Can you tip your face up a little so that the stuff doesn't run off? Yes, that's all right. You do see that I was bound to stop them arresting me, don't you?"

"Oh yes," said Elizabeth.

He drew back a little and looked at her critically.

"I hope I haven't made you too brown. You didn't say that 'Oh yes' as if you meant it. Here's your wig. It's quite clean inside. You said 'Oh yes' exactly as if you meant, 'You did it to save your own skin, you swab!' Is that what you thought?" He was adjusting the wig as he spoke.

Her eyes met his and fell. It was like being stared down by a terrifying stranger. His eyes were strange under the shaggy brows. But the voice and the hands were Stephen's voice and Stephen's hands. The voice was gentle.

"I expect it was bound to look like that," he said reassuringly. "Once I was arrested, you wouldn't have had a chance. Don't you see that? As long as I could keep on the right side of Petroff there were bound to be chances all the time. This is one of them. I couldn't have done anything if I'd been in prison too, or even if I'd been under suspicion. I had to go the whole hog. The great thing was to keep you out of the hands of the G.P.U. Once they've got you they never let go. Fortunately, Petroff wanted to run the show himself—if there was any credit going, he didn't want to share it. I told him you'd probably die just to spite him if he let you go to the political prison, so he wangled that. He really has got a special authority to deal with your case, you know, and I persuaded him to have you here so that he could deal with you all on his own without any prison officials to cramp his style. The fact is they want that process of Radin's, and if Petroff managed to get it out of you, nobody would ask any questions about how he got it. Give me that handkerchief from your neck—it'll help to keep the wig on."

He knotted it under her chin and then suddenly held up the mirror.

Elizabeth uttered a faint exclamation. She saw a face which she would not have known, framed in dark greasy hair just streaked with grey. Coarse eyebrows covered her own and concealed their delicate arch. A strip of very dirty sticking-plaster crossed the left cheek, whilst three large warts adorned forehead, nose, and chin.

"And now we've got to hurry," said Stephen.

He made a bundle of the newspapers, taking care that nothing fell from them. When he had pushed them into the stove and watched them burn, he came back to the table and began to put away all the things he had used. He was slipping the canvas roll into his pocket, when Elizabeth suddenly caught him by the arm. He turned his head, and so for a moment they stood and listened.

Someone was coming up the stair.

Chapter Eighteen

FIRM, LIGHT STEPS coming up the stair. No policeman on the habitable globe ever walked like that. Elizabeth's grip tightened as the footsteps ceased. There was a knock upon the door, and in the same moment the handle was turned and shaken, and Irina's voice said,

"Let me in, Petroff. Why have you locked the door?"

Stephen's hand came up empty out of his pocket. He put his arm round Elizabeth for a moment and, turning his face from the door, he laughed and said,

"Shall I let her in, Comrade?"

"Why have you locked the door?" said Irina outside.

Stephen released himself from Elizabeth, pushed her gently away, walked round the table without making a sound, and spoke in Petroff's rasping tones.

"Can't a man lock his own door? Tell her she can't come in!"

Irina raised her voice in some annoyance.

"Why can't I come in? You've got that woman there. Open the door! I want to speak to Stefan."

Stephen walked to the door and leaned against it. He sounded very persuasive as he said,

"Well, here I am. If you've got anything to say to me, I hope it's something nice."

"Why?" said Irina shortly. She twisted the handle again and rattled it.

The sweat stood out on Elizabeth's temples. At any moment she expected to hear the tramp of the police.

Stephen laughed a lazy laugh.

"Why? Why, because we've got a damned obstinate woman here, and I'd like something pleasant for a change." He dropped his voice and spoke into the crack of the door. "Irina—"

"What is it?"

"I want to come and see you."

"Do you?" Her tone was soft.

"When will you be in?"

"All the evening."

"Will you be alone?"

"Do you want me to be alone?"

"Well, what do you think?"

"I can be."

From the other side of the room came Petroff's voice again. The illusion was so perfect that Elizabeth started and looked round to see if the Commissar had broken in upon them. Petroff's voice said angrily,

"Go away—I'm busy! Don't you know when you're not wanted?"

And immediately Stephen was whispering at the door.

"You'd better go. We can't talk here. I'll come when I can."

There was a pause. Then Irina said softly,

"Come quickly."

They heard her step going away down the stair.

Elizabeth had not moved. Stephen whispering to Irina...Stephen asking her whether she would be alone...He was cheating her of course...Why shouldn't he trick her? Irina wouldn't know that it was a trick until he didn't come...In some queer way Elizabeth felt that she herself was being tricked. You couldn't trust anyone really. Nicolas Radin had taught her that.

Irina's last faint footstep died away. The house door shut with a dull bang.

Stephen turned round with a soundless whistle.

"That was a near thing!"

He took Elizabeth by the arm and hurried her into the back room. As her foot crossed the threshold, she felt the old sick fear. The light sprang on in the ceiling and she looked instinctively at the big bed in the corner. It was as if she expected to see the terrible old woman who had slept there—white scanty hair flying loose, thin lips drawn back in a sneer, jaws mumbling out cruel words, and red-rimmed eyes a-glitter with malice. Instead there lay propped up against the pillows a mummied Petroff, rolled up stiff and stark, with the sheet over his head. The blankets lay in a pile on the floor.

Stephen nicked the strongest with his knife to cut the hem, and then tore it into strips, which he knotted into a rope. Over the last knot he nodded to Elizabeth.

"Put out the light and shut the door into the other room."

With her hand on the switch, she saw the mummy heave. Then the darkness came with a rush, and immediately the wind blew cold from the opened window. Such a horror fell upon Elizabeth that she had no fear left for the drop to the yard. She had no thought left except to be gone from this haunted room. A weight of old, dead cruelty pressed upon her, and in the darkness Petroff writhed against his bonds.

She climbed eagerly out upon the sill with the blanket rope about her waist and met the bitter air with relief.

"Steady now," said Stephen, whispering. "Let your eyes get accustomed to the dark. There's snow on the roof below—that will help you. Get as far as the gutter and then let yourself down gently. It's quite easy."

At any other time she might have found it difficult. Now she only wanted to get away from that horrible room. The roof sloped below her. She let go of the sill and slid down with the sliding snow. She slid quite gently because of the rope, but when her feet found the gutter she had a sick moment of fear, because now she would have to swing out over the edge and hang dangling like a spider on a thread. Someone might look out of the window below and see her. Someone might look out of any other back window and see her. The knotted strips might loosen, or fray against the edge of the roof.

She lowered herself by her hands. They were so cold from the snow that as soon as her weight came upon them they lost their hold. She caught at the rope, spun giddily for a moment, and then came safely down upon the snow of the yard.

Stephen was after her in no time and they were running for the gate. It opened on a narrow alleyway, which they followed to a street of tall, dark houses.

"Where are we going?" said Elizabeth in a breathless whisper.

"To the station. We've made Tronsk a bit too hot to hold us."

Fear of the station surged up in Elizabeth. She had a picture of it in her mind as a wind-swept place beneath relentless arc lamps where the police of the G.P.U. scanned every passenger.

Stephen pressed her arm encouragingly.

"Don't worry—we'll get away before anyone finds Petroff. We shall probably catch something that was due an hour or two ago. They don't worry about time-tables in Russia. If it were summer, when everyone is travelling, we might have to wait a day or two to get into a train. It won't be as bad as that now, and we can thank all our stars they haven't got their internal passport system going yet."

Elizabeth drew away from him in the dark.

"What's the matter?"

She did not speak. She was tired, and bewildered, and afraid, and she could take no comfort from Stephen who had comforted her before. She was full of a cold grey anger which seemed to be soaking into her mind like sleety rain. A hot anger would have warmed her, but this cold resentment chilled her to the marrow.

Stephen slipped his hand through her arm.

"What's the matter?" he said again, and felt her draw sharply away. "Are you angry?"

"Oh no," said Elizabeth in a desolate voice.

"That means 'Oh yes,'" said Stephen. "I knew you were angry when you pulled your arm away. I won't touch you again, but you'd better tell me what I've done. It's going to be very difficult escaping with someone who is hating me like poison."

"I don't."

"I hope you don't. You sounded awfully like it just now. What have I done?"

The cold anger became suddenly hot. It loosened Elizabeth's tongue.

"Why did you ask Irina if she would be alone tonight?"

"Because I had to get rid of her, of course. You didn't think I was going, did you?"

"Oh no," said Elizabeth wearily—"I knew you weren't going. But Irina didn't. She'll sit there and wait for you to come. That's what I hate."

"Do you want me to call on Irina?" said Stephen. "I will if you like. We shall miss our train, but that won't matter, because you'll have been arrested again. They won't put you in the civil prison this time, and it'll end in our both being shot, but of course any of that would be better than keeping Irina waiting."

He spoke in a low matter-of-fact tone, but it came to her that he was angry too. For some obscure reason this made her feel a great deal better.

"You played on her being fond of you," she said.

"I had to get her to go away, didn't I? I've told you already that I've never made love to Irina in my life. If I've played a trick on her, she has only herself to thank. She's asked for it. When you fainted she laughed. Do you think I care what she feels or doesn't feel after that?" He caught her arm and tucked it under his. "For heaven's sake be practical! You can't quarrel with me now, because there isn't time. Wait till we're over the frontier."

He felt her quickened breathing. The frontier...Would they ever reach it? It seemed, like the line of the horizon, a distant goal which with every step receded instead of drawing near. No man ever reached the horizon, just as no man ever touched the rainbow's end. To Elizabeth the frontier seemed as unattainable. This time she did not draw her arm away. Instead: she said, very low,

"Shall we get there?" and at once was being scolded.

"Not if you talk like that—not if you even think like that. You'll never make a success of anything if you let yourself think about failing. Now I know that I'm going to get you over the frontier. I knew it the very first moment I saw you on the bridge. I could have picked you up and carried you over the frontier then and there. I've never had the slightest doubt about getting you away. I wish you'd clamp on to that instead of letting yourself get angry and afraid, and things like that. I'd rather you were angry than afraid."

Elizabeth was not angry any more, neither was she afraid. She was only tired.

They turned into the station approach.

"Now," said Stephen, "this is all going to be quite easy. Petroff wouldn't know you if he met you face to face." He dived into his pocket and brought out a hunk of black bread. "I want you to keep munching away at this till the train starts. Make it last if you can. I want you to keep a good wad of it in your cheek, then if anyone speaks to you, you can just mumble through it as if you'd got your mouth full. It's one of the best ways of disguising one's voice. I don't want to be seen with you on the platform, but I'll get the tickets. Don't appear to be hiding or anything like that. Keep near anyone else who is waiting and do as they do. Now you stay here till you see me come out on the platform, and then just trickle through unobtrusively."

The next hour seemed to Elizabeth the longest hour of her life. There was a shelter into which the half dozen people who were waiting for the train had crowded. Four of them were members of a peasant family consisting of an old grandmother, her son and daughter-in-law, and a girl of about sixteen. They sat on the bench surrounded by bundles. Why they were travelling and where they were going Elizabeth never discovered. The girl of sixteen was the only cheerful one of the party. She spoke to Elizabeth, asking her when she thought the train would come. At the mumbled reply she giggled and began to roll her eyes at a young man who sat at the end of the bench. He wore a collar and tie, and might have been a clerk. After a little while he changed his place and sat next to the girl.

The other passenger was an old man who looked like a Jew. He leaned forward upon a staff which he held between his hands. With his long hair and his long beard, and his long broken nails, he might have been Job, bereaved of friends as well as children. His eyes were sunk with trouble, he shook with cold and age, but in the curved nose and in the lines of cheek and jaw there lingered faint memories of that pride of race which the Jew never quite forgets.

The peasant family continued to talk about the train. It should have come four hours ago—no, two hours—no, six. It would be at least another three hours late. It might not come at all. If there had been much snow upon the line, perhaps it would not come. If it did not come till the morning, the old grandmother would be dead. She said so herself, and who should know if she didn't.

Presently Stephen came into the shelter. He stood near Elizabeth for a moment, and when he moved away, her ticket was lying in her lap.

The peasant girl nudged the young man she had been flirting with.

"That's what I call a proper man—don't you? Look at his shoulders! He could break you with one hand. What a pity he limps. Perhaps he has been a soldier. Shall I ask him? Soldiers are always ready to talk."

Elizabeth watched Stephen as he walked away. He dropped one shoulder a little and halted on his left foot. A stranger who saw him would remember a man with a limp. He talked for a while to one of the G.P.U. police and then walked on again.

The father of the peasant family rummaged in a bundle and produced a tin teapot. A meagre pinch of tea was put into it, and he went off to fill it with boiling water at the station samovar. He came back, and after a moment the G.P.U. policeman appeared in the shelter. He looked up and down the huddled occupants of the bench and fixed his attention upon the young man with whom the peasant girl was flirting. A few years before a collar and a tie were enough to damn any man. They marked the hated *bourzhui*, and caused all true Marxian comrades to see red. Now they were permitted even to the elect. Nevertheless the G.P.U. man frowned as he watched the girl and the young man taking alternative sips of tea from the same pannikin. Presently he broke in upon them.

"What's your name? Where are you going to? What's your work?"

The young man stood up and answered politely. In Soviet Russia no one offends the G.P.U. if they can help it. He offered information with both hands—his name, Vassili Ilinoff, his destination the new Collective Farm at Orli, where he was to act as storekeeper.

After a little of this the policeman was satisfied. His eye wandered over the others.

The peasant girl had pouted for a moment. Now she thrust her pannikin of hot tea at Elizabeth with a good-natured "Here—have a drink. You look cold. We shall all freeze if the train doesn't come soon." The tea was merely flavoured water, but it was scalding hot. Elizabeth took a grateful sip, and then wondered whether the stuff upon her lips would run. She was too cold to care. She went on sipping. The policeman had turned his attention to the Jew. The girl leaned towards Elizabeth, giggling and chattering, with a teasing eye for the young clerk, who was now crowded out.

"What do you think of that young man—the one that was talking to me? He has a sauce, I can tell you. I shan't talk to him any more." Here she raised her voice and looked provokingly over her shoulder. "He looks like a *bourzhui*—don't you think so? But that's a good job he's got. I'm going on to a Collective Farm myself in the spring." She giggled and looked over her shoulder again. "I shan't choose the one he's on, that's one thing certain." Here she looked round and gave a muffled shriek as she discovered that Stephen had elbowed the young man away and was pushing into the place between her and Elizabeth.

"Don't tell me I frighten you," he said. "Why do you waste your time with boys and old women? You don't look at all that sort of girl to me, I can tell you. Why, a girl like you could have any man she chose. But you know that already, don't you?" He turned to Elizabeth and snatched away the pannikin. "Look what she's left you—not too much. Get it filled up, and I'll help you to empty it." He went on teasing her and paying her compliments.

The G.P.U. man after asking the Jew a question or two had faded away.

Elizabeth wondered how long it would be before someone found Petroff.

The train came at last. Everyone got up and began to count bundles and to run to and fro in a distracted manner. The peasant family lost the old grandmother and rushed aimlessly up and down the platform looking for her. People poured out of the train, some because they had reached their destination, some because they thought that they had reached it, some to fill teapots at the ever boiling samovar.

It was Elizabeth who found the peasant grandmother ensconced in the corner seat of a carriage in the middle of the train. When the owner of the seat returned, there was a very loud and competent exchange of personal remarks. The rest of the family, attracted by the noise, surged into the compartment. The shelf-like sleeping berths above the seats were already full. So were the seats themselves.

Elizabeth crouched down on the floor beside the peasant girl. The grandmother, erect in her stolen corner, screamed out abuse in a shrill quavering voice, whilst the old man whose place she had taken continued his attempt to shout her down, vociferating that he had only left the carriage to fill his teapot.

Stephen had disappeared. A child on one of the upper shelves began to cry. The engine shrieked. The door of the compartment was wrenched open and banged again. Elizabeth looked up and saw Stephen's shoulders blocking the window.

With a jerk the train began to move.

Chapter Nineteen

IT WAS A horrible journey. The air in the carriage was at the same time icy cold and intolerably stuffy. The peasant girl, who sat next to Elizabeth, talked all the time, sometimes to her, sometimes to her father, mother and grandmother, sometimes to Stephen at the other end of the compartment. She had the high nasal voice of the Russian woman. When for a moment she ceased to talk, it was to giggle or to nudge Elizabeth.

"Are you a gipsy?" she said. "You look like one. Can you tell fortunes? I wish you would tell me mine. What did you really think of that young man who was talking to me? Do you think it would be pleasant to be married to a storekeeper on a Collective Farm? Do you like the name of Vassili? I can't bear it. And shall I tell you why? I have a cousin called Vassili, and he made love to me till I had to run away. I would never marry a man called Vassili—not if he went down on his knees to ask me."

Here she looked round to see whether the young storekeeper was listening. When she discovered that he was not even in the carriage, she pouted and flounced.

"No, I wouldn't have had him for worlds. I don't like those little men really. A gipsy told me I should marry a big black man and have seven children, but that is all nonsense. I shall not have a child at all unless I want to. Have you any children?" She giggled and screamed across the compartment at Stephen. "Did you hear what I said—about the gipsy—did you? You weren't meant to. You shouldn't have listened."

Stephen edged his way towards them. It was difficult to move without treading on someone, because not only the seats but the whole of the floor-space was crowded. He arrived, however, and achieved a place upon the floor by dint of letting himself down and shoving.

The peasant girl giggled all the time.

"Did you think we wanted you over here? That's where you made a big mistake. You weren't meant to hear what we were saying. And if the gipsy did say I should marry a big black man, you needn't think it's going to be you. There are more big black men than you, aren't there?"

Stephen bent his head.

"Tell me what the gipsy said."

"In front of all these people? I'd be ashamed."

"Oh no, you wouldn't."

"Oh yes, I should."

The voices were going through Elizabeth's head. She was in a terribly cramped position, and the grinding and clanking of the train seemed to shake her very bones. Presently Stephen pushed between her and the girl. Somehow he had made a little more room and she could stretch out her feet. Somehow too she found that she could lean into the angle between his shoulder and the seat. He put a hand behind him, felt for her, patted her, and pushed up a thick fold of his sheepskin coat to serve as a cushion.

The girl went on talking. Sometimes he answered her. Their voices became low and confidential. The old man who had lost the corner seat had resigned himself. He squatted on the floor, his head nodding on his breast. In the place which she had annexed the peasant grandmother slept with her mouth open, snoring rhythmically on a high-pitched note rather like that of an oboe with a slightly cracked reed. The girl's father and mother slept. The child who had been crying whimpered now and again.

Elizabeth leaned back against Stephen's shoulder and felt herself slipping into a thick drowsy mist.

She began to dream that she was alone in the midst of a vast snowy wilderness, just one black speck on an endless dazzling waste. It was terrible to be that black speck and yet to be alive. She tried to walk through the snow, but her feet had frozen fast. Then there came the whirring and clanging of great wings. They made a wind. It drove the snow in stinging clouds. The wings hovered over her with an intolerable humming noise, and she saw that they were the wings of an enormous aeroplane. Petroff leaned down out of it and caught her by the hair. She was carried up, and up, and up, and she knew that presently he would let go of her and she would fall into the unimaginable depths of the snow.

She gave a sobbing cry and woke up. The noise that she had heard was only the clanging and thudding of the train. Her feet were numb with cold. She was leaning against Stephen's back. She straightened herself up and moved her feet. The candle which burned under a glass shade in the ceiling showed that all the passengers were asleep—all except Stephen. As soon as she moved, he put his hand behind him as he had done before and patted her arm.

The peasant girl had at last stopped talking. She had gone to sleep with her head on Stephen's shoulder. A little shiver of disgust ran over Elizabeth. She drew away and leaned against the seat. The train chugged on.

She fell asleep again, but not as deeply as before. It was like lying in a shallow stream. Sometimes the water drowned sense, and sight, and hearing, and sometimes it ebbed away. At these times light filtered through her eyelids. She was aware that the train had slowed, had stopped, was going on again. Sounds came to her. Then the water flowed again, and she went down into it and lost everything. Bits of broken dreams came and went. Once she was back at school, doing a sum on the blackboard. When she looked at it, it was Nicolas Radin's formula, and she heard Nicolas say, "You promised." Once she was in a dark cellar, shut in alone, with the house fallen into ruins overhead. Then in the darkness

Stephen touched her hand, and the fear was gone. She had been most horribly afraid, but at the touch of Stephen's hand the fear was gone.

She could have stayed in that dream, but it broke in a red glow. She was standing with Stephen before an immense jewelled ikon, and a priest was marrying them. Stephen was Red Stefan again. Everything in the dream was red—his hair, his beard, his blouse. They were in a church, but it was on fire, and the fire roared so loud that she could neither hear the priest's words nor their responses. Then Stephen put out his hand to give her the ring, and a ray of blood-red light struck down between them like a sword.

She woke up with her heart beating hard and her lips dry. The train was slowing down. She moved her cramped limbs and wondered where they were and how long she had been asleep. The train had stopped before; she was vaguely aware of that. Once, twice, three times—she did not know how often, but she thought they must have been travelling for hours. She was so stiff...

Stephen was moving beside her. He had shifted the peasant girl, who sprawled fast asleep with her head against the skirts of a woman on the seat. He got to his knees and touched Elizabeth warningly. As she leaned towards him, he put his lips to her ear and said,

"We get out here."

Then he was on his feet, pulling her up. Without his hand she would not have been able to pick her way among the sleepers. From the middle of the carriage he swung her up and set her down again by the door. The train was still moving slowly. As he opened the door, there was a long piercing blast from the engine, followed by the hiss of escaping steam. Stephen took Elizabeth under the arms and dropped her down upon the snowy track. Next moment he had shut the door and followed her. The train moved slowly on. A few hundred yards away the lights of a wayside station broke the dark.

"You're not hurt, are you?" He was helping her up.

"No."

"I don't think anyone saw us go. They were all sleeping like pigs. Lord—what a fug there was in there! Are you gassed?"

"I had horrible dreams," said Elizabeth.

"I don't wonder. The air will do you good. Now we've just got to climb this bank and keep along behind it. Thank goodness the snow hasn't drifted. We haven't got far to go."

"Where are we going?"

She did not really mind. She hated and despised herself for it, but she didn't really mind where she went as long as she was with Stephen. The knowledge of this came to her in a burning flash as she asked her question. It was her pride that burned. It flared with a short, fierce flame as Stephen said cheerfully.

"Oh, just to a house in the village. It's only a step. I've got out this way before when I didn't particularly want to be seen. The train always slows down just outside the station. By the way, my name's Nikolai here. I think you'd better be my widowed sister Anna. It doesn't matter much, because the people in the house we're going to can be trusted. You're not the first refugee I've run across the frontier."

That short, fierce flame died down. She was only another refugee to him. He would get her over the frontier because that was his business, and then he would go on his way and forget that she had ever existed. What a bitter, weary fool she was.

She spoke quickly to break the picture in her mind.

"Are we near the frontier?"

"As near as I dare take you. But there's no chance of getting over it anywhere near the line of rail. We shall go on by sledge to-morrow."

They had come to the outskirts of the village. The snow on the ground seemed to give out a light of its own. Strange to have that ghostly light to guide them, with the sky so black above. The houses of the village were like bee-hives thatched with snow. Elizabeth had the feeling that she had walked out of the world into an etching.

Stephen stopped at the third house and knocked, not upon the door, but upon one of the little windows that flanked it. Rap—

rap—double rap—double rap—rap—double rap—rap. He waited a moment and then repeated this. In the short silence that followed, the whistle of the engine came to them and the chug-chug-chug of the departing train. As the sound died away, the house door was opened a chink and a grumbling voice said,

"Who's there?"

"Nikolai," said Stephen, and at once the opening widened and let them through.

The door was shut behind them and barred again. A flicker of light appeared, and the smoke of an oil lamp went up in a reek of soot.

An old man with a puckered face made a scolding sound as he adjusted the wick.

"Marya has no sense with lamps. When she trims them they always smoke. When I trim a lamp it does not smoke. Women are no good at these things." He raised his voice a little. "No woman can trim a lamp properly."

By the smoky light Elizabeth saw a movement on the platform about the stove. A woman's voice said,

"What's that?"

"The lamp's smoking again," said the old man.

A middle-aged woman sat up and pushed back her hair.

"Is that Nikolai? Because if it is, you're a fool to show that light. What a time of night to come here!"

She got down off the stove, and came towards them, showing a broad good-humoured face above square shoulders and a short, sturdy frame. At the sight of Elizabeth she clicked with her tongue against the roof of her mouth.

"Lord have mercy—who's this?"

"You can call her my widowed sister Anna," said Stephen. "And you can give her something to eat and drink, and then you can let us sleep. Wait a minute and I'll just make sure that the light doesn't show from outside."

He stepped out into the snow and was back again in a moment.

"It's all right."

"Of course it's all right!" said the old man grumbling. "Should I have lighted it if it wasn't all right?"

After a meal of hot cabbage soup, black bread, and cheese produced by Stephen the lamp was put out again and they slept.

Elizabeth did not dream any more. She felt safe and warm, and her sleep was deep.

Chapter Twenty

IT WAS STILL dark when Stephen woke up.

"I'm afraid we've got to start off again. I want to get away before there's anyone about."

"How are we going?"

"I keep a sledge and a horse here. I've been up and down this way for years as Nikolai. I used to go round all these villages persuading people to go on to the Collective Farms. Did you see me speak to the G.P.U. policeman at Tronsk? He comes from these parts, and would swear I was a red-hot Communist and a most useful comrade. It's a bit of a strain leading a double life, but if you do happen to want to disappear, it's useful to have another skin to slip into. There's a pretty good Collective Farm not ten miles away that I helped to organize."

"Are we going there?" said Elizabeth.

He shook his head and whispered in her ear,

"We're going to the frontier, and the sooner we get there the better."

They drove out of the village in a dusk that was just beginning to break. Snow had fallen during the night—"And that means that no one will know where we left the train last night."

As the dawn came, Elizabeth saw a landscape broken by clumps of trees which here and there thickened into woods. There was an even grey sky overhead. The wind had dropped, but it was cold enough. She sat wrapped in sheepskins and wondered how often Stephen had driven this way before, and with whom. She had settled it with herself that she was just one of the refugees whom he smuggled across the frontier. He did it because it was his trade. If they were women, he looked after them kindly, warmed them when they were cold, fed them when they were hungry, and rescued them when they were in danger. When he thought she was frightened he had patted her arm or her shoulder. She wondered whether he had done that to all the others. Probably. It was just his way of reassuring the silly frightened creature whom he happened to be looking after. She had found it rather an endearing way, but it ceased to be endearing when it ceased to be Stephen's way of comforting *her*.

She said after a long silence, "How many people have you taken over the frontier?"

He looked round at her with a laugh.

"I don't know. A good few."

"Men, or women?"

"Both—but more women than men."

"Young, or old?"

"Oh, mostly youngish. It's a bit too rough for the older ones. I did take an old lady over once, but I swore I never would again. She didn't really want to leave Russia at all, and every time we stopped she wanted me to turn round and take her back again."

Elizabeth let that pass. She was not interested in the old lady.

"Are they all your widowed sisters?" she asked.

Stephen laughed again.

"The old princess was my grandmother. She didn't like it a bit."

"He won't talk about the young ones," said Elizabeth to herself. She became horribly conscious of her disguise. She ought to have been able to laugh it away and be herself in spite of grizzled elf-locks, a plastered cheek, and warts on her face, but she couldn't. It was a dreadful thing to lose one's sense of humour. Quite suddenly she felt as if she couldn't bear those warts any more. She turned on Stephen with a sparkle in her eye.

"Did all the others have to be disguised?"

"More or less."

"Am I more—or less?"

"Oh, more. I made a particularly good job of you."

"Then they didn't all have warts on their faces?"

"No—it wasn't necessary." He stared at her. "What's the matter?"

"I hate them!" said Elizabeth vehemently. "Can't I take them off? No one knows me here."

"No, you can't take them off. They change you a lot. You'll have to stick to them till we are over the frontier. Why do you mind?"

"Because they change me."

"Well, there's no one to see you," said Stephen kindly. "I shouldn't worry if I were you."

"Oh, I'm not worrying," said Elizabeth.

Her voice had an odd choked sound, because she was angry and yet she wanted to laugh. Her sense of humour couldn't be quite dead yet, or she wouldn't have wanted to laugh. Of course it didn't matter to Stephen what she looked like, or how many warts she had on her face. Why should it? In point of fact it did not matter to Stephen at all. It did not matter to him what Elizabeth looked like. It would not even have mattered to him if the warts had been real warts instead of little coloured lumps of plasticine. His own picture of her was much too firmly fixed in his mind for any outward appearance to affect it. She stood in an inner shrine before which there burned a steady, changeless flame. He had no idea of why she should be troubled. Of course make-up wasn't particularly comfortable. You couldn't wash your face for one thing. He decided that this was what was bothering her.

"You'll be able to have a bath when we get to Warsaw," he said.

Elizabeth drew back into the sheepskins and shook with painful laughter. At Warsaw she would be able to have a bath. She would probably have to say good-bye to Stephen in Warsaw. He would have finished his job, and there would be nothing to keep them together. He could wash his hands of her, and she could wash her face.

She was silent for the rest of the way.

They passed no one at all during the first two hours, but after that they met one or two sledges. At midday they reached a village and there stopped. They were to spend the afternoon and night there and then go on again.

The house into which Stephen took her was a fairly clean one. He was greeted with noisy affection by a little girl and boy who appeared to be twins, and more soberly by their mother, a grave-faced woman with a baby in her arms. Her husband came in presently. He seemed very pleased to see Stephen. He was, it appeared, the person he most wanted to see. He had all but made up his mind to go on to the Collective Farm. What did Nikolai think about it? What was the use of staying on here?—"I ask you, what is the use? If we have a good year, the government takes so much that so far as we are concerned it might just as well be a bad year. And if it's a bad year, what is there for us to do except starve? And if anyone puts a little bit away, he's a food-hoarder and there's no mercy for him." He shrugged his shoulders. "Now wouldn't it be better on the Collective Farm? You don't starve there. The children would have enough to eat. I say we had better go, but Stasia says no. What do you say?"

"You'd be better off on the Farm," said Stephen.

Stasia's eyes dwelt on him for a moment. She shook her head and looked down at her baby.

"There!" said the aggravated husband. "Look at her! That's what she does all the time—just shakes her head and won't say why. If I've told her once, I've told her a thousand times how much better off we should be on the Farm."

Stasia shook her head again.

"It's no use, Ilya," said Stephen with a laugh. "When a woman has got her mind made up there's an end of it."

The two men went on talking. Stasia rocked her baby. Presently the children ran off to school.

As the afternoon wore on, three or four people dropped in— Stasia's father and mother, and her young brother Peter, a lad of eighteen. The father was a jolly man with a free tongue, the mother a dried wisp of a woman.

The boy Peter plied Stephen with questions about life in the towns. What was it like in Moscow? Could one get a job there? He was sick of village life and would like to go into a factory. Wasn't it a fact that the proletarian in the town was much better off than the peasant? It was the old grievance, with a personal edge to it.

"Why should I plough, and sow, and reap to fatten someone in a factory? I'd rather work in the factory myself and have someone ploughing and sowing and reaping for me."

His father clapped him on the back in mock anger.

"So your mother and I are to work that you may grow fat away in Moscow? That's a good joke! But I tell you what you shall do—you shall go into a boot factory and make boots for all the village. We'll manage to do without you if you'll do that."

Everyone began to talk about boots—how hard they were to get, and how soon they wore out.

In the middle of this the door opened again and there stood on the threshold a short, thickset young man with cropped hair. He was dressed like a peasant, but he wore spectacles with thick lenses, through which he looked with an air of some authority.

"The new schoolmaster," said Stasia in a low voice. She sat dumb whilst Ilya welcomed him loudly.

"Come in, come in! We're all friends here. You must meet my friend Nikolai. He's staying with us for the night, he and his sister." He turned to Stephen. "This is Anton Glinka who is waking us all up. It is he who has made Peter want to go into a factory. I won't say anything about what he has made me want to do, because of Stasia there." He winked at the young man as he spoke.

Everyone laughed except Stasia, whose colour rose. She pressed her lips together and looked down at her sleeping baby.

Anton Glinka sat down beside Ilya. His eyes, behind the thick lenses, were turned here and there. He had a curious way of looking at people as if his eyes made a pounce and then remained fixed. Elizabeth felt an extreme dislike of being looked at in this way. When he spoke, she disliked his voice. He had, it appeared, been to Orli and back. He must have been in one of the sledges which they had met. He had an abrupt manner and a harsh, dogmatic way of speaking. There was a woman teacher who had had to carry on the work of the school in his absence. He spoke of her with a lofty indulgence, supposing that she would have done her best. He had gone to Orli on important Party business.

Here he squared his shoulders and looked for Stephen to make some comment which would show that he had been impressed. Stephen immediately responded with an admiring glance.

Anton Glinka went on talking.

"Whilst I was there a broadcast message came through—a special broadcast. It is what I have always said—every village should have its wireless installation—every village in the Union of Soviet Republics. Orli has one. But why haven't we got one? We ought to have one. If I had not gone into Orli to-day, we should have missed this message."

"You don't tell us what it is," cried Ilya.

"That's a good joke!" said Stasia's father, laughing heartily.

The faint beginning of a shudder touched Elizabeth. From her place between Stasia and the old woman she looked round the circle. An oil lamp hung on the wall. It cast heavy shadows. Elizabeth sat with her back to it, but the schoolmaster faced the light, which was reflected from his glasses. As he turned this way and that, the reflection shifted. Sometimes when he moved quickly it looked as if his eyes were on fire. He had straight black brows above those fiery eyes. His lips were thick and shapeless.

Elizabeth felt the shudder touch her again. Why couldn't she look at Stephen, or at Ilya, or at the jolly old man, or at the lad Peter?

All this went like a flash. When Anton began to speak she knew why she had had to look at him.

"A joke?" he said, and stared the old man down. "They don't broadcast jokes. And it won't be a joke for the ones that are wanted, or for anyone who has helped them to get away—not that they have any chance of getting away, with a description of them wirelessed to every station."

"Still you don't tell us about the message," Ilya complained.

Elizabeth became aware that she was trembling. She could keep her face from showing anything, and she could force her arms and shoulders into rigidity by locking her hands together, but her knees shook, and as she sat on the rough bench her knee touched Stasia's knee. If she drew away from Stasia, she would be touching the old woman. If someone must feel the tremor which shook her, let it be Stasia, quiet and kind, and not her bitter-faced mother.

"Oh, the message?" Anton Glinka's voice rasped like a saw. "There are two *bourzhuis* who are wanted by the police—counter-revolutionaries and enemies of the state, both of them. A man called Red Stefan, and a woman called Elizabeth Radin. I have their descriptions written down, and so have a thousand other people. What fools people are to think they can escape! It's not very likely that they would come here, but you can never tell. Forewarned is forearmed. As Lenin says, the unknown enemy is the dangerous enemy."

"Now he is going to give us a lecture on Lenin," said the old man, nudging his son.

No one returned his wink, because they were all watching the schoolmaster. He unfolded a piece of paper and bent it over to catch the light. Then he read in his rasping voice:

"The man:—Over six foot in height and very powerfully built. Red hair and beard. Bright blue eyes. Bronzed complexion. Age about thirty. The woman:—Five feet five. Slight build. Black hair. Grey eyes. Good teeth. Small hands and feet. Small triangular scar on the back of the left hand. Age about twenty-four."

Elizabeth's hands were clasped upon her lap. They were pressing down upon her knees in an effort to stop that betraying tremor. She did not need to look down at her hands, but she did look down at them with a sick involuntary glance. The left hand was uppermost, and the scar showed faintly through the brown stain that Stephen had used. It would be Petroff who had remembered the scar. His mother had struck at her with her scissors, and he had seen the wound heal and leave that little three-cornered mark. She shifted her grip and covered it.

No sooner had she done so than her fear increased. She ought not to have moved her hands. It was the last thing she ought to have done. If the schoolmaster were watching her he might think... She looked up and saw his eyes fixed upon her. Behind the thick lenses they had a cold, unwavering stare like the eyes of a fish seen through the plate-glass of an aquarium.

For a moment Elizabeth felt as if she were going to faint. Then Stephen broke in with a hearty laugh.

"They won't get far, those two. A man who's got red hair ought to be careful about getting into trouble. He's a marked man, and with a description like this out against him anyone who sees him half a mile away can't help smelling a rat. Oh no—he won't get far, you'll see."

He began to tell a story about a man who had stolen a horse.

"Down in the Ukraine it was, about five years ago last summer. There were three horses he might have taken, and what does the fool do but take the one with the white star on its forehead. Well then, as soon as the description was out, there was everyone looking for that white star, whereas if he'd stuck to a plain brown or black, he might have got away with it—you never can tell."

"You came from Orli?" said the schoolmaster abruptly. He addressed Elizabeth, but it was Stephen who answered.

"Yes, this morning."

"And before that?"

"From Moscow." Again it was Stephen who spoke.

The schoolmaster turned and looked at him.

"Does your sister never speak?"

"Oh, sometimes—sometimes," said Stephen, laughing.

Stasia's father threw back his head and laughed too.

"That's a good joke! Don't you call that a good joke, Ilya? She's a woman, isn't she? And he asks if she can talk! I call that as good a joke as I've heard. Can she talk indeed! It's easily seen you're not married, schoolmaster."

Anton Glinka took no notice. He asked Elizabeth directly,

"Is your husband alive?"

Without looking up, Elizabeth said, "No."

"And when he was alive you lived in Moscow?"

Elizabeth said, "Yes."

"What was he, this husband of yours?"

Now he and everyone must see how she was trembling. What a poor weak fool she was to shake at a word and betray Stephen. It didn't matter about herself, but it mattered about Stephen. She was betraying Stephen. She sat there dumb, and heard Stephen answer for her.

"Ah!—you'd better ask me about that. Her husband? Poor Anna! Look how she shakes at the very sound of his name. You shouldn't torment her with your questions, because she's silly in her head and strangers frighten her." He dropped his voice to a confidential tone. "Do you know who she was married to? You'll never guess. Why, to a Chinese—one of those Chinese executioners. Li Fan Tung was his name. A great big hulk of a man and as yellow as corn. No wonder she shivers and shakes when anyone asks her about him. Yellow as corn and eyes like slits, and one of those big curved knives at his belt, and a revolver on the top of that. He'd come home to his dinner and tell her about the people he'd shot—thirty and forty in a day—all counter-revolutionaries, and a good riddance of course, but it put Anna off her food. A woman hasn't the stomach for that sort of thing. I can tell you he gave one the creeps. And why she married him nobody knows. But she was always a bit weak in the head—I suppose she couldn't say No."

The whole circle stared, fascinated, at the widow of a Chinese executioner. Only Stasia leaned sideways and put her baby down on Elizabeth's lap.

"Would you like to hold him?" she said.

The baby was soft and warm, and very deeply asleep. Elizabeth put an arm about it, and felt safer. She could even begin to be angry with Stephen for saying she had been married to a Chinaman.

"And he is dead?" said the schoolmaster.

"A month ago," said Stephen. "Someone shot him in the back on a dark night, so I had to go and fetch Anna away. We are going to the Collective Farm at Rasni. That's the life—isn't it Ilya? All working together, with the State behind you. What's the good of straining and sweating to wring a living out of a paltry acre or two? On a Collective Farm you can plough a hundred acres with a tractor and not feel tired at the end of it. The food's good too, and you get first chance with boots and clothes. It's only what's left over that comes to the villages." He went on talking about the Collective Farm at Rasni.

The schoolmaster listened, frowning. Presently he went back to the piece of paper from which he had read the broadcast message. When Stephen stopped, he turned it again to catch the light.

"Six foot in height and very powerfully built—"

Chapter Twenty-One

LATE IN the evening when the guests had all gone and the children were asleep, Elizabeth had a word with Stephen. He had been out with Ilya to see to the beasts, and she came across to the door and leaned against it, not speaking at first but looking at him, her eyes bright and angry. On the platform of the stove Stasia was feeding her baby, her shoulder turned to the room and her head bent. Just so might Mary have watched her child. To all intents and purposes they were alone.

"What is it?" said Stephen.

Elizabeth leaned on the door.

"That man—suspected us."

Stephen nodded.

"It doesn't matter. We'll be gone before dawn. By the time he finds out that we're not at Rasni we'll be over the frontier."

"Shall we?"

Their voices came and went with the least breath of sound. If Stasia had listened, she would have heard nothing. But Stasia was not listening. She was letting her love flow out to her baby. She had no thought for anyone in all the world beside.

"Shall we?" said Elizabeth.

"Of course we shall. I told you that before."

They were so close together that with the least movement she could have touched him, or he her. Neither of them made that movement. A bright anger sprang up in Elizabeth like a bright, brittle flame. She said a little breathlessly,

"Why did you tell that horrible story?"

"What horrible story?"

"Why did you say I had been married to a Chinaman?"

The expression in his eyes changed. There was a fleeting touch of amusement which melted into concern.

"Did you mind?"

"Of course I minded! It was horrible!"

The amusement was there again.

"Well, I'm sorry—but you were giving yourself away. I suppose you know you were shaking."

The flame of anger died. She had so nearly betrayed them both.

"I tried not to."

"Well, I had to say something to account for it. I'm sorry you minded the Chinese executioner. I thought I invented him rather well. You see, the important thing just then was to produce something that would take the wind out of the schoolmaster's sails. A Chinese executioner was a whole heap more exciting than a broadcast about a couple of *bourzhuis*. People in a village aren't really much worked up over *bourzhuis*, but they like stories of what goes on in Moscow, and the more blood and thunder the better."

Quite suddenly Elizabeth's eyes laughed up at him. They at least were not disfigured. When she laughed, they were very starry.

"I'm so tired of being weak in the head," she said.

Stephen's eyes smiled back at hers, but behind the smile he was serious.

"You ought to throw yourself into your part."

"Into being weak in the head?"

He nodded.

"You'd find it much easier. You ought to think of yourself as Anna—rather a poor thing and weak in the head. You want to let it soak into you, so that you're not in danger of giving yourself away like you did just now."

"I was afraid," said Elizabeth with wide blank eyes on his. The laughter had gone out of them and they were not starry any more.

Stephen patted her shoulder.

"There—that's just what I mean. If you were my widowed sister Anna, there wasn't anything to make you afraid. You were afraid because in your own thoughts you were letting yourself be Elizabeth Radin. That's fatal if you want to carry off a disguise—it makes the wrong atmosphere."

A quick little devil commandeered Elizabeth's tongue.

"Am I to remember that you are my brother—all the time?"

Stephen refused to be drawn. He said,

"If you did, you wouldn't worry about little things like having warts on your face or a Chinese husband. They'd be part of your disguise, and they'd help you to feel safe and not get into a panic."

Anger and laughter contended in Elizabeth. Laughter won.

"You call those little things!" she said, and with that the door was pushed open and Ilya came in.

There was no more opportunity for talk with Stephen. They sat about the stove, and he told stories and sang songs. Elizabeth went over the little scene in her mind—not the words, but the swift current of emotion which had run between them all the time. It was as if they had been facing one another across swift flashing water, glittering, darkening, swirling over unknown depths and flinging up a light inconsequent spray of words. It wasn't the words that mattered, it was this strange current that ran between them. She felt it all the time. Did Stephen feel it too?...Stephen? Oh no—why should he? He was too busy with being Nikolai—and her brother. It would be against his principles to remember that he was Stephen and she Elizabeth.

She went to sleep without any more comfort than that.

Chapter Twenty-Two

ELIZABETH DID NOT know how long she had been asleep when something waked her. There was no light in the house. Someone was moving in the dark. The sound that had waked Elizabeth came again, a tapping on one of the two small windows which flanked the door. Then the door itself was opened a cautious inch and a breath of icy air came through the chink, and at the same moment she was aware of Stephen brushing past her and going towards the door.

It was Stasia who had opened it. Elizabeth caught her whispered word as Stephen joined her. Then the chink was widened. The cold blew in, and when the door was shut again there were three of them whispering there in the dark. Her heart beat heavily. She sat up, listening, but the whispering had no words for her. It was like a rustling of leaves—a senseless, wordless rustling which mixed confusedly with the children's breathing, with Ilya's snores, and with the hammering of her heart.

Over by the door Stephen said, "What is it?"

And Stasia, with her hand on the bolt, answered, "It is Peter." And with that she drew back and let him in.

They stood so near together that they were touching one another, all the three of them, like the three sticks of a tripod, heads close, lips moving over words that were more breath than sound. First Stasia: "Oh, Peter!" Then Stephen: "What is it?" And after that Peter, breathing deep because he had been running, and shivering with cold and excitement:

"Anton Glinka!"

Stephen had a hand on the boy's shoulder.

"Steady! Take your time."

"There isn't any time! You must get away—at once!"

Stasia shrank and trembled. They were so close that her tremor shook them all.

Stephen said, "Quiet, Peter, and tell me."

"Yes—yes—it is Anton!" he said.

"What does he say?"

"That you are *bourzhuis*—that it is you—that are wanted by the police. He says—she has the scar on her hand. He says—he saw it."

Stasia drew in her breath. Stephen said,

"Don't be frightened, Stasia. It doesn't matter what he says. We'll be gone by cock-crow."

Peter caught his breath.

"You must be gone before that. He has been round to every house. Not ours—he knows better than that—but everywhere else. Boris came and told me. He said, 'Tell Nikolai to be gone before the moon is up. Anton will raise the village. He means mischief. Tell Nikolai to cut and run.'"

"Before the moon is up?" said Stasia faintly.

Peter shivered under Stephen's hand.

"Boris is right—Anton means mischief. He is like a wolf on the trail. His kind are all like wolves."

Stasia shuddered from head to foot.

"*Wolves—*" she said, and the three of them stood there silent.

It was Stephen who broke the silence.

"What does Glinka mean to do? Did Boris say?"

"He has got at least a dozen who will join him, perhaps more. They're coming now—at once—as soon as they have stopped talking about it. They will search you both and take you to Orli to answer for yourselves there. You know best whether that is safe for you, Nikolai."

Stephen's laugh just stirred the silence.

"Not as safe as it might be." And then, "We must go."

Stasia said again the word that she had said before—a word with a shudder in it:

"*Wolves—*"

Sitting up in the dark on the other side of the room, Elizabeth felt Stasia's fear come flowing towards her like a cold draught. She had not heard what Stasia had said, or what any of them had said, but she felt the fear. Then, very faintly, she heard Stephen laugh, and the fear went past her. She could not hear what he was saying, but she was reassured.

A moment later he came over to the stove and said,

"Are you awake?"

"Yes," said Elizabeth.

He knelt down close to her and spoke again.

"We've got to move on. Peter has come to warn us. It's the schoolmaster of course. He's roused the village. We must get away before they come and take us. Will you get up? I don't want to wake Ilya. He and Stasia can say we slipped away while they were asleep."

It was the strangest and most hurried flight. There were no more words, only a groping to find her shoes, her coat—and the door opening twice, once to let Peter out, and again for her and Stephen. Stasia pressed her arm as they touched in the dark, and then they were outside in the snow and the door was shut.

It was not so dark here as it had been in the house. The snow lighted them, and the sky was bare and starry with no more than a belt of cloud at the horizon. Elizabeth stood in the yard behind the house and watched the sky whilst Stephen brought out the horse and harnessed him to the sledge. The stars were very bright and the air was still. The belt of cloud to the east was luminous. If there was going to be a moon, it would help them on their way. She thought it was a long time since she had seen the moon or the sun. She thought it was a friendly thing to see the stars.

And then Stephen was ready. He tucked her in and led the horse out of the yard. He jumped in beside her and took the reins, and they were off—down the long village street, past the dark houses, past one house which was not dark, and out on the open snowy road. There was no tinkling of bells to proclaim their flight. They drove with muffled harness. The snow deadened the sound of the horse's feet. Only when they were clear Stephen broke into a laugh.

"Schoolmasters talk too much," he said. "Did you see the house with the lighted windows? I think Glinka and his friends were there, talking about how they were going to arrest us. Peter's a good lad. We'd have been caught if he hadn't come to warn us. I hope he won't get into trouble."

"Do you think he will?"

"No—he's rather a protégé of Glinka's. He'll be in bed and asleep, and not know anything until he's told. Stasia will do the same, and Ilya really won't know anything, which is much the safest plan."

"Will they come after us?" said Elizabeth.

Stephen laughed a little grimly.

"I don't think so. People hereabouts don't care for travelling at night."

"I wonder why," said Elizabeth vaguely. And then, "Will they come after us in the morning?"

Stephen cracked his whip.

"It won't matter if they do."

"Why?"

"The morning's a long way off, and we shall be a long way off by the morning."

Elizabeth looked to the east. The morning was far away. It was not the sun that was rising now, but the moon. Already the sky above the clouds was transparent and faintly golden. Presently the rim of the moon showed clear. It came up full like a bubble of fire, in colour at first an orange-red, which changed imperceptibly through orange to gold. It seemed as if the gold were draining away from it into the sky. In a little while it was all quite gone and the moon was white among the stars.

It was at this time that they entered the forest. Elizabeth saw it first as a shadow below the cloud-belt, then as a black mass coming nearer and nearer. They passed its outposts—stark clumps of trees standing up in the moonlight; thickets bent under a weight of snow; a tangle of bushes with the glitter of frost on them; more stark trees; and at last the forest itself.

The trees were very tall. The trunks ran up on either side to a black roof of pine branches. Here and there the moonlight barred their path, here and there it lay like a silver pool in a clearing, once and again it flooded a stretch of the forest road, but for the most part they drove in a shadowy gloom which made everything seem unreal.

Unreal. The word crept into Elizabeth's mind and stayed there. An unreal world, frozen into the semblance of reality. At any moment it might flow away from them, dissolving as ice and mist dissolve. They were past midnight, or it might have vanished at the stroke of twelve. No, midnight was the hour that ushered enchantment in. It was cock-crow which would break the spell. Meanwhile it stayed about them a glamour of frost and night.

When the gold had drained out of the moon the last trace of living colour died. Only black and white were left. Black, and white, and all the mysterious gradations through which light lapses into darkness.

Elizabeth began to try and find means for these strange, half luminous shades. Black, and white, and silver. Ink, and snow, and ebony. Grey velvet, and black velvet, and white velvet. Diamond, and pearl. Jet, and crystal. Bone—white scraped bone—moonbleached bone. Tears, and ivory, and the black of black deep water.

"What are you thinking about, Elizabeth?" said Stephen without turning his head.

"I was thinking about all the black and white things in the world," said Elizabeth. "But there aren't enough of them. This is all black and white—a hundred kinds of black, and a hundred kinds of white. I can't get names for them."

"Are you cold?"

"Cold is one of the white things," she said with a little shuddering laugh.

"Why did you shiver?" said Stephen. "Are you afraid?"

"Fear is one of the black things," said Elizabeth. "No, I'm not afraid, Stephen."

That wasn't the way one talked in real life. It was like an answer in a dream.

They went on driving between the black walls of the forest. Its dark rafters stirred above them in a wind which was so high over head that it never touched the sledge. It moved those high, solemn branches. Sometimes a ghostly snow-fall cascaded down, sending out a spray which flew up against their faces like the tangible breath of the frost. The roar of such a fall and the movement overhead were the only sounds which came to them from beyond. There was

Grischa the horse and their two selves, three living beings, moving, alive and sentient, through this strange world in which there was no other life, no sound or movement of any other living thing.

Elizabeth did not know how long they had been driving when the first sound came to them. She turned her head and listened until it came again, a thin, high sound more like the echo of a sound than a sound itself.

Stephen looked over his shoulder and said,

"An owl."

Ahead of them the trees were thinning away. They came out upon a clearing dimly bright with the moon. The snow crisped and glittered under foot. The forest walled the clearing in, and the owls hunted there. They were half across it, when Elizabeth turned her head sharply because another sound had reached her—not a sound of the upper air like the owl's cry, but a faint far off whine or howl. She held her breath a little to listen, and caught the sound again. It was like a dog baying the moon, but a long, long, long way off. And then all at once it was nearer, and nearer again. And it wasn't a dog, but a wolf.

No, it wasn't a wolf. It was Stephen playing a trick on her, trying to frighten her as he had tried to frighten Yuri on the day they drove away from Tronsk in the early morning. How could he be so stupid as to think that the same trick would serve him twice? Perhaps he had imitated the owl's cry too. No, he hadn't done that, because she had seen the spread of the great soft wings, white and silent as snow in the moonlight—seen them dip and glance, and rise again, and pass shadow-like into the shadows.

A long howling note came from the forest they had left. All at once Elizabeth was angry. She called out,

"Don't do it! Why do you do it? I hate it!"

Stephen nodded without turning round.

"Stupid of me—wasn't it? I'm sorry, Elizabeth."

"You've frightened the horse," she said in an indignant voice.

"He'll get us there all the quicker," said Stephen with half a laugh.

Grischa had reared and started. Stephen made no attempt to hold him in. He called him by name, spoke to him in Russian terms of endearment, and let him take his own pace.

As they reached the farther side of the clearing, Elizabeth saw the owl again. It swooped, light as thistledown and soundless as air, swooped and rose. It must have missed its aim. Its floating cry had a harsher note. Suddenly it was gone. She turned and looked back across the empty clearing. The moon was bright upon the snow. The forest road in front of them was dark and deeply shadowed. She looked back into the light.

And very far away, at the far edge of the clearing where the trees ended and the shining snow began, she saw a black moving speck.

Chapter Twenty-Three

ELIZABETH STARED at the moving speck. It was a long way off and very small. The far end of the clearing was a quarter of a mile away. She could see the path of their sledge across the snow. The trees stood all round, and the moon shone down. There was just that one black moving thing on the snowy trail. No, there was more than one. She drew in a long cold breath as she counted up to seven, and then stopped, not because there were no more of those black moving things to count, but because the rest ran close-packed, a moving mass, a—what was the word that she had already used in her own mind?—a pack.

She turned to Stephen and saw him looking over his shoulder, past her. Then his eyes came back and met hers.

"Wolves," he said. "Don't bother."

"I'm not bothering," said Elizabeth. She felt a certain excitement, but no fear.

Stephen was watching their road now. He spoke without turning his head. There was always a chance of this, especially on a moonlight night.

"But you really needn't bother—we'll beat them all right. There's a place where we can shelter if we're put to it. Can you shoot?"

"Yes," said Elizabeth.

"I hope you won't have to, but you'd better have one of the revolvers. I took Petroff's, and I've got my own, and I always carry a rifle on this run. Even if they catch us up, we shall beat them. They don't like firearms. What sort of shot are you?"

"Only fair."

He took a revolver out of his pocket and gave it to her. He had the rifle slung at his back peasant fashion.

"Don't fire at anything you can possibly miss. Don't fire at all if you can help it."

Elizabeth looked over her shoulder again. The trees had closed them in. The clearing lay behind. Looking back at it was like looking out of a dark cage at a stretch of silver sand. Only it wasn't sand, it was snow, and over the snow came the wolf-pack hot on their trail. As she watched, the trees drew close and hid the clearing. She turned, and Stephen spoke again.

"Stasia didn't want me to bring you. Ilya had told her there were wolves about. I told her you would rather meet the wolves than Petroff. What would you have said if I had asked you?"

"Why didn't you ask me?"

"What was the good? I knew what you would say. I didn't want to frighten you. There mightn't have been any wolves, then you would have been frightened for nothing. Most of the things one worries about never happen.

Elizabeth leaned forward with her hands clasped on the revolver.

"How did you know what I would say?"

"Well, there wasn't much choice, was there? Glinka and his friends would have haled us off to Orli and handed us over to the G.P.U. We'd both have been in the trap. I couldn't have helped you. Petroff would have had his knife well into us both. I don't think we should have had a chance in a thousand of getting out alive. I'd rather race a wolf-pack any day myself, and I was pretty sure you would too."

A broad belt of moonlight lay across their path. They slid through it and were plunged in darkness again. Over her shoulder

Elizabeth watched the shining patch. If she could watch it out of sight and lose it, still white and uncrossed, it would mean that they were gaining on the wolves. The road drove straight into the forest. She could see the light for a long way. But before she was expecting it the pack poured into sight. Just for a moment she saw the wolves quite plainly—one running ahead, then two or three, and then the pack. The moonlight shone on them, and then shone only on the trampled snow. They were all in the dark together now.

For the first time she felt a stirring of fear. The palms of her hands tingled. It was as if the moonlight had been a barrier between them and the following fear, and now the barrier had been crossed. The fear had crossed it and was gaining upon them in the darkness.

As if he discerned her thought, Stephen said,

"We'll do it all right. We haven't much farther to go."

"Where are we going?"

"There's a hut in the forest—I use it sometimes. One of Paul Darensky's foresters used to live there, but he's dead long ago."

She echoed the name in surprise.

"Paul Darensky—your step-father?"

"Yes. It used to be his land. I know every yard of it."

He spoke to the horse again, encouraging him. And then they were off the road and following a narrow track that went deep into the forest growth. Just at the turn the trees stood back and the moonlight lay in a pool of light.

Once more Elizabeth looked back. This time Stephen looked too, and this time they had not run fifty yards before the wolves came into view.

Stephen cracked his whip and shouted. Grischa bounded forward. The wolves like shadows melted again into the darkness, but now it seemed to Elizabeth that she could hear them. It might have been only her own troubled blood that beat against her ears, but she thought that she could hear the sound of panting breath, the padding of those tireless feet, and the drip of all those slavering jaws. How much had the wolves gained since the turn, and how near were they now? The trees stood close, and darkness covered them. It was the dark that was so horrible. To strain eye and ear and yet to achieve neither sight nor sound, to feel a chill of the blood at every blacker shadow and yet to know that the fierce surge of the pack might come upon them unawares—these things called up that last desperate reserve of courage which lets go of hope and steadies itself to face the end.

If there were light...Horrible to die in the darkness. Horrible to go down under a smothering rush and die in the dark. Light—light—light...Light to know what they had to meet—light to aim by—

She was on her knees, with the encumbering sheepskins pushed away and the revolver in her hand. A single ray of moonlight touched the path. As they went swaying and bumping through it, she saw just for one instant Grischa's head with the ears laid flat—straining. Then Stephen, standing up with the reins in his left hand. And then the dark again. And over her shoulder she saw by the same gleam the pack not twenty yards behind.

Stephen looked round and back again.

She said, "They're very near." And as the words left her dry lips, she saw the moonlight shine through the trees ahead.

Stephen spoke without looking round.

"We're there. The hut is just ahead of us. When I pull up I want you to jump and run for the hut. There's a wooden bar that lifts up. Get the door open, run right through into the inner room, and shut yourself in. I want to save Grischa if I can, but I don't want him to kick your brains out."

"Stephen!" said Elizabeth imploringly.

He cracked his whip and shouted at the top of his voice. The sledge creaked and lurched. The pace increased, the trees thinned away, letting the moonlight through, and with a last desperate rush they came out upon a clearing bright with untrodden snow. Not thirty yards away was the forester's hut, like a beehive thatched with snow.

But the wolves were nearer than that. The leader ran beside the sledge level with Stephen where he stood with the reins in his left hand and a revolver in his right, whilst around and behind the sledge the pack closed in. As the wolf leapt for the horse's flank, Stephen fired at him. He fell rolling and snapping in the snow, and in an instant the others were upon him. Stephen fired twice more into the tumbling, worrying mass. Grischa reared and sprang forward.

They were within a stone's throw of the hut, but the chase was up again. Elizabeth fired at the nearest wolf and saw him check. Her hand was steady and she had stopped being afraid. Stephen shouted to her, and she turned, ready to jump. With both hands on the reins he pulled the terrified horse back almost on to his haunches and called out,

"Jump!"

As she raced the few yards to the hut, terror raced with her. To be caught here defenceless in the snow, to go down under the pack, as she had seen those wolves go down...She said, *"No!"* and did not know whether she said it aloud or not. And then her hands were tearing at the bar and thrusting open the door.

She was inside, in a sudden blackness darker than anything in the dark forest, stumbling forward with outstretched hands and the door open behind her. For a moment the terror had her by the throat. Then her hands touched a doorpost and she was in the inner room with the door in her hand. She had done what Stephen had told her to do, but she hadn't done all that he had told her. He had told her to shut herself in. How could she shut herself in whilst he was still outside? She was sickeningly afraid, but she was more afraid for Stephen than for herself. There was a bolt under her hand, but she could not drive it home. What good would it do her to be safe unless Stephen were safe too?

She held the door a handsbreadth open and looked through the outer room to the outer door. It stood wide, opening inwards. The doorposts framed a white shining panel of snow and moonlight. She saw that first. Her ears were full of the shrill whinnying of the horse and the sharp crack of the revolver. She could see only that empty shining panel. A horrible snarling and worrying turned her sick. She had a moment of agony. And then the revolver cracked again, and into that empty shining panel there came the head, the tossed mane, and the wild hoofs of the rearing horse. They crossed the picture, flinging madly up, and down again.

She saw Stephen—his hand at the horse's head, his great shoulders straining. Then the doorway darkened and was blocked as he dragged Grischa down and over the threshold.

Elizabeth thrust her own door to and leaned against it. He was inside. Nothing else mattered. She leaned against the door, and presently slid to her knees, because the floor was tilting and the darkness was full of fiery sparks.

She did not lose consciousness. She heard another shot. She heard Grischa stamp and plunge. She heard the slam of the outer door and the rattle of heavy bolts shot home. After that, Stephen's voice soothing the horse.

Chapter Twenty-Four

WHEN HE CALLED her name, she was still half kneeling, half sitting with her forehead pressed against the rough unpainted wood of the door. It was pine-wood, for a faint aromatic scent still came from it and one of her hands was a little sticky as if it had touched resin. It was odd that she should notice things like that. She was conscious of the piney smell, and of her sticky fingers. But for a moment she could not find any voice with which to answer Stephen, nor did it seem as if she could get upon her feet.

He called again, this time urgently.

"Elizabeth—are you all right? Where are you?"

She drew in a long breath. Surely with as much breath as that she should be able at least to say his name. She said it in a wavering whisper which hardly carried a yard, yet through the closed door Stephen heard. It may be said that it took a most horrible load off his mind. If Elizabeth had not done as he told her—if she had remained in the outer room—if the horse had kicked her...All these suppositions were dispersed by that very faint, wavering "Stephen."

Grischa was quiet now, though still sweating and trembling. Stephen stood gentling him. He said,

"Elizabeth—are you all right?"

"Yes."

It was not a yes that carried much conviction. Stephen frowned in the dark, but he let it go.

"You can come out now. I want to put Grischa in there. Turn to the right as soon as you get through the door. Feel your way along the wall until you come to the stove. Climb up on to it and then you'll be out of the way. I'll get a light as soon as I've shut Grischa in."

Elizabeth got to her feet. Her knees still shook, but the floor had stopped tilting. She did exactly what Stephen had told her to do and, having reached the stove, sank down there and waited.

Stephen spoke to the horse and fondled him. Grischa blew into Stephen's hand, after which he allowed himself to be led into the inner room. It was not the first time that a horse had been stabled there. Stephen fastened the halter to a peg and came back again, shutting the door behind him.

Presently a match flared. It pierced the darkness with its sharp orange flame, gave Elizabeth a momentary picture of Stephen bending over a rough table, and went out. With the next match she could see him coaxing a frozen wick. In the end he got the lamp to light. It was a wall-lamp with a tin reflector. He hung it from a nail in the party wall and proceeded to light the stove. There was wood piled ready in a corner of the hut—logs, and branches of resinous pine which burned up quickly. The worst of the icy cold began to pass. Elizabeth had not known how very cold she was until it began to pass. She felt forlorn and useless. There did not seem to be anything that she could do.

Stephen moved to and fro, large, competent, and cheerful. From a cunningly devised hiding-place behind the stove he produced materials for a meal—cubes of solidified soup to be boiled up with snow water, bully beef, and bars of chocolate. When he opened the door to fill a bucket with snow, Elizabeth shuddered, but not with cold. He was out and back again in a flash. He laughed as he set the bucket down and shot the bolts.

"They're sitting round with their tongues hanging out. I'll have a shot at them presently. There aren't more than half a dozen of them left."

Elizabeth crouched down against the stove. It was beginning to get warm, and she needed warmth. She felt most forlorn, cold, and uncomforted. Stephen was a hundred miles away and more concerned with his horse than he was with her.

He set the bucket of snow by the fire to melt and disappeared into the inner room, where she could hear him rubbing Grischa down and talking kindly to him. He came back with another bucket for some of the water. She could hear the rustling sound of hay being stirred and pulled about. Grischa was being fed and watered. She could hear Stephen praising him for saving their lives. He was a kind master to his horse. It was she who was a hundred miles away and on the far side of a gulf which seemed to widen continually. It came to her that the gulf was of her own making. If she had trusted Stephen instead of believing herself betrayed, there would have been no gulf. She had believed her eyes and her ears instead of believing her heart. It was her own fault.

But Nicolas had betrayed her.

What had that to do with Stephen? She ought to have known that it was not in Stephen to betray a trust. He had risked his life to-night to save his horse...A shiver ran through her.

"Are you cold?" said Stephen kindly.

She started. She had not heard him come in. The cold was about her heart. The warmth of the stove would not help that kind of cold. She said,

"No."

The snow in the bucket had melted. Stephen tipped some of the water into a tin can, put in the soup cubes, and set it on the hottest part of the fire. Then he touched Elizabeth's hand, and found it icy.

"Why did you say you were not cold? You're frozen. It's a pity about that good rug I had on the sledge. We could have done with it in here."

"What has happened to it?"

He laughed.

"Oh, they've eaten it hair and hide. They don't leave much, poor starving brutes. Never mind—the soup will warm you."

He had her hands between his own now, rubbing them. He was being kind to her as he had been kind to Grischa. If she had any pride left, she wouldn't want his kindness. She had no pride. His hands warmed hers. His kindness comforted her. When he had finished with her hands, he rubbed her feet. After which he gave her scalding soup in a wooden bowl and told her to drink it up.

It did not occur to him for a moment that she was unhappy. She had behaved with great coolness and courage, she had shot one of the wolves, and she had done what she was told. The last was the greatest virtue of the three. Once they were safe in the hut there was nothing for her to worry about. He was concerned that she should have some hot soup as soon as possible, but having made provision for this by lighting the stove and setting the bucket where the snow would melt and the water heat, he had naturally to get on with the job of making Grischa comfortable. He was distressed that Elizabeth should be so cold, and that her voice should sound so faint. He regretted the sheepskin rug very much, but there was hay to spare in the inner room, and he would be able to make her quite a comfortable bed. The hay would, of course, have to be dried before she could sleep on it, but that would be easy as soon as the stove got heated up. That Elizabeth should fancy him estranged or offended had never once entered his head. His love for her was so much a solid and unalterable fact that he had never considered it possible that she did not know of it. It would have been against his code to make love to her while she was under his care. He had simple, definite views about that sort of thing. She was his star, and his love, and when the right time came he would tell her so. He did not consider that this was the right time.

And Elizabeth, with her pride in the dust, drank her scalding soup, and was grateful because he had been kind.

He made her eat bully beef and a stick of chocolate.

"When did you have chocolate last?" he said as he gave it to her.

Elizabeth managed to smile. He was so evidently proud of his chocolate. It was, in fact, something to be proud of. Such things are scarce in the Union of Soviet Republics. She said,

"I don't know—a long time ago—before I died and came to Russia."

Stephen looked at her for a moment out of those bright blue eyes of his. They made her forget the lank black hair and the darkened skin. When he looked at her like that he was Red Stefan again. She loved him with all her heart. If she had been dead, she was alive again. *But it hurt to be alive.*

"Are you dead?" said Stephen.

She nodded because it wasn't very easy to speak.

Stephen went on looking at her for about half of an unbearable minute. Then he said, "You talk a lot of nonsense, Elizabeth," and went off into the inner room to fetch the hay which had to be dried.

Elizabeth was ready for him when he came back. He shouldn't have to tell her a second time that she talked nonsense. She asked him where he got his chocolate and his bully beef in just the voice which she would have used in that far-away world where some people shopped at Fuller's and some at Rumpelmayer's. He smiled at her over the hay which he was spreading on the warm stove.

"I do a bit of smuggling every time I come over."

"But how do you get the things across? I thought they searched everyone."

"They don't search me," said Stephen cheerfully.

"Why not?"

She was prepared to hear that he was a Frontier Guard. It really seemed quite possible.

"They don't catch me," said Stephen with a grin.

"Suppose they did catch you?" It weighed on her mind that she was a danger to him.

"They'd shoot me first and search me afterwards. But you needn't worry—they won't catch me."

When the hay was dry, he heaped it into a comfortable bed, made her lie down, and covered her with his coat. It must have been about five o'clock in the morning when she sank into a light, uneasy sleep.

It was a sleep in which dreams and odd dream-like wakings came and went. At one moment she rode with Stephen over a pathless waste of snow. He held her in his arms, and the horse flew like the wind. There was a roaring in her ears, and when she looked back she could see a torrent of fire blown furiously up behind them by some unseen storm. It blew as the wrack is blown from a tempestuous sunset. Great banners of flame were flung up against the sky. A river of fire came rolling on, and as it came it threw up flights and drifts of singing sparks. Then straight upon that, and without any apparent break, she was looking across the hut and watching Stephen shave. He had his pocket mirror propped up on the table. The oil lamp with its tin reflector shone down on him. It went through her mind that the fire had not reached them after all, and she slipped into another dream in which she and Stephen were skating hand in hand down a broad river of ice to a glassy distant sea. The swing and rhythm of their pace was like the flight of birds. And then again, without any conscious waking, they were in the hut and Stephen was dyeing his hair. He had taken off the wig and the false eyebrows and he was staining his own hair black with some stuff out of a bottle. She was sleepily impatient for him to finish with it. She wanted him to take her hand again and skate with her down the river of ice to that far, shining sea.

The dreams kept on coming and going. Sometimes they were terrible, and sometimes they were foolish, and sometimes they were sweet. In one most comforting dream Stephen looked into her eyes and said, "You talk a lot of nonsense, Elizabeth." She had no idea why she should find this comforting in the dream, because when Stephen had said it to her waking it had wounded her very much. But in the dream it did not wound her; it comforted her. Perhaps it was because in the dream his eyes had smiled into hers.

She woke with a start to find that the lamp was out, and that the small window framed a square of cold daylight. Stephen had waked her. He had a hot drink ready, and more food. He told her that she had slept for six hours and that it was past midday. The wolves were gone, and they must take the road again.

After that there was the business of getting off. The traces had to be mended, the firearms reloaded. Stephen took what remained of his store of food and packed it on the sledge. The hut had been very dark, for the tiny window was frozen over. When they came out into the cold daylight, Elizabeth saw that he really had discarded his wig. The closely curling black hair and the strong sweep of black eyebrow achieved by the dyeing of his own hair made him look much younger than he had looked as Nikolai, and quite a different person from Red Stefan. She thought, "If it wasn't for me, he'd be safe. No one would know him."

They had to retrace their path of the night before as far as the forest road. As they started off across the clearing, Stephen said regretfully,

"I would have liked to have altered you, but I didn't know what to do about it."

It was as if he had read her thoughts, which were saying all the time, "You're a danger to him."

She said, "Why?" just for something to say. She knew well enough that she was a danger to him. The thought never left her except when she was angry, and that was a short respite, because she could only be angry with him for a very little while. It was a hot anger while it lasted, but she could not make it last.

"Why?" said Stephen. "Oh well, you know, a wig is a most awful give-away. If it comes to being searched, you're done. I never use a wig when I've got time to do things to my hair. If I have to use one, I get rid of it as soon as possible. Of course it's much easier to change a man, because a beard makes such a tremendous difference. But you needn't worry—you'll be all right. You don't correspond in the least with the broadcast description, and we'll be over the frontier before that ass Glinka can follow us up."

The frontier—the rainbow's end—the ever shifting goal—the unattained and unattainable—a line men draw on maps—a line between life and death, between safety and danger...

Across the chill melancholy of these thoughts Stephen's words: "What are you thinking about?"

"Oh, nothing," said Elizabeth.

"Well, that's not much good, is it? It's not true, either. You were thinking 'I wonder if we shall ever get to the frontier.'"

Melancholy was in her voice as she said,

"Not quite."

"Well then, it was 'We shan't ever get there.' Wasn't it?" He turned to look at her with a flash of white teeth and a challenging sparkle in his eyes.

All at once the frontier ceased to be unattainable. She felt ashamed of her fears.

They passed from the clearing into the narrow track down which they had fled with the wolves behind them. It was very dark under the trees. After the brilliant night the sky had clouded. They came to the place where they had left the road, and drove on through the forest. The snow over which they drove was untrodden. Since the last fall nothing had passed this way. The whole forest might have been dead and the snow its winding-sheet. There was no wind and nothing stirred. It was most bitterly cold.

"Snow coming," said Stephen. And then, "Don't worry—we haven't far to go."

Chapter Twenty-Five

IT WAS early dusk when they came to what remained of Paul Darensky's house. Elizabeth never forgot her first sight of it. They came out of the trees and saw it standing above its snow-covered terraces with a belt of dark forest at its back. Then a turn of what had been the drive, and the upper windows were against the sky.

Elizabeth caught her breath. It was like seeing a face turn into a skull. The house was dead and eyeless, the windows smashed and the roof gutted. As they drew nearer, she could see that one whole wing had fallen in. In the front not a pane of glass remained unbroken.

It was an easy house to enter, though the great door was, most ironically, shut and barred. There had been some attempt to fasten the shutters of the ground floor rooms, but it was not hard to find one that had been overlooked. Stephen knew his way. He lifted Elizabeth up to a snowy sill, held a loose shutter aside for her, and there they were, in a room much darker than dusk, that smelled of cold mouldering ruin.

He took her briskly across the bare floor and into what seemed to be the great hall of the house. Their steps echoed upon stone, and the echoes went whispering away to a great height overhead. It was quite dark in the hall. Elizabeth hated the echoes.

He hurried her on. She would have walked through worse places with his arm about her. They turned, their feet left the stone, and then Stephen's torch flashed out and showed a small octagonal room. It had been panelled in white, each panel the frame of an exquisite flower-piece. Even now Stephen could not enter it without seeing the delicate artificial setting which Paul Darensky had prepared for his bride. Fay Darenska had fitted very well into the picture. But where Stephen had that momentary flashing glimpse of his lovely butterfly mother in a French fairy-tale room Elizabeth saw only dust and decay—the smashed chandelier, its gilt stem blackened and pushed awry and not one lustre left to make a rainbow of the moving ray; panelling dirty and defaced; shutters fastened indeed, but with here a long splinter and there a gash, as if an axe had been used upon them.

The gilded furniture was all gone—couches and chairs with spindle legs and pale brocaded cushions. There had been a white bear-skin in front of the hearth, an ormolu cabinet on either side of the two long windows, and a mirror with a faceted rim which hung between them. There had been curtains of ivory brocade patterned with wreaths of flowers and small shining birds. There had been a great many little tables. Now there was only a massive wooden bench, too large for a peasant house, too hard to be worth the labour of chopping it into firewood. It stood across the shuttered windows as if it had been pushed there to bar them. Stephen indicated it by directing the ray of his torch upon it.

"I must take Grischa down to the village. There's a man there who looks after him for me. He'll get him for keeps this time, but of course he doesn't know that. I won't be longer than I can help."

Elizabeth's blood went cold with horror.

"You're going to leave me here?"

"Well, I can't take you to the village—can I?" said Stephen reasonably.

Elizabeth said, "Oh!" It was really a gasp of protest. He met it kindly but firmly.

"You mustn't be seen, you know. I'm quite well known here—so is Nikolai. At the moment I am Mikhail, who is Nikolai's younger brother. We're a good deal alike—brothers often are. It would be frightfully silly to let anyone see you. Besides you'd have to walk half a verst through the snow, and you don't want to have to do that. I should walk about a little here and get warm if I were you. I'll make a fire as soon as I come back. I won't be longer than I can help."

Elizabeth said nothing. It was no use saying anything, because he was gone. The light of his torch went first, and then he was gone and she was alone in the dark. She could hear his footsteps getting fainter and fainter. Then they died away.

It was a most horrible moment. The room was quite, quite dark, and everything was still. The house was dead, and had been dead for a long time. She stood in the middle of the floor and pressed her hands against her lips to keep herself from screaming. If she screamed now—at once—Stephen would come back. *She mustn't scream.* If she screamed, Stephen would despise her. He would be quite kind to her, but he would despise her. It would be better to die of fear than to know that Stephen was despising her.

After a minute or two she let her hands fall. It didn't matter now whether she screamed or not, because Stephen wouldn't hear her. She felt her way to the bench and sat down. It was all very well to say walk about and keep warm. If she was moving herself, how could she hear whether anyone else was moving too—any *one*, or any *thing?* The horrible thing about an empty house is that you are never quite sure that it really is empty. Sitting there in the dark, Elizabeth found herself straining her ears for the sounds which might be hiding behind the silence. At first she could hear nothing. A house that is lived in has always some sounds. At first the dead house seemed to have none.

Then sounds began. They were so faint that as each one ceased, she could not have said for certain that she had heard anything. Something rustled a long way off—something creaked—something moved with a gentle flowing sound—paper stirring in the draught—old broken shutters settling—snow on the broken roof moving, sliding.

And then suddenly a crash that sent echo following echo through the house.

Elizabeth crouched down on the bench, her heart thudding. There were so many echoes, and they took so long to die. The house that had been so silent seemed all at once to be whispering round her. Whispering just on the edge of sound. Whispering up in the rafters, where the dark night looked in through gaps in the roof. Whispering through the icy corridors and the desolate untenanted rooms in which people had loved, and hated, and been afraid. Now there was only Elizabeth Radin, a stranger and very much afraid. An icy sweat came out on her temples. The darkness seemed moving towards her with all those stealthy sounds.

There was a lapse of time. She steadied herself. The sweat dried. Her hands relaxed their agonized grip of the bench. What she had heard was the fall of broken masonry brought down by the weight of the snow. What else could it be? By daylight, nothing at all. In this dark loneliness, any fear-suggested horror.

If she sat here and listened, she would go on hearing things. To listen for sounds which are not there is one of the ways to madness. Stephen had been perfectly right when he said "Walk about and keep yourself warm." Only he might have made it "Walk about and keep yourself sane." Stephen was always right.

A spurt of anger behind the thought got her on to her feet and started her pacing the room. To be always right—was there a more enraging faculty in the world? Was it a faculty, or a virtue? If it was a virtue, it was certainly the most disagreeable of all the virtues—a tyrannical prig of a virtue, the sort of virtue which makes you want to go and wallow in vice.

Elizabeth walked up and down, and thought how much she hated prigs, and tyrants, and people who are always right. And then the heartening spurt of anger died and left her cold. What a fool she was! She couldn't even be angry with Stephen for more than five minutes. It was just as well their time together was nearly over. The words went stabbing through her mind. Not to see Stephen any more—not to have him to be angry with—not to know whether he was alive or dead..."He'll write. Why should he write? I'll ask him to write."...And have him forget, or do it once or twice and be bored..."I can't let him go." "You've got to let him go..."

She stood in the middle of the dusty floor and pressed both hands down over the pain at her heart. The house began to whisper round her again.

Chapter Twenty-Six

STEPHEN CAME ACROSS the hall and called her name from the doorway.

"Elizabeth—are you there? I've been as quick as I could. I hope you're not frightfully cold. I've got some wood and we'll soon have a fire."

She could hear him dragging the wood in—branches. And then a clatter of falling logs. She felt her way to the bench and sat down again. The rush of relief and joy with which she had heard his step really frightened her. What was she going to do when he went away—and didn't come back?

There was a crackling of paper from the hearth. *Paper*. How had he come by it? A match spurted, and a little creeping edge of flame ate flickering into the darkness. She could hear Stephen blowing at it. The paper must be very damp. It smouldered, died, and revived again. A sudden flare showed her the shape of his head and shoulders, and the black arch of the open fireplace. Then with a rush the flame sprang up.

The paper was wall-paper, old and tattered. The fire twisted it, and as it caught, for an instant the long dead pattern showed against the glow. Roses that had been red burned crimson once again. Then the pine-branches crackled and snapped. Bright firelight filled the room.

Stephen dragged the bench over to the hearth for Elizabeth. He continued to feed the fire, whilst she sat forward with her chin in her hands watching him. After the strain, the fear, the rush of joy, everything seemed to have come to a standstill. She was tired and content. The future concerned her as little as the past. She had been cold, and she was warm. She had been alone, and Stephen was here. She had been afraid, and the fear was gone.

She watched Stephen make up the fire. It filled the room with a warm glow. In this rosy firelight the painted panels recaptured some of their old grace and beauty. She said,

"Was this your mother's room, Stephen?"

"Yes. It used to be pretty. A bit gim-cracky, you know—all gilding, and little tables, and fluffy cushions. I was always knocking things over. But it suited her. It's bare enough now—isn't it?" He straightened himself up by the fire and touched Elizabeth on the arm. "Come back here a little and I'll show you something."

When they were in the middle of the room, he pointed to the chimney breast. There was the open hearth with its blazing fire framed in carved alabaster, and above a narrow shelf, in the midst of the white panelling, a picture. Everything else was gone, but the picture still looked down on the ruined room. Shadows veiled it. Elizabeth could see no more than that it was a portrait. Then the ray of Stephen's torch touched it, and she saw that it was a portrait of Fay Darenska. She looked very young. She had a girl's slim body and a girl's unshadowed eyes. They were as blue as Stephen's. But her hair wasn't red, it was gold. She stood smiling out of the picture with rosy childish lips. There was a row of pearls about her throat. A second row touched her breast, and a third hung almost to her knee. A white fur wrap was slipping from her shoulders. The ray passed to and fro, bringing out the pale rose of the dress, the delicate flesh tints, the shimmer of the pearls, the whole aspect of smiling youth.

"How young!" said Elizabeth.

Stephen nodded beside her.

"She really looked like that. But she was thirty when that was painted, and I was ten years old."

The light slid down across the pearls. Fay and her pearls...Such frail things to have survived so great a ruin...

Stephen answered her thought as if she had spoken it aloud.

"Look!" he said, and turned the ray to the edge of the picture.

There was no frame. The portrait had been painted upon the central panel above the hearth.

"If it had been an ordinary picture, they'd have torn it down when they murdered Paul and wrecked the house. Someone did throw a knife at it. There—you can see the mark, just at her knee. It looks as if she had torn her dress—doesn't it? Well, the man who threw the knife slipped and fell. They'd been down into the cellars and they were all roaring drunk, so the wonder was not that one of them fell, but that any of them managed to keep his feet—only it just happened that when this particular man fell he broke his leg. After that no one would touch the picture, so there it is. If it was a canvas, I'd have got it away long ago, but I can't manage that panel."

"What happened to the pearls?"

Stephen switched off the torch. Fay Darenska and her rosy dress and her pearls went back into the shadows. The firelight glowed, faded, and glowed again. There was a little pause before he said,

"Funny you should ask that."

"Did you mind?" There was a quick compunction in her voice. "They're so lovely—and I just wondered—what happened to them."

"I should like to know," said Stephen soberly.

"Don't you know?"

They were suddenly so intimate that there was no longer any question of his minding what she asked.

He shook his head.

"I thought they'd been looted. But the other day when I was in Paris I ran across a man who was staying here with Paul just before the crash. He said Paul knew it was coming, but he wouldn't get out—said he didn't fancy being an *emigré*. That was so like Paul."

"Well?"

"Well, Paul gave him a message. By the time he thought of delivering it I was off the map, and he'd forgotten all about it till I ran into him in Paris."

"What was the message?"

"An odd one. He swears Paul told him to tell me that my mother's pearls were where she had always kept them."

"Don't you know where she kept them?"

"That's just it—she didn't keep them anywhere. She wore them always, day and night."

"What do you think he meant?"

He hesitated for a moment and then said,

"Well, it sounded as if he'd buried them with her. He might have done it—I never saw them after she died."

A bright flame shot up in the fire, and for a moment the pearls caught the light. Then they were gone again. Elizabeth shivered.

"Well, that's that," said Stephen. "Now come along and warm yourself and have something to eat. I'm afraid it'll have to be bully beef again."

"Is it safe here?" said Elizabeth when they had camped down before the fire for their meal. It was quite a good meal, because there was tinned soup as well as the beef.

He laughed a little at the question.

"It depends on what you call safe. If you don't have a fire and something to eat, you'll die—and that's not safe. On the other hand I don't think anyone can possibly get here after us until well on into to-morrow. You see, this is how I figure it out. Glinka wouldn't get going until daylight. I've thought about it a lot, and I'm pretty sure he'd go back to Orli. Of course he *could* follow the track of our sledge and come after us here, but I'm pretty sure he wouldn't."

"Why?"

Stephen ticked the reasons off on his fingers.

"One. It's not a run anyone in that village is specially keen about—the wolves got two men last winter. I'm considered—or rather Nikolai is considered—the sort of fool who'll do it once too often. I don't think Glinka would be much of a hand with a rifle, and I don't see anyone lending him a horse for the job or being keen on going with him. That's three reasons. And the fourth is that he hasn't got any authority. No—I think he'll go into Orli, say he suspects us of being the two people who are wanted, and then see what happens."

"What will happen?"

Stephen laughed.

"Well, they may tell Glinka to go and boil his head, or they may raise a posse and come chasing after us. It won't matter to us which they do, because we shall be in Poland by then."

Elizabeth's heart jumped. She said in a low voice,

"Suppose Glinka didn't go to Orli. Suppose he did get a horse and come after us."

"Well, he'd be here by now, or else the wolves would have got him. I'm not worrying about Glinka."

After a minute or two Elizabeth said,

"What about the people in this village?"

He laughed again.

"They think we're smugglers, Nikolai and me. They believe firmly in us both. I'm quite sure it has never occurred to anyone in the village that they've never seen us together. They'd probably be quite ready to swear that they had. They've heard us talking in the dark. Smugglers always come and go in the dark."

"Heard you talk?"

"Nikolai and me—or let's say Nikolai and Mikhail. I can do different voices, you know, and make them sound as if they came from different places. It's quite useful sometimes. So there it is, we come and go and they don't ask any questions—there are pickings you know. If Glinka did manage to get here, I think the chances are that he might be quite roughly handled."

Elizabeth shivered.

"Are you cold?"

"No."

"Because I'm afraid we can't stay here."

She looked at him with something like dismay. The black night—the snow—the cold—the forest—wolves...She said on a caught breath,

"Are we going on to-night?"

"Suppose I say Yes?"

"I hope you won't."

"But suppose I do?"

She managed the ghost of a smile.

"Then I suppose I'd come."

"Come along then," he said and took her by the arm.

"What—now?"

"Well, I don't think we ought to stay here."

In the firelight she could see a dancing light of mischief in his eyes.

"Where are we going?"

"Across the frontier," said Stephen with a note of triumph in his voice.

She had not known that they were so near, and her heart leapt. Of course the crossing would have to be at night. Cold, darkness, and danger—nothing mattered if the goal was really in sight. Eager words came stammering to her lips.

"The frontier! Stephen, are we so near?"

"Come and see," said Stephen.

He swept her into the hall. Its cold silence met them on the threshold. Their feet made ghostly echoes on the stone flags. He flashed his torch to show her what a huge cavern of a place it was. The great stone stair rose up to a gallery. He turned the torch upon it, and she saw how it was littered with fallen masonry.

"The hall is much older than the rest of the house. It's a feudal hall with a seventeenth-century house built round it. Paul's several times great-grandfather had a French architect over. He was a most intelligent and cultured person, and a patron of the arts, but by all accounts you didn't have to scratch very deep to find the Tartar. He had one of his serfs knouted to death in this hall. Paul wasn't very fond of the story, but it happened."

"What had the man done?" said Elizabeth. No wonder the house had felt horrible.

"Oh, he was a groom. He'd lamed the prince's favourite horse, I believe."

They crossed the hall and passed through a gaping doorway into a long stone passage.

"Where are we going?"

"To the kitchens."

"Do we go out that way?"

"We don't go out," said Stephen.

"What do you mean?"

He said, "Wait and see," and with that they came to a heavy door hanging drunkenly from wrenched hinges. The lock had been smashed and then burnt out. The wood showed pitted and blackened in the ray of the torch. Beyond, stone steps went down and out of sight.

"The cellars are as old as the hall," said Stephen.

Elizabeth stared into the black depths.

"Are we going down there?"

"It's not as bad as it looks."

They went down fifteen steps, and were in a vaulted hall, stone paved and quite dry under foot. The air was heavy and cold. Stephen took out a piece of candle and lit it. The yellow flame burned unstirred by any draught. The place was very big, and seemed all the bigger for the shadows which thronged it. That the wreckers had been here was very plain. Doors to the right and left had been smashed, casks rolled out and broken, bottles splintered. The stone under foot was deeply stained. Elizabeth hoped, shuddering, that the darkest stains were wine, not blood.

"They made a pretty fair mess of things," said Stephen dispassionately. "Paul was most awfully proud of his cellar. Some of the wine was absolutely priceless." He laughed a little. "They just smashed everything and wallowed. Well, here we are."

The last door on the left had been dragged right off its hinges. It lay where it had fallen, and they had to step over it to enter the cellar it had guarded. It was a small place with an arched roof and a row of wine-bins running round three sides of it.

"Look out for the glass," said Stephen. He held the candle up to show the littered floor.

There were smashed bottles everywhere. The candlelight picked up the shining splinters and the jagged edges of larger fragments.

"This was the old madeira," said Stephen. "Paul's grandfather laid it down. If anyone had told him his serf's grandsons would drink it, he would have had a fit. He was a bit of a connoisseur. Well, they found the madeira, but here's something they didn't find. And that's a thing I've been thankful for ever since."

He stood the candle on the side of one of the bins and went into the far corner of the cellar, where he carefully moved some of the litter aside, shifting it this way and that with his foot. Then he seemed to press downwards with considerable force, whilst at the same time he grasped the corner bin with a hand on either of its wooden sides. With a grinding sound the whole bin swung out, disclosing a narrow arch some four feet in height. He laughed, let go, and turned round upon Elizabeth.

"There's our road into Poland," he said.

Chapter Twenty-Seven

ELIZABETH PUT out a hand to steady herself. She took a step nearer the wall, and a piece of glass under her foot cracked and splintered. She looked at the black mouth of the arch and said,

"Poland?"

Stephen nodded. He was dusting his hands and picking up the candle.

"The house is just on the frontier. Thank the Lord no one knows about this old passage. Paul told me the last time I saw him, and my word, it's been useful."

Elizabeth looked at the black arch with a sort of fascinated horror. There was the way to safety and freedom. *A horrible way.* Its dank breath sickened her. She said faintly,

"Who made it?"

"Well, I gather there was an old passage running from here to a sort of shrine or chapel, but the chapel fell down and a good deal of the passage fell in. Then when Paul's great-great-grandfather built on to the house, he had men down from his estates in the north and he had the passage cleared out and rebuilt. The men who did it were told they'd lose their tongues if they talked, and the secret never got out. I don't know why Prince Boris wanted the passage restored, but I believe he was a desperate intriguer, and I daresay it was useful. Anyhow there it is. It's about half a mile long and it's in quite decent repair. It comes out on the Polish side of the frontier in the ruins of the old chapel, and it has been an absolute god-send to me."

"Are we going now?" said Elizabeth.

All her life she had had a horror of just such a place as this. It was like the horror of a nightmare. Dark passages—low passages—dark cramping walls, and a low slimy roof—places where you could not lift your head, or breathe, or see the terrors that pursued you. There was always a pursuing terror, and you could not run from it, because the roof closed down.

When Stephen said "Come along," she took a step forward, but her face was suddenly so drawn that he said,

"What's the matter?"

She found herself looking at him with entreaty.

"It's the passage—"

"What's the matter with the passage?"

His voice made the nightmare seem farther off. He patted her shoulder encouragingly.

"It's not as bad as it looks. I have to look after my head the whole way, but you'll be able to straighten up as soon as you're through the arch. I'll go first with the light. I always take a candle through here in case of bad air. It's a good danger signal."

"Is there bad air?" said Elizabeth by the arch.

"Not now. There are ventilating shafts. Some of them were blocked, and I had to clear them out. Now stand just where you are while I shut the door."

She was about a yard inside the arch, and she could stand upright, though she guessed that there was very little room over her head. She saw Stephen with a candle in his hand replacing the broken glass which he had pushed aside in order to open the secret door. Then he caught hold of the bin and swung it back. The door shut with a click and he squeezed past her, holding up the light.

The passage stretched away before them. After a yard or two there were some steps, seven or eight of them, taking them still farther down under the earth. The steps were of stone, and the passage was floored, and walled, and roofed with stone. It was like being in a great stone drain. The air had an odd dead feeling. It was not nearly so cold as it had been in the house or even in the cellar.

A yard or two beyond the foot of the steps a second passage ran away to the left. The candle-light hardly penetrated its blackness. Elizabeth looked, and looked away quickly. She had a feeling of the earth pressing down on them, over-weighted by the ruin of Paul Darensky's house.

"Where does that go to?" she said in a voice that would not rise above a whisper.

"Guess."

"How can I guess?"

He laughed.

"It wouldn't have suited old Boris to have his secret visitors trekking through the cellars and the kitchen premises. Publicity was about the last thing he wanted. That passage comes out in the room we were in."

"Then why did we come round by the cellars?"

"Well, the passage isn't too safe. There is a wooden stair, and some of the steps have gone, but at a pinch it might have come in handy. If Glinka had rolled up unexpectedly, there was our bolt-hole. That's why I chose that room."

"Where does the passage come out?"

"Behind my mother's picture. The panel opens like a door. No one has ever found it."

So Fay Darenska stood guard over Prince Boris' secret door... Elizabeth wondered what kind of visitors had come through it— hooded, cloaked, perhaps a little breathless from the darkness and the danger. She wondered if any of them were women. She wondered whether she could love any man enough to go to him at night through these dark passages.

They had gone a little way past the second passage, when Stephen uttered a sharp exclamation and stopped. He held up the candle, and Elizabeth looked over his shoulder. Her first impression was that there was a wall in front of them, and then she saw that it wasn't a wall of any man's building. The candle-light was stopped by a ragged fall of earth. The black arch of the passage was blocked. The roof had fallen in.

Stephen stood quite silent for a moment. Then he said in his most ordinary voice,

"I'll have to clear it away. I hope there isn't a great deal of it. Do you mind holding the candle?"

She took the candle, and was told not to worry.

"I don't suppose it's very much." He was taking off his coat and rolling up the sleeves of his blouse. "Here—you'd better have my coat to sit on. I tell you what I think has happened. I think some of the falling masonry from the house has come down on the roof of the passage and made it cave in. I always thought it might happen some day. Bits of the west wing keep on falling. Don't bother—we'll get through all right."

After a preliminary survey he went back to the cellar for tools. He suggested that Elizabeth should stay where she was, but when she refused, he agreed that she might make herself useful by carrying things.

"When they passed through the secret door she had the feeling that they had turned their backs upon the frontier. What was the good of it being only half a mile away if the way was blocked by who knew how many tons of earth?

Stephen collected a couple of iron bars, an old shovel, and some sacking. Then they returned to the passage and he fell to work. She had wondered about the sacking, but she soon discovered its use. The earth that was cleared had to be dragged away and spread out upon the floor of the passage. It was weary, heavy work. They strained and sweated, and at the end of three hours the way was still blocked. They knocked off then, ate a brief meal in the cellar, drank snow water, and returned to the passage to lie down and take a few hours of uneasy sleep.

Chapter Twenty-Eight

"How LONG will our food last?" asked Elizabeth.

They had waked, toiled, eaten, rested, and toiled again. She had lost count of the time, but the day must be far spent. They were resting when she asked her question, sitting on the mud-heap on the floor of the passage.

Elizabeth ached in every limb. Her hands were scraped and sore from the rough sacking and the rougher stone and earth. All day long she had been piling earth upon the sacking and dragging it away. They had come now to the point where they could not afford to raise the floor any farther. The earth had to be dragged into the branch passage and spread out there. She could not tell Stephen how much she minded having to go into that darkness. Every time she came there stumbling and panting with her heavy load, this horror of the darkness met her, and every time she had to go a little farther away from Stephen and the candle-light by which he worked.

Now they were resting. A meagre portion of food had been served out. A can of snow water stood between them. Elizabeth asked her question:

"How long will our food last?"

"Oh, long enough," said Stephen with cheerful vagueness.

She did not press the point. What was the use? She didn't really want to know just how desperate a case they were in, but that horror of the dark made her say quickly,

"We shan't run out of candles?"

He shook his head.

"Oh no—they're all right. I've got two whole ones left, and an end or two besides."

Elizabeth gave a sigh of relief. She pushed back her hair, lifted the can of snow water, and took a long drink. She had discarded her wig hours ago, and the sweat of her labours had removed the sticking-plaster, and most of the make-up with which Stephen had disguised her. The warts which had so outraged her feelings were gone. When she had drunk, she wetted a corner of the handkerchief which she had been wearing about her head and bathed her face with it.

Stephen laughed at her a little.

"You can't pass for a gipsy now."

"I wasn't a gipsy. You never meant me to be one. I was Nikolai's sister Anna, and now—"

"Well?" said Stephen. "What are you now?"

"I don't know. What am I?"

His eyes dwelt on her for a moment. Then he said in a matter-of-fact voice.

"You're a very good caddy. I expect we ought to be going on again."

They went on. Elizabeth's head swam and her hands shook. Every time she dragged her load of earth along the passage she said to herself, "Just this one, and then I'll tell him I can't go on." But when she came back with the empty sacking the words repeated themselves, and her shaking hands began to gather the earth and pile it on the sack. She came to a dazed state in which she only knew that she mustn't fail Stephen. She must pile the earth, and drag the sack, and spread the earth, and go back again for more—pile, drag, spread, and back again—pile, drag, spread—pile, drag, spread.

Sharp through the daze in which she moved cut Stephen's voice: "We're through!"

She must have been standing with the empty sack in her hands, because when he came climbing back across the rubble, the sack had just fallen in a heap at her feet. Her hands were still stretched out as if they held it, but her eyes were blank. She did not see him, because the passage was suddenly full of mist, but she felt his arms come round her and swing her off her feet.

"Elizabeth—we're through! It's going to be all right. I say, you're not going to faint—not now—not when it's going to be all right? *Elizabeth!*"

Elizabeth let her head fall on his shoulder. She was no longer faint. The mist had cleared. Her heart was beating wildly. If she said that she wasn't going to faint, Stephen would put her down—or would he? She wasn't sure. She didn't want him to put her down. She drew a long sighing breath.

"Elizabeth—"

She turned her head a little. There was a torn and gritty blouse under her cheek. Stephen's eyes looked into hers. They held a triumphant sparkle.

"You're not to faint—there's no time. Are you better now?"

Elizabeth closed her eyes. Perhaps this was the only moment in the world when Stephen would hold her like this. If she said she was better, the moment would end. His arms were round her because she was faint, and not because he loved her. What was the good of it? He didn't love her. What did it matter whether he held her or not? She opened her eyes and said,

"I'm all right."

He put her down at once, but kept a hand upon her shoulder.

"You're quite able to walk?"

"Oh yes—it was nothing."

"Well, sit down for a minute—there on the sack. I think we can crawl through the hole I've made, and I think the passage is all right beyond. I'll get you some water, and you can sit quiet whilst I just go up into the house for something."

Instead of sitting down she caught him by the sleeve.

"Back to the house? Oh *no!*"

"I shan't be five minutes. You just sit down and rest till I come."

Elizabeth gripped him with both hands.

"Why are you going back? Please, *Please* don't!"

"I shan't be five minutes."

"But why?"

"Well, it's my mother's pearls. I've just had an idea about them. It came to me like a flash whilst I was howking away at that beastly landslide. It won't take me a moment just to go and see if I'm right."

"The pearls?" said Elizabeth in a tone of dismay.

To go back, when the way to safety lay before them—to go back into that horrible house! The ruin and the desolation of it pressed in upon her.

"Yes. It came to me all in a moment—why Paul sent me that message, and what he meant by it."

"The message?"

"To say that the pearls were just where they'd always been. She always wore them, and I thought he meant that he'd buried them with her. Stupid of me, because if he had, why should he wait till everything was crashing to send me a message about it? No—I think I know what he did with them, and I was a mug not to think of it before. I think he hid them behind her portrait. I can't go away without just having a look to see if they're there."

Elizabeth still held him with both hands.

"You think they're behind the picture?"

"I think they may be. Anyhow, I'm going to see."

"Then I'm coming too."

"You'd much better stay here. The passage isn't really safe."

"I'd rather die than stay here by myself," said Elizabeth.

There was so much conviction in her voice that he laughed and patted her shoulder.

"Then you'd better come. I always told you I wasn't going to let you die."

When they turned off at the branch passage her spirits began to rise. It was, after all, impossible to go away without finding out about the pearls. And there was no risk. They would not have to come out into the open.

"We won't chance the way we came, just in case there's anyone about," Stephen said.

No, there wasn't any risk...

The passage ran up a slight incline for some way. Then there was a mouldering wooden stair. Stephen went first, testing each step and treading as near the edge as possible. He lifted her over a gap or two and came scrambling up behind her. The passage now became very low and narrow, with a stone wall on one side and wooden panelling on the other. Presently there were steps again, not quite so ruinous.

Stephen held up the candle to show her a knob and bolt this time.

"That door comes out on the big staircase just where it turns. It was convenient to have a lot of bolt-holes."

The passage bent sharply to the right, and a little farther on there were some more steps which went down. At the foot of these steps there was a curious circular turn, with the passage very narrow indeed.

"We're skirting the chimney," said Stephen, and they came out into a small square chamber. There was barely standing room.

Stephen put the candle into her hand and touched the wall which barred their way.

"The back of the picture," he said.

Elizabeth held up the candle in her right hand. Her shoulder touched Stephen's arm as they stood. It was a very narrow place, with an old, heavy smell of soot and rotting wood. They could just stand in it and stare at the back of Fay Darenska's picture. On the other side of the panel she stood, perpetually smiling and young, in her rosy dress and her pearls. But on this side there was no youth and loveliness; there was only a dusty oblong of rough unpolished wood. Stephen looked at it for a moment. Then he tapped upon it. Elizabeth felt him start. The candle flickered.

She said, "What is it?" and at once he caught her wrist and threw the light sideways on to the edge of the panel.

"Look!"

Elizabeth looked. The edge was raised about three quarters of an inch, throwing the panel into relief. He swept the light up, down, and across. Everywhere the panel which held the picture stood up from those on either side.

Stephen let go her wrist, and tapped again.

"It's hollow," he said. "I wish Paul had told me how to open it. I expect there's a catch, if I can find it. Just give me that candle for a moment."

Half way down the left-hand edge there was a wooden knob, but when Elizabeth pointed to it he shook his head.

"That only opens the panel. I want to get the back off it."

He moved the light to and fro, and presently came to a halt before a knot-hole in the wood.

"It's probably here," he said, and gave her the candle again. "I think you'll have to go into the passage whilst I see what I can do. If the back does come off, you might get hurt."

There was, in fact, no room for more than one person if either the panel or the back of the panel was to have space to swing into the tiny chamber.

Elizabeth stood in the mouth of the passage with the candle in her hand. She saw Stephen crook his finger into the knot-hole and pull. Something creaked. He said in a quick whisper, "It moved," and pulled again. And with that the back of the panel came out in a cloud of dust and sent Stephen stumbling up against the chimney wall. The noise in that narrow space was like the sudden noise of a train in a tunnel. Stephen's exclamation and the splintering crash of the wooden back as it grounded upon the stone floor echoed and re-echoed with a most terrifying loudness.

Elizabeth put a hand to the wall of the passage to steady herself. She heard the echoes die away behind her, and she heard Stephen say,

"Sorry—my foot slipped." And then, half laughing, half dismayed, "If there's anyone on the other side, they'll probably think it's the devil coming down the chimney."

They stood listening, but no sound came from beyond the panel. Stephen propped the great piece of wood against the chimney wall and beckoned to Elizabeth. If there had been little room before, there was still less now.

The back of the picture leaned behind them like a shutter. Its removal had left a shallow cavity extending to within a couple of inches of the edge of the panel. About five feet from the floor two little hooks had been screwed into the thick wood, and from them there hung, milk white amid the dust, the three gleaming rows of Fay Darenska's pearls.

Elizabeth caught her breath. So that was what Paul Darensky had meant. The pearls were where they had always been. On the front of the panel the painted pearls lay softly on Fay's soft neck— fell to her breast—dripped to her knee. And here on the reverse side, in dust and darkness, the real pearls hung, pearl for pearl, in the same position. There was a touch of madness in Paul Darensky's thought—a touch of morbid romance—a great heart-break.

The candle shivered in her hand. The light flickered on the pearls. Stephen leaned forward, lifted them, and held them up.

"Do you like them?" he said.

"They're beautiful."

He said, "Yes," and before she knew what he was going to do he had slipped them over her head. Something burned the back of her neck—a cold burn, not a hot one—ice burns. That would be the diamond clasp. Pearls were warm. Their milky smoothness touched her throat and slid down it to her breast. The long row swung a little and then came to rest against the coarse stuff of her skirt. What a change after Fay's rosy satin!"

With all these thoughts in her mind she leaned against the wall and opened tragic eyes upon Stephen. He looked back at her. She might have read the worship in his eyes, but that wide gaze of hers was on the past—on the dead woman who had worn the pearls—on her dead lover's heart-break.

He took her left hand and laid it against his cheek for a moment. Then he turned back to the panel.

"We mustn't stop. I'll just see if there's anything else."

He took the candle from her and once more passed it up, down, and across. From the right-hand hook a string hung taut. When he pulled, it came up with a little bag of dusty muslin at the end of it. He gave her back the candle, cut the string, and untied the knot which closed the bag. For a moment he looked frowningly at his own hand and what it held. Then he shook the bag out over his palm.

Four rings lay there under the candle-light. They rolled a little, and he cupped his left hand to hold them—a square-cut emerald, a diamond solitaire, a great pearl set in diamonds like the moon in a circle of stars, and—a wedding ring.

"Her rings," said Stephen. And then, "Poor old Paul...Well, we'll have to be going."

"What time is it?" said Elizabeth.

In all this strangeness she had taken no count of time. There had been no day to reckon by, only this flickering candle-light by which they had worked until they could work no longer and then lain down and slept.

Stephen turned his wrist.

"I don't know. I took my watch off whilst I was working. It's down there."

"Is it night or day?"

"Day, I think—afternoon—but I can easily tell."

He took hold of the knob on the left-hand edge of the panel.

"Stephen—what are you going to do?"

It was part of the strangeness that all their talk was in whispers—words more breathed than broken. It was almost as if they were hearing one another's thoughts. That was how people spoke in a dream—soundlessly, intimately. Oh, how after being so near, could they let one another go?

He had answered her question by twisting the knob. The panel moved outwards a bare half inch. Then he drew it back again.

"Put out the candle," he whispered. "If there's any daylight, it will show where the shutter's broken."

Elizabeth blew out the flame. The curled wick made a little glowing question-mark on the darkness. Then it faded and everything was black. She heard him move, and all at once there was a grey streak at the edge of the panel. It seemed no wider than a thread. The movement ceased. Then Stephen said, "It's all right," and the panel swung out, leaving a grey oblong between it and the wall.

The room beyond was in dusk. The splintered shutters let a little cold daylight through. She saw his head and shoulders black against it. And then all at once she heard him exclaim. It was the merest muffled ghost of an exclamation, instantly checked.

She said, "What is it?" and saw him turn with a quick shrugging movement.

"I've dropped my mother's wedding ring. It's so small, it slipped between the others. Will you take them? I'd like to find it if I can. I won't be a moment."

Their hands touched. She took the rings.

"Where did it fall?"

"Down into the room. I'm afraid it may have rolled." And with that he was through the half open panel and out on the mantelshelf beyond.

When Prince Boris had planned this secret door he had not neglected to provide an easy descent from it. On either side of the hearth the panelling was recessed to form a small niche or alcove at a height midway between the floor and the mantelshelf. In Fay Darenska's day the niches had held a pair of Dresden figures—on the right a Flora in a pink flower-bespangled dress, rose-crowned and holding a garland; and on the left Pomona robed in green, with vine-leaves in her hair, an apple in her outstretched hand, and her lap piled high with grapes, peaches, and apricots. Perhaps the figures had been there in Boris' time. They were fine dust now, blowing with the other dust through the ruined house. The niches remained.

Stephen stepped down by the right-hand niche, resting his foot where the Flora had rested hers in its rosy sandal. Another step took him down on to the hearth. His torch came out and he was flashing it here and there as he looked for the ring. It had shone bright enough on his palm. It should not have been hard to see on this bare, dirty floor. It would not have fallen among the ashes—he had heard it strike the shelf and roll. The impetus would have taken it away from the chimney-piece. It might have rolled right across the room...

He widened his search. Where the torn shutter gaped there was a pile of debris—dust, mortar, splintered wood, a lump or two of stone. He went over to the window and kneeled down, sorting the stuff over.

It might have been a minute, or it might have been a little longer, before he saw the ring. The ray of the torch glinted on it and then lost it again. The blows which had shattered the window had wrenched the panelling beneath, leaving a gaping crack where it should have joined the floor. It was from this crack that the gleam of gold had come. To reach it he had to crouch between the leaning shutter and the wall. As he focussed the torch and began to coax the ring out of a crack which would barely admit one of his fingers, his shoulder jarred the shutter and it fell. He felt it slide as the ring came towards him. The next moment the whole crazy contraption crashed down upon the floor.

Stephen scrambled to his feet with the ring in his hand. Except for a glancing blow on the shoulder he was not hurt. His torch was out. He heard Elizabeth say his name in an agonized whisper. And then, with the noise of the fall and of his own scramble amid the debris still in his ears, there came to him the sound of running, trampling feet.

Trampling feet in the hall. Trampling feet, and the rush of voices. It was like the sudden breaking of a storm.

He had taken but a couple of running steps towards the hearth, when the beam of a powerful electric torch struck him full in the face. In an instant the room seemed full of people. His hand went to his revolver and dropped again. Too many of them. He had bluffed his way out of tighter places than this...If he were shot, what would happen to Elizabeth?

He slipped Fay's ring on to the top joint of his little finger and called out in a surprised voice,

"What is it, comrades?"

Over his head he heard the click of the closing panel.

Chapter Twenty-Nine

THE PANEL CLOSED without any sound except that one faint click. On the inner side of it Elizabeth stood in an agony of fear and doubt. She had closed the panel. But had she closed it to save Stephen, or to save herself? She had ached a hundred times with the knowledge that it was she who was his greatest danger, but was it that knowledge which had made her hand go out and pull the panel to? Was it? *Was it?* Or was it just the coward's instinct to save herself? She didn't know. She stood in the dark with Fay Darenska's pearls lying over her heart as heavy as tears, and she did not know.

She had the rings he had given her to hold in her left hand. It was her right hand with the blown-out candle in it which had snatched at the panel and pulled it to. The candle had fallen—somewhere— here at her feet. But it didn't matter, for a candle was no good if you hadn't any matches. Stephen had the matches.

Stephen—

She had been shut in with her half stunned thoughts, but at his name she came back to the outer sense of things. She felt the sharp cutting edge of the big diamond where her hand was clenched over Fay Darenska's rings, and she could hear the voices in the room beyond. She could hear them quite clearly—a lot of angry men, a torrent of excited words. And then Stephen, quite cheerful and at his ease:

"But I'm not Nikolai."

"Here you—schoolmaster—Glinka—isn't he Nikolai?"

So it was Glinka who was here...A feeling of passionate rage swept over Elizabeth. She became less afraid. Her thoughts moved quickly. She had done the right thing when she shut the panel, because if the secret way had been discovered, there would have been no hope at all. Her mind cleared. If she had been taken with Stephen, she couldn't have done anything to help him, but as long as one of them was free there was hope.

She heard Stephen say, "I'm Nikolai's brother Mikhail. Everyone in the village knows me. What have you got against Nikolai anyhow?"

"Nikolai this—Nikolai that! We don't believe in your Nikolai!"

Then Stephen again:

"But everyone knows us here, I tell you."

She heard Glinka break in angrily.

"Where's the woman you were passing off as your sister? If you're not Nikolai, where is he, and where's the woman? We followed the track of their sledge, I tell you, and it brought us straight here. What are you doing here if you're not Nikolai?"

Out in the room Stephen shrugged his shoulders. There was a Red Guard on either side of him. Two more confronted him, with Glinka between them. The man with the torch had turned it out. Now that the shutter had fallen, there was enough pale wintry daylight to serve. Facing Stephen, Glinka faced the light. It showed the uncertainty in his eyes. He was not sure that this was the man whom he had seen in Ilya's hut. This man seemed younger. His hair was short, he was less swarthy. His voice was different—a higher, younger voice. A man can cut his hair and change his voice...But then where was the woman?...He wasn't sure.

His uncertainty made an atmosphere of which Stephen was intensely aware. He said with half a laugh,

"What am I doing here? No harm. I camp here sometimes when I'm passing through. There are fewer fleas than there are in the village, and I've a tender skin." He pointed to the hearth. "There's one of my fires if you don't believe me."

A half burnt log lay across the cold ash. Everybody stared at it. Then they all looked back at Stephen.

"If Nikolai is your brother, where is he?" said Glinka angrily. "He had a woman with him, and I say that he is a *bourzhui* and a counter-revolutionary who has been going by the name of Red Stefan, and that the woman is an English *bourzhui* called Elizabeth Radin whom he has helped to escape from prison, assaulting the Commissar Petroff and carrying her off. A description of these two people has been broadcast, and I immediately suspected that the woman with Nikolai was disguised. She would not speak or give an account of herself, and when I spoke to her she trembled."

"Fancy that!" said Stephen. He winked at the Red Guards. "She didn't know her luck—did she? Anyone can tell he's a schoolmaster. I wish I could talk like that."

One of the men laughed, and Glinka spat with rage.

"Where's Nikolai?" he shouted. "Where's the woman? Where's the sledge? I tell you we traced it here!"

Stephen changed his expression. The laughter went out of his face and a deep melancholy took its place.

"The sledge is in the village. As for Nikolai and my sister, the wolves got them."

The men looked at one another. It was true that the sledge had been chased by wolves. The tracks showed that.

Glinka gave a furious, scornful laugh.

"And the horse brought the sledge here and told you what had happened, I suppose!"

Stephen gazed at him sadly.

"No, no, no, Comrade Schoolmaster. Grischa is clever, but he cannot talk. I will tell you how it all happened. May I do that, sergeant?"

The sergeant at Glinka's right gave a brief nod. Like the other Red Guards he wore a long, heavy military overcoat and a peaked cap with a red star in front.

"Say anything you like," he said, "but if you tell lies, it will be the worse for you."

"Oh, I shan't tell lies," said Stephen. "Never waste a good lie when the truth will do just as well—eh, Comrade? Besides, if you've been over the track you'll know whether I'm speaking the truth or not. Well, this is just what happened. Nikolai got a message to go to Moscow and fetch away our sister Anna because her husband was dead and she's always been a poor thing who couldn't shift for herself, so we thought we ought to look after her, and Nikolai went off to Moscow. He took the horse and sledge as far as Orli, and he dropped me at the old forester's hut. If you tracked the sledge, I expect you came on it."

"What were you doing there?" said Glinka.

Stephen winked at the Red Guard who had laughed.

"Shall I be put in prison if I say I was snaring hares? Mind you, I don't say that that was what I was doing, but I might have been."

"Go on," said the sergeant.

"Well, there I was anyhow, and you needn't worry about what I was doing. Then a couple of nights ago, just as I was beginning to wonder where Nikolai was, he came driving hell-for-leather across the clearing with the wolves after him. I heard him shout, and I ran out with my rifle. Between us we managed to get the horse clear and the three of us into the hut."

"The three of you?" said the sergeant.

Stephen flung out his hands.

"The three of us—Nikolai, and Grischa, and myself."

"Where was the woman?" shouted Glinka.

Stephen looked down at the dusty floor.

"When I asked him that, he didn't answer me. I said, 'Where's Anna?' and he didn't answer me. I said 'Didn't she come with you?'"

He had them all spell-bound, waiting for the answer. When he had kept them for a tense half minute, he went on, his voice low and shaken.

"Nikolai said, 'Yes—she came.' Then I said, 'Where is she?' and he said, 'The wolves got her.'"

Even Glinka shrank back a little. There was a pause. Then one of the men said,

"He threw her out?"

"I didn't ask him," said Stephen very low. He brushed his hand quickly across his eyes. "I gave him some food. Presently we slept. I don't know how long it was. I woke up because the door banged. Nikolai was gone. I looked out and I could see him running over the snow. I called to him, but he went on running. The moon was very bright—I saw the wolves on his trail. I shut the door again. What could I do? He had gone mad—I couldn't save him. In the morning I took the horse and sledge and came here."

The guards exchanged glances. Such things had been known to happen. The story tallied with the tracks in the snow.

"And what brought you here?" said the sergeant. Then, in an altered voice, "Here, let's have a look at your hands."

Stephen held them out—broken nails, earth-grimed fingers, the incongruous glint of Fay's wedding ring.

"You've been digging," said the sergeant. "What's that ring on your finger? What have you been up to? You'd better own up."

Stephen made a shrinking movement.

"Digging?" he stammered.

The sergeant came up to him with a menacing expression.

"Here, turn round to the light and let's have a look at you!" He took him by the shoulders and swung him round to face the gaping window. "Digging?" he said, and looked at the hand which had touched Stephen's gritty blouse. "Well, I should just about say you *had* been digging! Look at your clothes! Come, come—what have you been up to?"

Stephen looked down at his dirty hands.

"I got wood and made a fire," he said.

"That cock won't fight," said the sergeant. "What's the good of telling lies? If you're this Red Stefan we're looking for, your number's up anyhow, because we've got someone down at the village who can identify you—come all the way from Tronsk on purpose. If you're what you say you are, of course that needn't worry you, and we can have a talk about this digging business." His eyes were on the glint of the ring.

Stephen hung his head in apparent confusion. Up and down all over Russia there were stories of treasure buried or hidden. Such treasure certainly belonged to the State. But there was a gleam in the sergeant's eye. Even Glinka listened instead of talking. Treasure is sticky stuff to handle. With any chance of handling it, they would not be in a hurry to remove him to the village.

"Tie him up!" said the sergeant. "I can see he's a slippery fellow. Just his hands—he'll want his feet to walk with presently. And you two get that shutter up to the window and light the fire! We needn't freeze whilst we're waiting."

Stephen held out his hands with a sheepish air. What a fool he had been to let himself be trapped like this! Someone from Tronsk to identify him...Petroff? Good Lord—that was going to be awkward. He wondered if there was any odd chance that Petroff wouldn't recognize him. He rather welcomed the tying of his hands. If he was tied up, they might not keep so close a watch upon him. If he pitched a tale about a treasure, could he get some of them out of the room? That was what he wanted—to get them out of the room. Half a minute would do the trick. He measured the distance with his eye as he sat on the bench with a guard on either side of him. One stride to the hearth, a foot on the niche, another on the mantelshelf, and the panel shut between him and the room...

There were at least three people too many to make it possible. If he could get rid of Glinka, and the sergeant, and the guard who had laughed, he thought he could account for the two lads on the bench. As to his hands being tied, they were tied for just so long as he chose and no longer. It would take someone a great deal cleverer at the job than a Russian peasant to tie any knot that he couldn't get out of just when he wanted to. A useful accomplishment, and well worth the time he had given to acquiring it.

He looked down at Fay's ring and considered what sort of yarn he had better spin. He didn't want to be taken out of this room, that was the worst of it. Yes, that was the worst of it, because sooner or later it would be bound to occur to somebody that the ground was frozen hard, and that if he had been digging, he must have been digging underground.

He began to consider leading the whole party down into the cellars and trying to give them the slip there. Half a minute's start would be enough. The bother was that he didn't see his way to getting that half minute's start. There were a damned sight too many of them, and he simply couldn't risk being shot, because of Elizabeth.

"Thinking it over?" said the sergeant's voice. "If you know what's good for you, you'll own up."

The shutter had been propped into position. Someone had produced a lantern and set it on the mantelpiece. The fire had begun to burn.

Stephen shrugged his shoulders. Beyond the sergeant he could see Glinka staring at him with an angry, puzzled frown. He could think of no story that would serve him. The situation smouldered, and might at any moment go up in flames. He thought he would strike a match and see what happened. He looked up with a grin.

"If you've got someone who knows this Red Stefan of yours, why don't you trot him out? If he's down at the village, why not get a move on and take me there? He'll soon say he never set eyes on me before in his life, and everyone else will be able to tell you all about me." He laughed a little. "And I can tell you just what they'll say—'A bit of a rapscallion, but nobody's enemy except his own. Never did an honest day's work in his life, but a good fellow all the same. Tells a good story and sings a good song, and gets a good welcome wherever he goes.' That's what they'll tell you, sergeant."

"He wants to get you away from here," said Glinka in an angry whisper.

"We're staying here," said the sergeant.

Stephen looked impudently at Glinka.

"Schoolmasters know everything—don't they? What does it feel like to be so clever?"

"Where did you get that ring?" said the sergeant.

Stephen changed his tone.

"I picked it up—honest I did—just now, in the corner of the room. I saw something shine, and there it was, in that crack under the window. And while I was trying to get it out the shutter came down *blip*, and there we all were."

"He's telling lies!" said Glinka violently.

Stephen winked at the sergeant.

"That's not a lie—that's the truth. If I was telling a lie, I could tell a much better one than that. I told you I could tell a good story. Would you like to hear the one about the Commissar who lost his clothes? Or shall I sing you a song?"

"No!" shouted Glinka.

"Then I will," said Stephen, and burst forthwith into song. He pitched his voice higher than he had done as Nikolai. He sang to a wild, ringing tune:

"I went to the fair of Kazan to see
If the strongest man would fight with me.
Hola!
I broke the head of the strongest man,
So now I'm the cock of the town of Kazan.
Hola! Hola! Hola!

"Why don't you stop him?" stormed Glinka.

The sergeant looked at him sourly. The man was a nuisance—a prying know-all of a fellow—a damned nuisance. Why hadn't he stopped in the village? Then they could have got down to this treasure business, he and the men. He damned Glinka for a meddler.

Stephen went on singing:

"I went to the fair of Kazan to see
If the prettiest girl would fancy me.
Hola!
The prettiest girl she squealed and ran.
So now I've no use for the town of Kazan.
Hola! Hola! Hola!

As the last "Hola!" died away, there was a sound in the hall beyond the open door—the sound of footsteps on the stone flags. They came on lightly and quickly. Everyone turned and looked at the empty arch. The footsteps left the stone and crossed the wood of the fallen door. In the next instant Stephen's bound hands clenched one upon the other.

Irina was coming into the room.

Chapter Thirty

BEHIND THE PANEL from which Fay Darenska watched the room Elizabeth waited. Her first sharp agony of fear had lessened. The dreaded sound of a shot had not come. As long as they did not shoot Stephen or take him away there was hope. She steadied herself with the thought that she must be ready. Stephen might want her help, and she must be ready. Her hand was still clenched over Fay Darenska's rings. The diamond had been cutting her palm for what seemed like a very long time. She heard the men talking and she heard the fire crackling below her on the hearth.

When Stephen began to sing she relaxed a little and opened her hand. Her palm was bleeding. It felt damp and sticky. She took the rings one by one and slipped them on, the pearl and the diamond solitaire together on her left hand, and the big emerald on her right. She pushed the long rope of pearls down inside her blouse with the other two rows. Then she drew a long breath and looked about her.

The narrow place was quite dark except for a single glimmer to the right. Just beyond the panel which held the picture there was a knot-hole in the wood. It was no bigger than a shilling and the light that came through it was of the faintest, but if she could get close up to it she would be able to see what was happening in the room beyond.

Very slowly and carefully she moved to the right until her eye was on a level with the hole. No doubt it had been convenient to leave a spy-hole in order that Prince Boris' visitors should make sure that he was alone before they opened the secret door.

Elizabeth pressed her right hand against the wall and looked into the room. She saw Stephen on the bench between the two guards, and the sergeant and another guard warming themselves. She looked right down on the back of the sergeant's neck as he stooped forward over the fire. She looked down on the top of Glinka's head and the sullen set of his shoulders.

And then Stephen stopped singing and they all looked at the door. She did not hear the footsteps, but her heart began to beat heavily. She did not know what they were all waiting for, but its approach made her feel sick with terror.

Then she saw Irina.

She came through the broken doorway and stood just inside it looking into the room with its mixture of firelight and candle-light, and dusk. There was a man with her—someone from the village. He had brought her here because she insisted. Now he hung back, having no wish to be mixed up in affairs of state.

Irina stood looking into the room. The play of light and shadow confused her after her passage through the darkness of the shuttered house. She saw at first only a group by the fire. Then the group split into Glinka, the guards, and the man who sat on the bench between two of them. She began to come slowly across the hall, whilst they all looked at her—all except the man on the bench. His hands were bound, and he looked down at his bound hands.

So it was Irina and not Petroff—Irina come all the way from Tronsk to identify him...He wondered if they would shoot him out of hand. He looked at her without appearing to look, and saw how pale she was—pale not with any faintness or fatigue, but with the burning pallor of emotion. Her eyes blazed. Her lips were a scarlet line. She had opened her sheepskin coat at the neck, and he could see the throat muscles tense and straining.

She came to the end of the bench and stood there, her head a little thrown back. When Glinka began to say something she ignored him.

"You have been a long time," she said to the sergeant. And then, "Who is this man?"

The sergeant coughed, drew himself up, and put his cap straight. He was conscious that Irina was a handsome young woman, that he resented her presence, and that he must be careful to keep on the right side of her. A complicated frame of mind and bad for the temper. He spoke gruffly.

"Well, that's for you to say, isn't it, Comrade?"

Irina kept her eyes upon him. Big blazing eyes he thought them, but his own taste was for something softer—a bit more melting, as you might say. Anyhow, damn women when you were out on a job. Why couldn't she stay down at the village until she was wanted? He saw the treasure-hunt receding.

"Who is he?" said Irina in an odd shrinking voice. She had seen broad shoulders and a black cropped head. Stefan's hair was red. Yet something pulled at her heart. She said "Who is he?" and waited for the sergeant to answer her.

He said with a good deal of impatience,

"Comrade Glinka says he's this Nikolai that we're hunting, but *he* says he's only Nikolai's younger brother, Mikhail. And it doesn't matter a damn which one of them he is so long as neither of them's Red Stefan—and that's where you come in."

He swung the lantern down from the mantelpiece and held it so that the light fell full on Stephen. "Here—stand up, my man, and let her have a look at you! Now, Comrade, here you are—and here he is. If he's Red Stefan, you've only to say the word. If he isn't Red Stefan, I don't care a damn who he is, and I don't suppose you do either."

Stephen stood up when he was bidden. A tight place—a most uncommon tight place. Well, well—*"de l'audace, de l'audace, et toujours de l'audace."* A sound fellow Danton. He looked straight into Irina's eyes with a smile.

There was a pause. For two women it seemed as if everything in the world had stopped. Elizabeth could see Stephen's face, but not Irina's. She saw him smile with his eyes. She waited for the word that would be his death warrant. Everything stopped whilst she waited—even her heart, even her breath, even fear.

Irina looked into Stephen's eyes. They smiled. It was whilst they smiled that for her the world stood still. She wished that it might never go on again, for then she would have no choice to make...If she said that she did not know him, he would go away and she would never see him again. If she said he was Red Stefan, he was as good as dead. She pictured him gone away. She pictured him dead. A man who went away could come back again. The dead never came back.

"Well?" said the sergeant.

"Where is the woman?" said Irina quickly.

She had not said that he was Red Stefan. She had not said that he was not Red Stefan. If he was alone, perhaps she would let him go. But not with Elizabeth Radin. It would be easier to see him dead than to let him go to Elizabeth.

"What woman?" said the sergeant.

She turned on Glinka.

"You said there was a woman with this Nikolai. Where is she?"

"He says the wolves got her," said the sergeant.

"My poor brother Nikolai and the woman—the wolves got them both," said Stephen in a mournful voice.

Glinka came pushing in, beside himself with impatience.

"But you haven't said who he is! You ask where's the woman, but you don't tell us about the man."

"Now, now, schoolmaster," said the sergeant—"this is my job, not yours." He turned to Irina. "It's my job, and he's no call to take the words out of my mouth. But we all want to know, do you recognize this man, or don't you? There, you've got it in a nutshell—is he Red Stefan, or isn't he?"

A gust of rage whipped the colour into Irina's cheeks.

"Well, here's your answer!" Her voice rang in the empty room. "Red Stefan? No one but a fool would ever have thought he was Red Stefan!" She flung round on Glinka, who recoiled in physical fear. "Only a fool would have thought it! And only a double fool would have dragged me here whilst the real man got away!" She stamped her foot with violence and repeated, *"Fool!"*

The sergeant looked relieved. Glinka was getting it, not he. When she had stormed herself out she would go back to the village and they could get on with this treasure business. He supposed they would have to let the schoolmaster come in on it, if only to stop his mouth. When Irina drew an angry sobbing breath, he said briskly,

"Then you don't know him, Comrade?"

Irina stamped again.

"I never saw him before in my life!" she said.

This suited the sergeant's book well enough. If the man wasn't Red Stefan, there was an end of it—so much the better for him, and so much the better for everyone else. Irina had had her say, he and the men had done their duty, and Glinka was a meddlesome busybody. And that was the one thing he had felt sure about all along. Let the man stick to teaching his village brats and be damned to him. He squared his shoulders and addressed Irina.

"All right, Comrade, that settles it—you don't identify him. Very well then, we needn't keep you. You'll be more comfortable in the village." He lifted his voice and hailed the nervous peasant by the door. "Hi, you there! Get a move on! The Comrade has finished her business here, and you'd best be getting along whilst the daylight lasts."

Irina turned an angry stare upon him.

"And you stay here?"

"We stay here."

"Then I stay too." She sank down on the edge of the bench and called to the peasant, "You heard what the sergeant said? Hurry along, or the wolves will get you. We're staying here."

There was a silence of dismay. The peasant looked from one to another and then slipped away, glad enough of the excuse.

Stephen laughed a little.

"And what about me?" he said.

The sergeant made the best of a bad job. He knew an obstinate woman when he saw one. Since Irina meant to stay, she must either be squared or hoodwinked. It could be done.

"Aren't you going to let me go?" said Stephen.

He got the sergeant's most martial frown.

"None of your lip, my lad! You haven't told us how you came by that ring yet—not to my satisfaction anyhow. Unlawful possession of a gold ring, and making up a silly lie to account for it—that's what I'm charging you with. Now you listen to me—and Comrade Irina will bear me out, and so will the schoolmaster—treasure belongs to the State."

"Treasure!" said Irina contemptuously.

Glinka's eyes sparkled.

The sergeant repeated the word in a weighty voice.

"Treasure. I say this man's found treasure that belongs to the State, and that being so, we've got our duty—we've got to make him say what he's found and where he found it. Now you, Mikhail or whatever your name is, own up! You've found a treasure."

"You're joking, sergeant."

"It'll be no joke for you," said the sergeant grimly. "What did you find, and where did you find it? Come—find your tongue, or we'll see what a touch of fire will do to make you speak."

Behind the panel Elizabeth straightened herself. The hand on which she had been leaning was numb, but her mind was suddenly quick and clear. She knew exactly what she must do, and she knew without a shadow of doubt that she would be able to do it. First three silent steps to the left and her hand feeling for and finding the knob which opened the panel. She had to set the door ajar, and she had to do it very steadily in case anyone in the room beyond should see—anyone except Stephen.

Her right hand was too numb. She couldn't depend on it. She put her left hand on the knob and turned it a fraction of an inch at a time until she could feel that the catch was free. Then she pushed the panel outwards for about a quarter of an inch and released the latch again. It caught on the wood instead of sliding into its groove. At a touch the door would open.

Stephen saw the panel move, and had a sickening throb of fear. What was Elizabeth doing? The movement was so slight that even his sharp eyes could not have sworn to it if he had not been looking that way—measuring the distance—whilst the sergeant expatiated upon the most effective methods of making refractory prisoners find their tongues.

The movement ceased, but he thought that the panel was ajar.

Ajar. What did that mean? Had it been done to attract his attention? Had it—

He continued to gaze abstractedly over the sergeant's shoulder.

Elizabeth lifted her hand from the knob. The panel stayed, neither open nor shut. A touch would open it, a touch would close it. It stayed. The faintest, narrowest thread of light just showed at its edge.

She turned from this thread of light and moved soundlessly towards the open mouth of the secret passage. She mustn't hurry, because if she made any noise at all, it might kill Stephen. When the life of the person you love most in the world depends on your not making any noise, it is astonishing how quiet you can be. The strange clarity and calm that had come upon her gave her perfect control of every movement.

She reached the passage, and remembered that it took a circular turn to avoid the chimney. She kept the fingers of her right hand upon the wall and felt before her with her left. After the circular turn there would be steps going up. She felt for the bottom step with her foot and climbed up in the dark. It was very, very dark. The air was heavy with the smell of decay. At any other moment the place would have filled her with horror. To be alone in the dark in these old passages would only an hour ago have brought her to the edge of panic. You might die here and turn to dust before anyone found you. She had thought of that when she passed this way with Stephen. Now she thought only of Stephen, and of the sergeant's voice as he talked about torture.

She came to the top of the steps. Now the passage turned sharply to the left. Her hand moved up and down on the wall as she walked, feeling for a handle. Somewhere here there should be a knob and a bolt. Stephen had shone the candle on them as they passed, and she had remembered them when the sergeant began to talk about torture. Up and down, up and down went her hand. Sometimes the wood it touched was rough, sometimes her fingers slipped on it. Suppose she couldn't find the handle. Suppose she had passed it in the dark. Suppose—

The knob was under her hand.

She faced the wall and felt for the bolt. It moved a little and then stuck. She had to take both hands to it and wrench with all her might before it moved again. It creaked, and her heart thumped. That was stupid, because she was too far from the room for anyone to hear the creaking of a bolt.

It creaked again, and shot back, pinching her finger. She turned the handle, and the door opened outwards. Twilight filled the opening. It was at once a shock and a relief to find that it was not yet dark. It seemed so long since she had asked Stephen whether it was day or night.

The door opened on to the great stair just where it turned. She could see the heavy black line of the gallery above her, and the huge shadowed hall below. The door was like the door of a cupboard. It opened a foot above the floor, so that she had to step out over the panelling.

She was now on the flagged landing from which the stair ran down to the hall. There was dust and rubble everywhere—dust, rubble, and the great broken lumps of masonry which she had seen by the light of Stephen's torch when they had crossed the hall—how long ago?

There had been pillars guarding the stair, and a stone balustrade—thrown down and wrecked by the insensate fury of a drunken mob. One pillar was in fragments, the other leaned drunkenly against the wall with splintered capital and broken base. In the dusk all this ruin had a most terrifying aspect. It seemed as if the tilted pillar were in the very act of falling, as if the wall swayed and at any moment the roof might come crashing down. She really did feel as if the stone were moving under her feet. Perhaps it did move. Perhaps it was only she herself who was shaken by cold, and fear, and strain. It didn't matter. Even if the house fell in, she would do what she had come here to do.

If there was a sudden noise in the hall, the men who were guarding Stephen would surely come to see what it was. If she could make enough noise, they would surely come...

Just where the stair met the landing there lay a huge rounded lump of stone, part of the capital of the broken pillar. Elizabeth came across the landing and looked down at it. It was so near the edge that if she could move it ever so little, it must overbalance. But could she move it? She went down on her knees in the dust and pushed. She thought the stone moved, but she wasn't sure. She braced her feet against another piece of the pillar and pushed again.

If the broken capital had really been lying on the flat surface of the landing, she might have pushed and strained for ever, but in its fall it had smashed away the lip of the step. It hung there tilted, balanced, ready at the slightest shock to lose its equilibrium. Elizabeth's first push faintly disturbed this balance. Her second set the stone rocking. She put out all her strength, and felt it leap away from her hands as if it were some gigantic ball which she had thrown. It was all she could do not to follow it. She felt herself pitching forward, and just managed to save herself by clutching at the balustrade.

She scrambled to her feet, shaking and catching her breath. The great piece of stone had gone rolling and bounding down the stair. It smashed another step, broke through a fallen length of balustrade, and carrying dust, rubble and debris with it, crashed down upon the echoing flagstones of the hall. The noise in that silent place was overwhelming. The echoes came beating back against her ears and dazed her. She stood for a moment, steadying herself. Then she ran back across the landing to the secret door.

Chapter Thirty-One

IN THE octagonal room the fire blazed up. The sergeant glanced from his prisoner to the reddening embers and back again.

"Well?" he said.

Stephen was silent.

Irina stared at them both. She did not mean to allow Stephen to be tortured, but the nearer he came to it the more he would have to be grateful for when she stepped in with a flourish of trumpets to save him. There was a smouldering anger in her eyes—anger with Elizabeth, who had escaped; anger with this stupid bully of a sergeant; and deepest anger of all with Stephen, for whom she had lied, and who sat there looking as if he didn't care a fig for any of them. It wouldn't do him any harm to be taken down a peg or two.

Stephen, on his part, had no intention of being tortured. For one thing, he wanted his feet to walk over the frontier with. Burnt soles would be extremely inconvenient. No—the minute things really began to get hot he would have to pitch that tale about the cellars and trust to luck and his wits for a chance of getting away. Meanwhile he kept a still tongue in his head and looked over the sergeant's shoulder.

The panel had not moved again. But it had moved; he could swear to that. It had moved outwards, and it had not moved back again. Therefore it was ajar.

At this point he thought he had better answer the sergeant with becoming politeness.

"You, and your rings and your treasure!" he said. "What's the good of my telling you anything? You don't believe me when I tell the truth. Do you want me to make up lies?"

"Better not, my lad—I can tell you that."

Stephen changed his tone.

"Look here, sergeant—if I tell you the truth, will you let me go?"

The sergeant swore.

"If you don't tell me the truth, I'll burn the hide off you!"

"No need," said Stephen. "Now look here, sergeant—what I told you was the truth, but I'm free to admit that it wasn't the whole truth. I did find the ring in that crack under the window, but that wasn't the first time I'd found it."

Irina set her chin in her hand and scowled. The sergeant swore again.

"Now we're getting at it! Go on."

"You'll let me off if I tell you? Well, I really found it first down in the cellar."

And with that the top of the broken pillar overbalanced as Elizabeth thrust at it for the third time. The noise of its crashing fall filled all the house with clamouring echoes. Glinka, nearest the door, ran to it and shouted that the roof was falling in. Irina, the sergeant, and the guard who had been making up the fire followed him, but the men who sat on Stephen's either side held their ground.

Glinka had run out of the room and out of sight. Irina and the sergeant were a little beyond the doorway, still visible as shadows in the dusk. The guard came to a halt a yard or two beyond the threshold. Stephen had his moment, but he also had two guards to reckon with. As they both craned forward, intent upon what was happening in the hall, he slipped his hands free, took them by the scruff of the neck, and brought their heads together with a vigorous bang.

One stride took him clear. The slumped bodies had barely reached the floor before he had his foot in the niche which had held the rose-crowned Flora. A second step, and he had reached the mantelshelf, and even as the guard beyond the threshold turned bewildered, to see two men lying in a tumbled heap instead of three sitting quietly on a bench, the panel had swung out and back again and Stephen was fastening the catch on the inner side.

Elizabeth moved in the darkness of the passage with a beating heart. She had shot the bolt between her and the landing. Now her foot felt for the steps, now she went down them, one hand on the wall and one stretched out before her. She could not see anything at all. She could hot hear anything either except the beating of her own heart.

And then suddenly in the dark her hand touched Stephen's face. She did not cry out, but she gave a very faint gasp, and in a moment his arms were round her and he was whispering in her ear, first her name, and then,

"How clever of you! It did the trick all right! But I don't know whether anyone saw the panel shut. They didn't see it open." He laughed a little. "Have you got the candle?"

"No—I don't know—I think I dropped it."

"It doesn't matter—they left me my torch. We'd better run for it."

Without more ado they ran—up the steps, past the door on the landing—down more steps, and through the lowest, narrowest part of the passage, with stone on one side and wooden panelling on the other. The ray of the torch flickered and danced before them. They came to the ruinous wooden stair which led to the cellar level.

Stephen stood still to listen for a moment. Then he said, "Quick, Elizabeth!" and took her down the stair as he had brought her up, trying each tread before he put his weight on it and swinging her over the gaps.

As they ran down the incline beyond, the first sound that was not of their own making reached them—the confused and hollow sound of following feet.

"All right," said Stephen—"we've got them beat." And with that their feet were on the earth they had dug out.

They came into the main passage and ran down it. Stephen focussed his torch on the rough tunnel which pierced the fall of earth.

"Quick!" he said again, "you first! There's just room!" And Elizabeth found herself on her hands and knees crawling into a thick, clammy darkness.

It was the worst moment of all. Her body filled the hole, so that the light could not help her. The loose stuff gritted and slid beneath her as she crawled. The roof let down a continual shower of pebbles and earth upon her hair, her face, her neck. She did not know how long the tunnel might be. If it fell in upon her, she would be buried alive. It might fall in and crush her, in an instant. That would not be so bad. But if it were to pin her here alive—or come down ton upon ton between her and Stephen...A terror such as she had never known swept over her at the thought. She felt, or imagined, a tremor that shook the whole earthy mass.

Then, as she crawled, Stephen's hand touched her foot. The nightmare lifted a little. She blinked the earth out of her eyes and suddenly found her head and shoulders free. Next moment she was out of the tunnel and scrambling to her feet in the passage beyond. She leaned against the wall, pushing back her hair, and drawing a long sweet breath of relief.

Stephen followed her.

"Lord—what a tight squeeze!" he said.

Then his torch went on and the ray swept to and fro overhead. She heard him give a whistle between his teeth and, looking up, she saw how the roof of the passage sagged and bulged. Great cracks showed black in the ray. She thought she saw them tremble. Was it the light that shook, or was it she herself? She thought the wall shook too. She thought it moved when she leaned against it. This all in one flash of fear. In another flash the fear had become a certainty of terror. The wall bulged, and the cracks were widening. And then Stephen had her by the arm, and they were running faster than she had ever run in her life. His arm came round her, sweeping her along. She stumbled on the uneven floor and he held her up. She gasped and strained for breath, but he urged her on.

And then it came—the shaking and heaving of the earth, the horrible dull boom, the rush of driven dusty air, overtaking and half choking them. It came with its stunning noise, its merciless reverberations, its terror. It came, and passed. The sound of it died away. The earth was steady under them again. The walls stood, and the roof covered them.

Stephen stopped running and sent the ray exploring once again. There were no cracks here, no bowing of the arch, no horrible gradual slipping out of the true.

"That's all right," he said cheerfully. "A near shave—wasn't it? But nobody will follow us now. It's the west wing of the house coming down that's done it—too much weight on the roof of the passage. Well, there goes a very convenient back door."

They walked on in silence. Elizabeth felt dazed and weak. She walked on because Stephen expected her to walk on. If she had stopped, she would not have been able to start again. The passage went on, and on, and on. The air was heavy and cold. She went on walking.

Then they stopped. Stephen stopped, and as soon as he stopped, Elizabeth stopped too. The passage had come to an end. The torch showed old broken steps rising steeply upwards. Elizabeth looked at them and roused a little from the daze that hung about her like a fog.

"Are we over the frontier?" she said.

Stephen nodded.

"Yes, we're in Poland. The steps come out in the ruin of the chapel I told you about. The opening's very well hidden."

Elizabeth put her hand against the wall to steady herself.

"And then?" she said.

"There's a farm-house about a quarter of a mile away where the people know me. You won't find that too far to walk."

"And then?" said Elizabeth again. The words were so faint that he hardly caught them. She might have been speaking to herself—perhaps she was.

Russia was behind them. Their danger, their close companionship, the days and nights when he, and he alone, had stood between her and the nightmare that threatened—these too lay behind.

In front of them—what? Separations—a divided path...The future looked as cold as ice and as barren as the snow. She saw these things, like two painted pictures, in a moment of time.

Then Stephen was answering her.

"They'll set us on our way with a horse and sledge in the morning. They're used to my comings and goings, and they don't ask questions. We'll get to the railway and be in Warsaw by the afternoon."

Warsaw—civilization...She would have to get a passport—clothes...She remembered suddenly and bleakly that she hadn't a penny in the world. She leaned a little more heavily against the wall, and as she did so, the topmost row of Fay Darenska's pearls slipped from the torn collar of her blouse. She put up her hand, remembering. Stephen had given her the pearls to take care of—and the rings—his mother's rings. She must give them back again.

She lifted the pearls over her head and held them out. He had set the torch on a step at the level of his shoulder. The ray cut the darkness between them like a sword. The pearls dipped into the light and slid away to the shadows below.

"What's this?" said Stephen in a startled voice.

"The pearls. Will you take them?"

Her hands felt weak, but they were steady. She thanked God that they were steady.

"But they're yours," said Stephen with devastating simplicity.

Elizabeth's hands began to shake. Her whole body began to shake. She took a sobbing breath and tried to speak, but the words that should have come failed and became just a stammering murmur of sound.

Stephen took the pearls, knotted them in a dirty red cotton handkerchief, and dropped them into his pocket.

"I'll keep them for you," he said. Then all at once his voice changed. "Elizabeth—you did know that they were for you?"

She leaned against the wall. One moment not to have a penny piece in the world, and the next to be given the Darensky pearls. One moment to be poor and lonely, and the next to have Stephen's voice changing for her like this. She said,

"How could I know?"

Stephen put his arms round her.

"Didn't you really know? I knew the first time I saw you in that damned bread queue at Tronsk. I knew that I belonged to you, and I knew that I could make you belong to me. And when I found you on the bridge, I knew it all over again. You were all frozen and dead, but I knew that I could get you to come alive. I told you right away that I wasn't going to let you die."

"My face is dirty," said Elizabeth. "You mustn't kiss me with a dirty face."

"Mine's dirty too," said Stephen. "We'll get baths when we get to Warsaw, but I'm not going to wait to kiss you till then."

He kissed the eyes which he had always thought were like stars and the soft trembling lips, and then he set her down.

"I want to get you to the farm before it's dark."

"Won't it be dark yet?"

"Not quite."

"They won't come after us?"

"They can't. There's a great wire entanglement all along this part of the frontier, and we're on the Polish side of it."

He picked up the torch and began to help her up the steps—old broken steps and slippery at the edges. Elizabeth went up them in a dream. Stephen loved her. Stephen really loved her. They belonged to each other. Their love made a safe, light place about them. She would have walked with him through the loneliest, darkest place in the world without a tremor of fear.

They came to where the steps ended beneath a slab of stone. The torch showed a niche with a rude lever. As Stephen put his hand on it, he said,

"We'll get married in Warsaw. I should think it would take about three days."

Then, before she could speak, the stone pivoted and he was swinging himself through the opening. A sharp piercing air brought down a flurry of snow. Stephen took her under the arms and lifted her up and out. The stone fell back into its place.

It was late dusk. The sky was dark overhead. Black formless shapes of ruined arch and fallen pillar were about them. A glimmering snowfield stretched away on every side.

"Poland!" said Stephen.

THE END

Made in the USA
Lexington, KY
22 October 2016